Ray J. Abbott
9-5-54

TROUBLE IS A WORD SPELLED WOMAN

The deal was simply this: the Skaggs to supply the sheep and the money, the Fewkes and their friends to put up the guts and the gunplay.

"It don't hardly sound like enough to go to war over," said Frank thoughtfully.

"If we get by with it," rasped Jim, "we'll make more honest money in two years than the Gradens have made crooked in five! You ain't answered me, Frank. What cards you playin'?"

"The draw's down to me, eh? So what you think I'll do?"

"Throw in with us."

"You figure crazy. There ain't nothin' left in this world would take me back into the Basin."

"There is, Frank. You're forgettin' somethin'. Somebody, I mean . . ."

This is Old Jim Stanton's map of the Basin,
hand-drawn from partly failing memory and the
time removal of many years. It contains several
errors of the type quite common to such old-
timers and their conceptions of the land they
lived in. It is nevertheless the only document of
its kind left us, and in its principal information
is surprisingly accurate.

W. H.

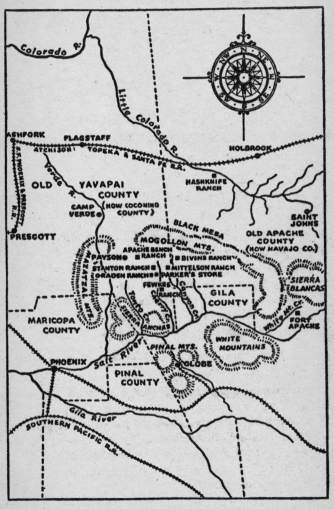

Early settler's map of Arizona Territory locating Peaceful Basin and the "dark and bloody ground" of its famed Graden-Fewkes vendetta . . .

"What horsemen are these?" asked Argensola.

"Those which go before the Beast of the Apocalypse," said Tchernoff.

"But the four horsemen?" persisted Desnoyers.

"They were preceding the appearance of the monster in John's vision . . . the first horseman appeared on a white horse. He was Plague. The second leaped forth on a flame-colored steed. He was War. And when the third seal was broken, John saw a black horse. He who mounted it was Famine.

"And there appeared a fourth, pale-colored horse.

"His rider was called Death . . ."

from *The Four Horsemen of the Apocalypse* by V. Blasco Ibañez

THE FOURTH HORSEMAN

Will Henry

A novel about old Arizona

THE FOURTH HORSEMAN
A Bantam Book

PRINTING HISTORY
Random House edition published May 1954
Bantam edition / July 1956
2nd printing .... July 1973
3rd printing .... May 1981

ISBN 0–553–14989–X

Published simultaneously in the United States and Canada

*Bantam Books are published by Bantam Books, Inc. Its trade-
mark, consisting of the words "Bantam Books" and the por-
trayal of a bantam, is Registered in U.S. Patent and Trademark
Office and in other countries. Marca Registrada. Bantam
Books, Inc., 666 Fifth Avenue, New York, New York 10103.*

PRINTED IN THE UNITED STATES OF AMERICA

12 11 10 9 8 7 6 5 4 3

Contents

Since the echo of its last shot that long-gone summer of 1887, Arizona's narrow-eyed oldsters have held that Peaceful Basin's famous Graden-Fewkes feud was a sheep and cattle war, started by the driving of the Skaggs Brothers' sheep over the Mogollon Rim and fought to the last, bitter death by the cattlemen of the Basin. They have always been, and still are, wrong.

In a sense, of course, the invasion of the Skaggs Brothers' sheep was a very real part of the war. But the fighting had far deeper and longer roots, stretching back through five years into the fall of 1882; and the sheep were only in the Basin for six brief months during the winter of 1886-87.

The real story lies in the hitherto unknown memoirs of the Basin's pioneer cattleman, James F. "Old Jim" Stanton. It is these memoirs, six time-yellowed letters and a faded map sent the author in 1951 by the old frontiersman's grandniece, Miss Oleta Brand Stanton of Hagerstown, Indiana, now deceased, which make possible the first full disclosure of the story of those missing years in the Peaceful Basin War.

That is the story of the Fourth Horseman. It does not begin with any animal, be it cow or sheep, nor with any man, be he cattle or sheepman.

It begins like the very first story ever told, and the very last.

It begins with a woman . . .

W. H.

Into the valley

A man will ride so far. He will come then, one lonesome sunset, to a time and a place in the trail from whence there is no turning, and no returning. He will find himself at last walled in. To the north and the south, to the east and the west. He will suspect then, where he is.

For a little while he will sit his horse, feeling behind him all the lost yesterdays, seeing ahead of him all the empty tomorrows. He will realize then, that for him there is no yesterday and no tomorrow, but only what little is left of today. When he feels that, he will no longer suspect where he is. He will know.

He is at the end of the trail.

In the mind of the weary horseman pausing atop the rimrock, eyes slitted to the westering sun, there was no confusion. He knew where he was.

"Peaceful Basin," the boy had told him. "If you make it away, Frank," he had said, "head south for the Basin. Look up Old Jim Stanton . . ."

Lifting the alkalied corners of his mouth in a grimace which never would have passed for a grin outside a Mescalero Apache camp, the stranger contemplated the sheer passage of the Mogollon Rim. The rim itself, a thousand foreboding feet in height, sprawled in a rough half-circle around the north and east sides of the Basin. The streams which watered the deep-hidden valley drained south. From that a man could guess they emptied into Arizona's famed Salt River, beside which, he knew, stood the territorial capitol of Phoenix.

He shook his head, the grin still twisting his wide lips. You couldn't call this goat-track break in the cliffs confronting you a trail, though the boy had done so in telling you about it. It was slashed into the raw rock as though some old fearsome god of the Navajo had thrust his skinning knife into the bowels of the Basin walls and ripped upward to their scalp lock of scrub pine in one angry belly-slice. But the boy had said it was the only opening in the rim for sixty miles, and a man could take it or leave it. At that, the chances of "leaving it" looked very good in any one of a dozen places easily seen from the big rider's dizzy lookout.

Clucking softly to the bay stallion, he sent him down the first pitch of the granite decline. The hour of easy choices was long gone for Frank Rachel.

The old man put down the ax, stepped away from the chopping block. He looked up the valley, squinting against the glare of the early sun. Shortly he moved behind the corner of the corral shed, reappearing seconds later to peer through the peeled logs of the fence adjoining it. The ax had been replaced by a rusty-snouted, 45-70 Springfield carbine. Eyes narrowed, he watched the approach of the solitary rider.

After ten seconds of study he was no more pleased with what he saw than he had been when he put down the ax for the Springfield.

Old Jim Stanton was no pioneer. His was the breed which went ahead of the pioneers, hewing out the trails for them to follow. He had lived beyond the frontier fringe all his life, and in this same southwest territory for better than forty years of that long span.

He had come to the Yavapai country only the year before, in '81, having been pushed off his Snowflake range in the Apache country to the east by the threat of another Chiricahua uprising. There he had traded his land holdings to the crowding Mormon settlers for twelve hundred head of prime cattle, himself moving on west in search of room to "swing his hat." He had found it here in Peaceful Basin. The native grass stood belly-high to a tall steer. Nothing grazed it off save the pronghorns and whitetail deer, and the whole rich range of it lay naturally fenced off; on two sides by the unbroken, cloud-high wall of the rim, on the third by a ragged string of distant, bare-rock peaks, on

the fourth by the southern-stretching desert of the upper
Salt River Valley.

Its winters were mild, its springs lush, its summers and
falls, shaded by its extensive stands of native pine and
cedar, relatively cool and free of the relentless sun blaze
which made a withered desert of so much of the surrounding rangelands. But chiefly it was the Basin's unknownness
and its hidden inaccessibility which made it such a jeal-
ously guarded treasure, and it was this last thought which
now crowded Jim Stanton's mind.

The old man nodded to himself. His right hand slid up
the worn butt of the Springfield. If a man like himself,
born to the territory, had spent forty years finding this
lost basin, no passing stranger was apt to ride into it by
chance.

Beyond that, a man did not need to have spent his
grown life watching distant dots across the mesa jog up
and turn into solitary, hard-eyed horsemen, to know the
cut of this one now turning off the valley trail and in toward his ranch.

He sat a horse like all of them, like a lean sack of loose
oats. His long legs reached straight for the ground in the
let-down stirrup leathers. Cradled under the offside knee
was the omnipresent Winchester. Slung across the cantle
were the trademark suggin and slicker, encompassing in
their slender girth all that the world held personal to the
man straddling the low-horned roping saddle.

Coming to his clothes, the pattern held. The overalls
were faded blue, low-hipped, shotgun-barreled as to leg,
and a man could bet his last yearling steer that their
waistband was stamped "Levi Strauss." The full, choked
tops of the Levis would be stuffed inside the pull leathers
of sixteen-inch Texas boots, and if those boots failed to
support cartwheel Mexican rowels, a man would lose his
second head of beef. The hat was out of the territory
Bible, a genuine Six-X Stetson, flat-crowned, four-inch-
brimmed, held on by a string under the chin.

He fitted all right, and yet he didn't. There was something missing. A standard item which should have been
there but wasn't. Something, the obvious lack of which,

despite the dust-covered denims and the high turned collar of the Strauss jacket, made this one look peculiarly naked.

Then Stanton had it, his forefinger crooking into the trigger guard with the nod. In a land where a man would as soon mount up without his pants as he would without his six-gun, this one rode Coltless.

He was of the breed though. Either that or a man had sure as hell lost his third cow.

"That'll be far enough . . ."

The flat statement caught Frank, making him curse. He pulled the bay in, tracking the voice to the lodgepole fence corner. Damn it, he hadn't seen the old coot. Slips like that could shorten a man's rope considerably.

"I'd like them hands crossed on the horn." The old man stepped around the fence, the big bore of the Springfield wandering the newcomer's belt buckle.

Frank nodded, let the reins slide. "They're crossed. You Stanton?"

"A name's a name," said the old man.

"Mine's Frank Rachel."

"One's as good as another."

"Try Johnny Fallon, then." There was an edge of grit in the dry dust of the suggestion. The old man held.

"World's full of Johnnies, Mister. Franks, too . . ."

Frank acknowledged the implication with a noncommittal grunt. He kneed the bay, quartering his offside toward the old man. Covered by the motion, his left hand slid from the horn into the onside saddlebag. "Catch!" he called, flipping the weapon.

Again the old man held. His eyes caught the sunflash of the big Colt as it turned in the air and lit in the dust at his feet. But his hands didn't vary their grip on the carbine, nor his eyes leave the big horseman.

"Where'd you get it?" he said sharply.

"Kid by the name of Johnny Fallon give it to me. 'You'll need a passport for Peaceful Basin,' he says. 'Use mine.'"

"What else 'he says'?" Frank saw the rim frost edging the old man's eyes.

"Not much," he shrugged. "Man doesn't waste wind with a .44 rifle slug in one armpit and out the other."

"Lungs?" The frost broke to the quick pain of the question.

"Both. He was already bled out bad when I rode onto him. Lasted maybe two hours."

"How come you to ride onto him, Mister?" The frost again.

"I'm ridin' the highline down from the North . . ."

"Figured that." The interrupting nod was short.

"Don't break in on me, old man," the return nod was shorter, "it ain't polite.

"Like I said, I'm ridin' the ridges. I seen this posse along about dusk, and I seen it wasn't mine. Pretty quick I spot their game. He's maybe three, four miles up on them. Bad hit, plain enough, by the way he was sacked in the saddle. He was makin' up my ridge and I seen where I could cut him before they did, if he held out and the daylight didn't."

The highline rider paused, letting his listener's jerking head-nods catch up.

"I cut him all right, but the posse had closed up and the light was still holdin'. I roped the kid on his hoss and hit on down the ridge, gettin' what I could out of both ponies."

"They seen you? You, I mean."

"I allow they did, old man."

"But you and Johnny got hid out before dark?"

"Still on the ridge," Frank nodded. "They had only to bottle both ends and wait for sunup."

"The boy go hard, Mister?"

"Not too. He was dream-talkin' toward the last. About the Basin here, and worryin' as to my gettin' took in for the job he'd done."

"Some bad of a job?"

"Some. Train, east of Tucumcari. This kid and four others. Amateurs. Busted a mail sack. The kid had some of it on him. Registered stuff mostly. They'll never learn. I put it under the rocks with him. Smoothed our tracks and led his hoss out along about moonup."

"Trouble then?"

"Two, three, down." The nod and grunt were terse. "I

tried holdin' wide for winghits but it's tricky in the dark. One of them hit the ground too soggy. The rest of them run me and the kid's hoss till daylight. I lost them in the malapai."

The old man chucked his head. "Them lava beds is hell on posses." He said it as though he'd been there. "That about it, son?"

The big rider didn't miss the little softness in that "son."

"About," he agreed. "They tailed me ten days. Lost them up north of Holbrook. Figured from the jumpoff that I had them out-hossed. Rode a wide swing to prove it."

He grimaced, hawking the alkali dust from the back of his throat. The cottony spittle lanced the dust alongside the gun at the rancher's feet.

"I'm near talked out, old man. Your turn, likely."

Stanton's jaw tightened with the nod. "Get down," he said, putting the Springfield against the fence as he picked up the fallen Colt. "Feed's in the shed yonder. Water tank's past them big oaks. Grub'll be ready when you are."

"Thanks," the short grunt demurred, "but I'm aimin' to talk one more little mouthful."

"It'll keep, Rachel." He glanced at the Colt in his hands, then stared down the long valley. "Up to now, the gun's talked for you. I give it to the boy when he was sixteen. Four years ago, May. He was my sister's youngest. Come to me when she died. I could never hold him. Wild, he was. Always fightin' the bit. The grub'll be ready."

"Suits me." He was turning for the shed. "A man talks better with his belly full."

"Either way he does," replied the old man cryptically. "Whether it's lead or beans he's got it full of."

Jim Stanton hefted the steaming pot. "Black?" he said.

"As possible," grunted Frank, closing his long fingers around the tin. Then, curiously, the first shade of a grin lifting the wide mouth. "It comes another color?"

"Suit yourself." He jerked a thumb toward the half dozen cans of condensed milk on the shelf back of the

Buck's range, and added defensively, "Damn it, it's only seventy-five miles to Holbrook!" Then, quietly, eyes squinting, "You had somethin' else to say out yonder." He kept the battered coffee pot suspended with the challenge.

"I'm done." The big rider turned on him, narrow-eyed. "Rode out, lucked out, trailed out. I've covered my tracks from Holbrook here, the best way I could. But they'll be waitin' outside. That was a mail job and they seen me with the kid. They've rode me down and I aim to stay down. Old man," the pale eyes were looking through him as though he weren't there, "I need a hole. You hear me?"

"I hear you," said Old Jim Stanton slowly. "I reckon you've found one."

"Black, then," said Frank Rachel, and there was no grin as the big hand came forward with the tin to meet the syrupy stream of the Arbuckle's.

The ten-minute silence which followed was broken only by the wolfish grind of famished jaws and repeated, sloshing gulps of the No. 2½ can which, born to seal eastern-grown tomatoes, now stood yeoman service as a Peaceful Basin demitasse.

The greasy slabs of yearling loin beef and the pint ladles of re-fried, red chili beans evaporated under the wordless assault. The old man, ostensibly straightening up the breakfast debris of the cook shack, took the opportunity for the first time fully to size his self-appointed guest.

It was a sizing well calculated to put the thoughtful chill of reconsideration on his tacit approval of the dead Johnny Fallon's pearl-handled passport.

He was a big devil, bigger by somewhat than you'd spotted him for, riding up. Over six feet by half a hand, the three-inch hike of the Texas boots put him to towering like a White Mountain ponderosa. Yet there was reason in a man's taking him for being smaller than that. It was the way he was built, "all of a piece," the old man was wont to call it, that fooled you. You could lay a double-bitted axhaft across those shoulders and not have yourself a decent handhold left on either side. You could, at the same time, throw a thirty-inch girth around that lean

belly and still have to cinch it up a couple of holes to
make it hold his Levis on.

In a land of spare men this one still seemed gaunt. Yet,
seeing the span of the big hands and what you could of
the linepost thickness of the wrists where they showed
past the frayed cuffs, you knew he wasn't the one the boys
would offhand take to calling "Slim." A shade winter-thin
right now maybe, but born a meat and bone and tendon
man. The kind who was mainly made of gray gristle and
red muscle meat, for all his schoolgirl waist and cat-dainty
way of moving around on foot.

When you got over the surprising heft of him, you got
around to the face. One look let you know that big, me-
dium or orphan-runted for body size, what was wolfing
down your beef and beans was a real *hombre duro*, a sure
enough hard man.

The old man had been looking at rimrock all his life.
He knew it when he saw it. He saw it now in the narrow
face of Frank Rachel.

It was a dry face, sculptured free of all the overflesh of
ordinary softness by a lifetime of southwestern rainwash
and sun blister. It was a face—no matter it looked strangely
pale at the moment—that would ordinarily be as cross-
checked and weathercracked of skin as any square foot of
the Basin's walls. And a face as high of cheekbone, oblique
of eye and impassive of set as that of any blood Chiricahua.
But when you had marked the Indian grimness of it, you
had gone as far as you could with the Apache part of it.
The peculiar coloration of the eyes, and of the hair,
stopped you dead.

The eyes caught you first, and for a moment you
couldn't call them. Then, of a sudden, you had it. When
you did, the hair fell into place, and you had everything
about him, and just what it reminded you of.

In the natural course of frontier events it wasn't given
to many cowmen to see a *real* one. Oh, plenty of the Mexican, or mountain, variety, with their little heads, dainty
faces and housecat manners. Sure, they were common as
clay, and about as dangerous. But a *real* one now, that
was something.

Old Jim Stanton had seen one. In a flea carnival wagon

over in Albuquerque one summer. Was it '68? No, that was the winter of the big die-off up by Dodge. Must have been '69. No matter anyway. So many years ago now that the track of them was long lost. Not the memory though.

Old Jim had stood and watched him for a full hour. All he had done in the livelong time of it was glide one way, then the other, face to the bars, eyes on the horizon. Looking at a man and through him. Seeing him, yet not seeing him. Conscious of every move that went on outside that cage, yet never swinging his gaze from the farthest, distant peak of the Sangres.

Those eyes had been as yellow and clear as the bottom of a sandpool in the Verde at low water, and as quiet, too. Yet they had been as restless and never still as the keep-watch swing of a hunting hawk. "Let me out," those eyes had said. "Open the door and let me out. I'll be your friend for life." Then, sweeping across the bars, over your head to the distant plains again, they'd whispered. "You do it and I'll smash your head like an eggshell. I'll knock you down on the first jump and kill you on the second. I'll be gone, and ever gone, and you the fool for letting me out."

The old man hunched his shoulders, as to a draft felt only by him. His eyes flicked to the stranger again, pausing on him only long enough to note the heavy sweep of the ash blond hair, the oddly dark eyebrows and pale lashes, the dried straw droop of the bleached mustaches. It was all there: the yellow eyes, the stiff roach of the wheaten mane, the motionless, wide line of the dark-lipped mouth.

Maybe human, maybe otherwise. It made a man's hide crawl either way. You looked at him now and you knew it.

You'd let a lion into your house.

Hunger, not of the belly kind

Peaceful Basin lay dark and still, waiting for the moon. Against the formless smudge of the ranchhouse the glow of the cigarettes rose and fell. They were flipped away to smolder in the dust of the ranchyard. Others, freshly lit, blue clouding and fragrant in the night quiet, took their places to limn the thoughtful faces of the smokers. The moon came, lipping the rim with silver. It spilled over into the Basin, picking out the ranch buildings, the corrals, the yard pines; standing them in bold relief against the blackness of the timber at the clearing's edge.

The men talked, first, as western men will, of the weather.

"Late fall usually this warm around here?" The big rider spoke softly, as men do when they have lived much alone.

"Well, yes and no." It was a topic near to the old man's heart. "If you mean the Basin, yes. We winter it better than most. They catch hell up on the Rim though. You take from Ashfork to Flagstaff, north, they get it heavy. Do some winter feedin' off and on, pretty regular. But down here she's half the time open from October to April. Cattle do fine, no matter."

"Hosses too, I reckon?" The talk shifted easily to livestock.

"There ain't a better hoss country. Lots of mineral in both grass and water. You ain't seen heavy bone on brood stock till you've seen these Basin mares. I got the only native bunch in the valley. Growed here by somebody ahead of me. The 'Paches burnt him out, whoever he was. You can see what's left of his place over west there in the Tonto Creek headlands. The bunch run wild, what the 'Paches left of them anyhow. Me and the boys brung them in with salt and sugar. You never seen such mares, Mister!"

He had deliberately laid it on heavily. He hadn't missed the careful way his companion followed each word once the talk swung to horses. And before that he hadn't missed the blood-fine lines of the bay horse the big man had ridden into the valley. Nor the fact that the bay was an uncut stud. He concluded now, his statement a direct question for all its casual ease.

"Not many rides a stud. And none I seen so far, a blood stud."

The stranger let the silence hold so long the old man grew uneasy.

Likely, he'd overstepped on him. This one, with his edgy, cold way of looking square through you, wasn't the man you made a profitable habit of outreaching. He was surprised then, when his words came at last. He knew too, when they did, that the big man wasn't only hungry for the beef he had just put in his belly. Nor for the smoke he now held so long and gratefully in his lungs.

"I'd allowed you'd marked the stud," Frank said softly, "and me along with him." He paused, dragging deeply on the cigarette.

"Old man, if we could see the whole blessed world spread out in this moonlight, right from where we're set-tin' on this stoop, we couldn't see another single thing rightfully belonging to Frank Rachel.

"But the stud is mine, you hear? Bought and paid for on top of the counter, twice over. Not lifted, not brand-run, not nothin'. He's all I got—man, beast or woman.

"He was took from me once . . ." Again the pause and the heavy drag. "Legal bill-of-sale stole and blotted on me. Old man," the third pause, "you read sign smart and sure. I seen you cuttin' trail on my face color. What would you say, if you was asked?"

The unexpected shift of the question stopped the white-haired rancher. His first thought was to back and look for cover. But there was that in this light-eyed young giant which called to a man over and beyond the fear he put in you. Jim Stanton saw again that years-gone carnival wagon in Albuquerque. His words came straight, even so.

"Color's fresh," he said. "More red than brown. You're old to the sun but it's new to you these past days. Somewhat and of recent late, I'd say, you ain't been in it."

"You'd say right." The bitterness stained like acid. "Two years, old man. Seven hundred days and better. Just walkin' and lookin'. Fed out of a pan night and mornin'. Watered once a day. Walkin' one way, walkin' the other way. Up the bars. Down the bars. But lookin', always, just one way —out."

The cigarette flipped spinningly across the yard to fall and smolder through the silence.

"They left the door open one night," he shrugged. "They knew where I'd head, all right, only they missed headin' me. I got the bay back and burnt the blotted bill."

"You left a receipt, I reckon?" The question showed its edge.

"Paid in full," nodded Frank. "Eyes wide, boots in place."

"It's how come you was ridin' the highline," said Stanton acridly. "Hossflesh comes high with some. You paid plenty."

"I paid what was askin'."

"But killin' a man . . ."

"I bought cheap there." He looked at Stanton. "The bay is mine. Croup, hock, foot and fetlock. You hear me, old man?"

The rancher nodded, not liking the soft ugliness of the question. "Sure, son. Likely it ain't the first time a man's died over a stole hoss."

"No . . ." the voice dropped softer still, "nor it ain't the last. If anything ever happens to that stud, you remember that!"

It was a clear threat, plainly out of time and place so far as Old Jim Stanton could see. There would come a time, and in this place, when it would assume monstrous proportions; when its ugly spark would ignite a flame which would make the name of Peaceful Basin a grim mockery wherever decent men might meet; when its resultant holocaust would destroy more human lives than any rangeland war in western history. But that time was not yet, and the old rancher merely nodded.

"I'll remember it, son. What was it now"—he led the trail carefully away from the bay horse—"that you wanted of me? You see that I'm old and that we ain't got no trouble here. You're welcome to stay. I owe you that. But I smell trouble, boy. You put the ache of it in my bones. What's in your mind that you ain't told me?"

"Nothin', that I ain't told you. I'm tired of runnin'. I want to turn around and rest, that's all." The admission came openly, no hint of harshness in it, but only a suppressed loneliness which cut deeper than any hard talk.

"You're right about me and trouble," he went on slowly. "It's born to some. There's men can live their whole lives and never lift a fist. Good men too, and men there don't nobody throw off on. There's others can't walk six feet from the hitchin' rack without somebody's sizin' them up. That can't ease up to the far end of the bar but what some local hero moves all the way down from the other end to make a show. A man's got an eye and a face for trouble and it's goin' to look him up every time. You meet some jasper and you nod and say good mornin' and he backs off and says that's a goddam lie, and there's your trouble. I been meetin' that kind all my life. It's been a fight—thumb in the eye, knee in the guts, Colt slug in the belly—ever since I was a kid. I tell you, old man, I ain't never had a friend."

"That's some of it," said Stanton thoughtfully, "but it ain't all of it. Friends ain't born, they're made. Your kind never takes the time."

"I'm aimin' to take it now." Frank eyed him a long time. "Old man, I want to stay here in Peaceful Basin. I want to live here and work here, and make a friend if I can." He hesitated, groping for words. Stanton said nothing, and he went on.

"I want to build, old man. My own house and sheds and corrals; hoss sheds and hoss corrals. I want to rack that Winchester up over the fireplace and only get it down if I want a saddle of venison or an antelope ham.

"I want to look up at a man ridin' into my place and to know who he is. To wave a hand at him, one that ain't filled with a gunbutt. To maybe laugh with him once in a while, or even to turn my back to him and not even think about it till some later. I want to get down off my hoss and stay down off of him. You know what I mean, old man?"

"I've been there," said Stanton shortly. "It's why I came here."

"I'll stay then, by God, I'll stay!"

Old Jim sensed the peculiar excitement in the soft oath. He knew, instinctively, how rarely the lightning of such emotions struck in this kind.

"I'll work, too." The excitement held. "I'll work damn hard. It'll be the first time I ever had a place of my own. Me and the stud . . ."

"Where'll you work, boy?" The interruption was carefully gentle. Stanton wanted to slow him down but didn't want to rile him in doing it. "Mine's the only big spread in the Basin. Otherwise, there's only Will Mittelson between me and Canyon Creek, Sam Houghton twenty miles southwest of my place, Charley Parker that runs the valley store below me, Al and Ed Ross and half a dozen others in the whole valley. They don't run five hundred head of cattle between them. I'm askin' you, boy. Where'll you work?"

"I'll work for you, old man. If you'll have me, I will." There was an intense, open appeal in the quiet words, and Stanton felt himself wavering. Still, he hesitated.

"By God, son, I'd like to, but . . ."

"Old man, you let me. *I'll be your friend for life.*"

The chill of the words and the sudden light of the pale eyes behind them struck Stanton. "Let me out," those other eyes had said. "Open the door and let me out . . ." He shook himself, not wanting to look back to those eyes again. He forced himself. Made the words come earnestly.

"I just can't do it, Rachel. I can't pay the hands I've got. I'm owin' them now, since last September."

"I don't want money!" The excitement grew, thrilling the old rancher with its strange, lonely rush. "I want mares. You understand that, old man? *Just mares!*"

"Mares? God Amighty, what for? You can rustle them right and left up on the rim. All the boys do. The whole mesa's lousy with loose hoss stuff."

"Not like yours. Not like this native Basin stuff. I seen them down in your pasture this mornin'. I want them big-boned, straight-legged ones. For me and the stud. Don't put off on me, old man. No money, you hear? A mare a month and found. I'll work that way for a year, you hear me?"

"I hear you," said Stanton. He felt himself suddenly moved beyond the uneasy borders of the fear put up in him by the gaunt rider. "A mare a month and found."

"My pick?"

"Of the bunch."

Hearing his own voice say it, Stanton didn't care. He felt, all at once, like throwing an arm around those spreading shoulders. Like putting a friendly hand to that broad back, quickly, impulsively. To let the man know that he was all right. That he had come home at last.

Even as the impulse struck him, the old rancher was taking another look through the evening darkness, watching the tall rider ease, catlike, to his feet and move away from the stoop. He knew then, that the impulse was a fool one, and false. He was thinking again now, while the big stranger was thanking him and turning away toward the horse shed and his precious bay stud, of just one thing: that red and yellow carnival wagon over in Albuquerque thirteen years ago; and of those gold-flecked, amber eyes looking clean through and away past him to the last far peak of the Sangres, high and blue and lonely up back of Santa Fe.

And maybe so, a friend

The old man awoke to find his "lion" gone, the "cage door" swinging idly open to mark his passage.

The pale-eyed rider had refused the use of the bunkhouse behind the cook shack despite Stanton's assurance the JS riders were popping brush for strays up under the north rim, and would be absent another three or four days. He had grunted his thanks and made off for the horse

shed with the evident intention of bedding down with his
mount.

It was this shed the rancher was now inspecting. He had
gotten as far as noting that both horse and man were gone
and that the loose straw in the loft was undisturbed. He
was in the midst of a heartfelt sigh of relief at being thus
so easily rid of his disquieting guest, when the soft voice
hit him from behind.

"Guess who?"

He came around, not liking to be Indian-stalked any
better than the average Arizonian. And nettled too, like
any old hand, that he could be.

"Not Frank Rachel," he said acidly. "That's as sure as
sheepdip stinks."

"A name's a name." The stranger, lounging easily
against the shed door, made rare use of his hard grin. "You
said it yourself."

"Well, it's a new day," grumped Stanton. "Where do we
go from here?" The old man's ire, bolstered by the broad
daylight and the token grin and easy attitude of his un-
welcome guest, lifted its lip to show a little hostile fang.
"I'm done tryin' to figure you. You look bad to me, boy,
and you feel bad. Why don't you and that rangey studhoss
move on and find yourselves another hole?"

"You talk too much." The grin was gone. "Let's ride."

"Where to, damn it?" He was still bridling. "That is, if
it ain't askin' too much."

"Look, old man, we made a deal. I said I'd be your
friend. Don't put off on me."

The pale eye were looking through and beyond him
again, and Stanton backed off.

"All right, where'll it be?"

"Upvalley, first. I want to meet your boys."

"Then?"

"That 'Pache burn-out. Where you got the mares."

"And?"

"The whole damn Basin. Every foot of it. Side basins,
creek cuts, benches, cross-ranges—all of it. A man's found
a hole, he likes to know how to get in and out of it, you
hear?"

"I hear." Stanton turned, his scowl growing. "Like you said, let's ride."

They struck northeast from the ranch, the going level and open until they hit the main fork of the creek and swung along its course. An hour's hard ride took them up the stream's rough bed to top out on its headlands under the towering north wall of the Mogollon Rim.

Here the land benched, spreading east and west high above the level of the Basin floor. While the horses blew, the old man flung his arms wide and south, indicating the vast tumble of the range below. The gaunt rider by his side followed each word and gesture in narrow-eyed silence, careful not to interrupt, like a man will be when he is meaning to miss nothing and memorize all of it.

"There's your Peaceful Basin," said Stanton abruptly. "I'd advise you to get it straight, right from where we sit. For hard looks or otherwise, boy, I don't aim to ride over it with you. You take a good look at it and I reckon you'll see I ain't puttin' off on you."

The narrow eyes swept the upflung, broken floor of the great valley. "I pass, old man. You give me the main lay. I'll ride it out on my own time."

Stanton eyed him, still frowning.

"All right, we're backed on the north rim. What you see, downvalley, is due south. Holbrook is off our left shoulder seventy-five miles northeast. There's one crack in the rim from that way and you used it comin' down. South, a little better than seventy miles, yonder there under the Pinals, is Globe. The valley opens on that end. You can get in and out fair easy. Payson is twenty-five miles over west there, off this near shoulder of the Mazatzals. Payson," he repeated the town's name, underlining his next words meaningfully, "is where this here Yavapai County's nearest law and order holds out."

His companion's eyes didn't leave the indicated range of the Mazatzals. He went on quickly.

"Them rough hogbacks to the southwest is the Sierra Anchas. That king mountain bustin' up out of them is McFadden Peak. We compass on it from any place in the whole Tonto Basin country.

"The creek we come up is the main fork of the Cherry. West fork branches below my place and heads out over behind me. The Cherry runs into the main Salt at the foot of the Basin, as does Canyon Creek over east there. West, you'll mark Diamond Butte. Past that is the headwaters of Tonto Creek and your 'Pache burn-out. Savin' for the upper box of Canyon Creek where the Bivins' spread is, that burn-out is the choppiest country flankin' the Basin." He paused, looking straight at the silent rider. "If a man was aimin' to hole up, he couldn't pick better."

Frank swung his mount. "It's good enough, old man. Let's move."

Stanton gestured westward. "The boys should be yonder, along under the rim a bit. Likely we'll hit them for noon dinner."

"Likely they'll be lookin' for us too." The slow statement was question-marked.

"Likely. They don't miss much," Stanton said. The way he said it brought Frank's eyes around.

"Meanin' what?"

"You'll see, Mister."

The old man's forecast was right as rim ice in November. The minute Frank laid eyes on the JS crew, "he saw."

There were three of them, brothers according to the little fill-in Stanton had given him on the ride over. They had come into the Basin six months after the old man, and hired on to him as common hands. There was a considerable clan of them, headed by the father of these boys. A couple of the latter appeared to be married and there were some young children. Outside of that there was an older girl, looking about twenty. Their names were Fewkes and the story had come in with them that the three boys and possibly the older girl were halfblood Modoc Indians, the elder Fewkes supposedly having taken up with a fullblood squaw somewhere in the Humboldt country of Northern California.

Sizing the present members of the Fewkes clan as he and Stanton now rode up to their noon fire, Frank figured that squaw-bred or pure-blood, these three would do better to side with than against.

They were lithe, cleanly made men; dark-skinned, green-eyed, black-haired. Two of them, looking to be the older pair, were darkly mustached. The other, youngest one, was clean-shaven. If there were an ounce of extra flesh shared by the trio, the spare-hipped fit of the jeans and the loose drape of the hickory shirts failed to show it. None of them wore beltguns. But it was worth remembering that in a country where they could know the next, nearest human being to be forty miles away, each of the three squatted to the noon fire with a late model '73 Winchester within instant reach.

The old man introduced them as Ed, Jim and John Fewkes; his own companion, for lack of more certain knowledge, as Frank Rachel.

The four acknowledged each other with a mutual, calculating nod. Ed Fewkes said, "Get down and come in." The younger brother, "We seen you comin'. Help yourselves." Jim Fewkes said nothing. And having said it, he looked at Frank long and slow.

Swinging off the bay to squat at the fire, the latter poured himself a can of coffee. While the old man fell to questioning his three hands on the progress of the gather, Frank watched Jim Fewkes. This required no particular sense of judgment. Of the three, the middle brother was plainly the one to watch.

He was slender in build, not missing six feet by half an inch. Peculiarly handsome, as were all three of them, Jim Fewkes fascinated a man where the other two only hung his eye long enough to warn him, then let go of it.

Where they were dark, he was darker. Where their hair fell straight and black to the faded collars of their workshirts, his lanked down glossy and thick as that of a winter wolf. Where their eyes were slightly oblique and of that murky green frequently seen in the Indian crossbreed, his were slant as a Mongol Hun's and of a peculiar turquoise brillance that defied the memory of any quite like them.

He moved around in a shadowy way that put you to watching his feet. And to nodding to yourself when you did. Where his brothers used the standard stockman's high-heeled boots, Jim Fewkes wore a set of soft-tanned Apache moccasins under the cover of his regulation Levis.

Frank's regard was being returned in kind. Not alone
by Jim Fewkes but by Ed and John as well.

While the three of them grunted their answers to the
old man, their swart faces swung continually to the new
rider. The latter, exchanging slow look for slow look, made
a mental note of one thing: they watched a man close and
hard but there was no challenge in the watching. There
was no invitation to get cozy either. Just the kind of watching one dog-wolf will give another when the meeting is
unavoidable and the trail tolerably narrow.

Frank felt the satisfaction of this grow quickly. The
Fewkes had looked him over, and he them. Nobody had
felt called on to make a show of it. Each and all, apparently, had seen what they had seen and bought it.

Long after he and the old man had left the noon fire,
he found himself thinking about Jim Fewkes.

There was gnawing inside of him the empty pangs of a
hunger which would not down. Not having felt it before,
a man couldn't identify it for sure. But he could guess at it.
And admit that he was hoping, along with that guess.
Unless something meanwhile went wrong to spoil it, the
brief meeting with Stanton's JS hands had put him, Frank,
onto good sign.

Maybe so, being that green-eyed breed felt the same way
about it, him and Jim Fewkes were going to be friends.

The lonely men

Stanton's fall gather had been good. As usual
with the autumn roundup a few big slick-ears, overlooked
in the spring gather, were popped out of the brush and
burned with a belated JS. Otherwise, the regular purpose
of the fall surround obtained: the cutting out of market-
able beef, two years old and older.

The old man had an Army contract with Fort Apache
over in the northeast corner of Maricopa County. Frank,
with Ed, Jim and John Fewkes, had made the hundred

and fifty mile drive with four hundred prime head. Frank
had worked well with the brothers and while the anticipated friendship with Jim Fewkes had not matured, a man
could feel that the latter, as well as Ed and John, had
tacitly accepted him.

Winter came to the Mogollons, glistened briefly up on
the higher rims, fell swiftly away under the early March
sun.

With the lengthening span of the sun-drenched April
days, preparations went ahead at the JS for the spring
branding. The vernal calf crop had signaled a mild winter
and correspondingly active herd bulls by tallying a whop-
ping 80 per cent. Two weeks would bring him and the
Fewkes boys close to six hundred calves to rope and burn.
If a man meant to take over that Tonto Creek burn-out
and get his horse spread going, he had best be about it.

Red Boy, the bay stud, had wintered off on the Basin
grass. Frank had meanwhile worked from the regular JS
saddlestring, giving the big stallion ample chance to fit
himself for his part in the Tonto Creek venture. The stud
had barreled out beautifully and as the winter coat shed
away a man could see he was as ready as he was ever going
to be.

Months back, a week or so after the fall gather, Old Jim
Stanton had come to Frank. Awkward about it as a cub
bear backing down a sycamore, he had grumped that,
"Seeing as how you're aimin' to get started from scratch, I
might as well give you a little advance in your wages."

The "little advance" had proved to be the old man's insistence that he pick his twelve mares then and there, that
they might winter in the fenced pasture with the stud.
"No point," he had scowled, "in letting them mares go
through fallow. Or get in foal to some scrub range stud.
Nor in wasting a whole winter and spring they could be
carryin' Red Boy's colts."

It had been his way, Frank knew, of paying off the debt
of Johnny Fallon's gun. He had simply nodded, "I owe
you one, old man," and gone about his picking.

Perched now atop the split log rails of the home pasture,
he soaked up the April sun, surveyed his sleek-coated seed
stock, found both warm and good. A man could feel he

hadn't squandered any time so far. The JS ran close to
three hundred head of horse stuff, half of them mares, the
rest gelded saddle stock. The working of this big bunch
had fallen to him. He had shown himself a remarkable
hand with horses and while the average wrangler stands
last below the cook in the southwest social scale, the work
he had done on the JS rough string had put him on a professional par with the highest caste calf roper in the Basin.
The valley men, on his sometime trips to Parker's Store,
had begun to nod when they saw him. Of late, a couple of
them had even clapped him on the shoulder and grinned
when they had met him. Yes, a man could begin to feel
that in Peaceful Basin anyway, he might at last begin en-
joying the trail in front of him without forever watching it
behind him.

The rusty scrape of the bunkhouse door brought his
head around. He watched Jim Fewkes move to the work-
stock corral, shake out his loop and snake it, underhanded,
over the head of his blue roan.

Frank slid off the fence, legging up on Red Boy. He
breasted the stud through the pasture gate, worked him
around the mares and headed them out. Fewkes joined
him below the ranchhouse, kneeing the roan up alongside
the stallion.

"I got a cute way into them Tonto headlands. Figured
I'd ride with you." He didn't look at Frank.

"Figured you would," the big rider nodded. "I'm
obliged."

The morning was well gone when they topped out on
the Tonto headlands. The last part of the way was up a
four-mile gorge, so narrow the mares had to move in it
single file. And so bad and cut up underhoof that half the
string were going sorefooted by the time they got out of it.

"The other way's easier," Jim said. "You come up from
the south slope below Diamond Butte. It's longer though.
There'll be times you'll want to remember this one."

They shoved the mares out and away from the canyon
head, spreading them over the heavy bench grass. Loosen-
ing their cinches, they slipped their bits and let their saddle mounts feed while they stretched and built smokes.
Neither spoke as both eyed the land before them.

This was the place, Frank decided. Here a man could stand with his back to the wall of the rim and look out on nothing, as Old Jim Stanton would put it, "But miles and miles of miles and miles."

The bench itself was nearly level. Beginning at the mouth of Dry Canyon, it ran north two miles and south three. It averaged nearly a mile wide for all of that length, with a drop-off on the Basin side of better than a thousand feet. If there was a trail up from the South as Jim had said, it was hidden and well hidden.

Frank looked across the waist-deep winnow of the bench grass. And across the scattered heads of granite which with parklike regularity lifted their piney crowns above the level of the little mesa. South, the still snow-capped crests of the Sierra Anchas thrust up against the raw blue of the spring sky. To the west, the naked red granite of the Mazatzals bulked hot and dry. Eastward and into the north, shouldered the heavily timbered scarp of the Mogollon Rim and beyond it, tumbled range on tumbled range, rolled the Sierra Blancas.

Ahead of them a short mile now, sunlit and still under the noon-high light, lay the charred footsills of the ranch-house. The corrals, yet standing and in good repair, lay behind the rocky rise upon which the forgotten settler had built not wisely but exceeding well.

The abandoned ranchhouse knoll commanded the full, five-mile sweep of the bench and in turn the southward-stretching haze of the entire Basin. It was a place of the wildest beauty, well fitted by a stupendous nature to stir the souls of silent, lonely men.

"We're home," said Frank Rachel softly. "Let's cinch up and move in."

His companion nodded, shouldered up his loosened girth, swung wordlessly into the saddle. They moved off quickly.

Jim Fewkes watched the big man riding ahead of him. He hadn't missed that "we" where a man might have said "I." He wondered now if his fellow rider had meant anything by it. And if so, just what.

In the back-of-beyond country, a man takes a long time

sizing. Peaceful Basin was behind the back-of-beyond.
Jim Fewkes had sized this one for six months. He shook
his head, putting down now what he had from the very
first: the strange belly-warming tug this big devil put to
work inside you. Not yet, he thought. In another six
months, maybe.

But not yet.

The six months came and went. Fall again lay crisp and
sere over the Mogollons. Frank Rachel had worked his
year for the JS; the happiest, best year a man could count
clean back to his bitter boyhood.

The mares were his, the "Apache Bench" ranch filed
on and title cleared. The little ranchhouse, bucksawed
and built plank for plank by his own hand, stood solid and
sure on the foundations so well laid by that first man there
ahead of him. Back of it, the peeled-log ramblings of the
hayricks, the feed and foaling sheds, and Red Boy's box
stall and stud corral showed a man what his first year of
lonely peace could sweat out of his own tall pines and red
granite field slabs.

Down the bench, sunbright and glossy against the grass,
his twelve mares stood in tail-switching content to the suck
of Red Boy's first foals. There were ten of the little hel-
lions, only two of the mares having failed to the stud's
cover. They were out-of-season rascals, naturally enough,
and would have to winter through on the bag. But a man
could look at his hayricks with their lodgepole snowbreaks
three-quarters around, and know it would take more snow
than the rim could hold to lose him any one of his
spraddle-legged babies.

Frank came out of the feed shed, bucking the hundred-
pound bulk of the oat sack and grinning across to where
Red Boy watched him coming over the top rails of the
stud corral.

Dumping the sack in an empty manger inside the box,
his fingers sought the tie-twine, worked out the pullstring,
ripped the sack open. He measured the two-quart scoop
to the brim, funneled it into the stallion's bin, the papery
disks of the rolled oats mounding up against the rough
wood. Behind him, the nuzzling stud moved in. He put

the arch of his crested neck playfully under Frank's reaching arm and bunted him hungrily aside.

Frank cursed him with clear satisfaction. He put a hard knee in his belly and moved him over, then squeezed along the logs and past the nervous sway of the satiny rump. At the last minute, the stud threw his quarters into the logs, playing at the daily game of "pinning the man." Frank was ahead of him, already squeezed clear. He hit him whackingly across the rump with his Stetson.

The big horse humped, tucking and swerving his haunch into the opposite wall with shed-jarring force. Rolling his eye whites wickedly, he neighed harshly and gruntingly. It was the rest of "the game," and the man cursed him with hard-grinned fervor.

Still, it was not the sound of the stud's eager challenge nor of the man's gladly answering profanity which followed the latter back out into the sunlight. It was another sound; a quick, clean, good sound, bell-like and startling in its unexpected richness.

It was the first time in five years that Frank Rachel had laughed.

Out in the daylight, again, he glanced toward the near pasture. Whistling shrilly, he swung his hat at the mares with a good-natured, "Hee-yahhh there! Damn you! Quit eatin' so much and move around a mite!"

The mares responded, prick-eared and nickering to the familiar greeting. Their heads came up and their plush-coated offspring scattered wildly in mock alarm as their dams trotted forward. Frank watched them a moment, then moved over to the sunny side of the ranchhouse and sat down.

As he built his smoke, he looked long and thoughtfully across the mile-high mesa of his domain. Then, with the deep, first-fragrant lungful of his lighting drag, he let his mind take him back over the six months which had gone since Jim Fewkes first brought him here in that April which already seemed as long ago as a man could remember—or would want to.

In the spring roundup on the JS, he and the other hands had put the old man's brand on better than six hundred calves, over four hundred of them bull calves that would

make good beef come the following fall of '83. He had
found the Fewkes top hands all around and felt they hadn't
found him far short of the same. Of the three, he had continued to favor Jim, and more and more the latter had
come to side with him. Let the work call for a split-up and
the slant-eyed middle brother had paired off with him
without any asking on either part. The others, Ed and
John, and the two new hands put on for the roundup,
shrugged off the unspoken partnership. It was natural.
On the range men did that, moved to one another and
sided-up without making speeches about it.

With the fall gather due, he had parted company with
the JS. The two new men, Tom and Judd Graden, lately
drifted into the Basin from Globe, had hung around the
ranch long past when there was any decent work to keep
them there. Accordingly, Old Jim, full up with hands, had
been glad enough to see Frank go.

The others hadn't been any too dewy-eyed about it
either, while for his own part he had managed to keep
his burden of grief pretty well borne up under. It was only
Jim Fewkes that had worried him.

The half-breed hadn't said a word when he left. He
hadn't, as a matter of fact, looked up from peeling out the
frog of his roan pony's foot. He had just let him ride out
of the yard and then when he was half a mile up the
valley road had waved after him, just once.

Frank had answered that wave eagerly. And had held
the bay stud in for a couple of side-switches to see if Jim
would acknowledge the answer. He hadn't and Frank had
turned for Dry Canyon figuring his year-long hope about
being friends with the breed was a dead hunch.

But a week later to the day—it was a Sunday like this
one, he remembered—the ewe-necked roan had ambled
up out of Dry Canyon to head in across the bench toward
where he was scything hay for the mangers. And this time
when he had waved, Jim Fewkes waved back.

And more. When he had come up, he'd slid off the roan
in that Indian-quick way of his, stared back for a length of
time which made Frank wonder if he wasn't aiming to
knife him for his year of trouble over him. Then, without
his knowing in a hundred years it was coming, Jim had

stuck out his hand stiff and awkward as a cigar store Mohawk.

Frank could still feel the warmness in his belly over that handshake. He remembered wondering then, as he did now, if that slim brown hand had ever been offered to another man. And doubting it, even as he wondered about it.

After that, no Sunday failed to pass but what the rat-tailed roan stood hipshot in front of the Apache Bench cabin. And with the swift, succeeding weeks Frank had found what he sought above all else.

He had found it in the pleasant, keen-eyed stalks for table game, sided by the silent Jim, in the brushlands under the mesa's edge; in the wild rides with the dark-faced breed along the main rim, cat-hunting, wolf-running or bear-trailing, pursuing that unholy trinity of varmints whose main appetite was weanling horseflesh; in the long, wordless hours of horseback exploration, following Jim into and out of every crevice in Peaceful Basin's back country. And in those briefer, happy times across the night fires when the coffeecan kept moving until it was drained of the last black dreg and the rushing spells of talk tumbled out, unabashed, as only they can between men who are at last alone with the night and the stars and the soft wind in the gramma grass, and with two bellies full of a word hunger many a long, hard-eyed year in the building.

In all these things then, and in a hundred more unmarked by conscious thought or deed, had big Frank Rachel found himself. And found too, that other thing for which he had so long searched in vain.

A man to be his friend.

Trouble is a word spelled woman

There was a peace then at last in the restless heart of the highline rider as he sat that final Sunday in the sun along the south side of his ranchhouse. Peace in his heart and high contentment in his mind. He had found a home and a friend. What more might the world hold for a lonely man?

A woman perhaps. Yes, a good woman. With some kids too, like as not. Sure, the kids would go right on Apache Bench.

The thought of the woman stirred briefly in him. It pulled in his lean belly and put the little muscle tremor to running his jaw the way it always did when he was in a tight spot and no way out save back of a gun. The way it had that night he had left Red Boy's illegal owner sprawled in his own ranchhouse door. The way it had that night he had run his way through the posse with Johnny Fallon's led-horse, and seen that third deputy hit the ground like a sack of sour mash. The way it had with a dozen other nights long before these, and with a dozen other figures just as sprawled and wet-sack limp.

He shook his head, putting the backtrail behind him. He smoothed the jaw twitch and eased the belly pinch.

What a man had done, he had done. There wasn't much he could do to change it. What little could be done had been done that year-ago sunset when trail's end had brought him to Peaceful Basin; when he had unhooked the guns and rolled them in his suggins and promised himself never to belt them on again.

It was all a man could do and he had to be content with it. Frank Rachel was. No man, least of all him, could help that uneasy stir in his loins or that nerve squeeze in his belly when he thought of a woman. Not when he had been two years and more without one. And all his years before that without a good one.

No, women were behind for Frank Rachel. Good ones or bad.

He had his ranch now, and his horses. He had a good name in the Basin, and the best man in it for his friend. The October sun was good, the autumn air wine-sharp with piñon and cedar. It was Sunday again. The whirring call of the mountain quail would be coming up Dry Canyon any minute and, back of it, Jim Fewkes on the ewe-necked roan. There would be some more talks. Some more

smokes. And a long going-on of the peace and contentment . . .

The whistle of the blue quail broke his reverie. He
grinned quickly, lounging away from the wall to wave at
the approaching horseman. Jim Fewkes came on. There
was no return of the wave. He brought the roan hard up
and stepped down off him, letting the reins slide.

"What is it?" he asked him quietly, his grin long gone.

"Trouble," the half-breed answered.

With the three words given and the one taken, peace
and contentment came not again for big Frank Rachel.

"How many head you figure we should have cut out for
the Army contract this past gather?" The asker was Jim
Fewkes; the reference to the JS fall roundup, just held.

"Contract still calls for four hundred prime don't it?"

"It does."

"Five hundred and fifty, six hundred anyway." Frank
watched him closely. "Why?"

"We cut three hundred and ten. Sixty head of those was
under the eight hundred pound limit and was cut back
into the brush. The old man was short a hundred and fifty
head and lost the contract."

"Who filled?"

"The Graden Brothers."

"The who?" Frank's question jumped.

"You heard." He kept it short. "Tom and Judd Graden."

"I thought they was ridin' for the old man."

"They was," said Jim succinctly.

"I'm listenin'."

"Right after you pulled out they located below the old
man. Ten miles southeast, north side of the creek. Built
a cabin and filed on the land. They stayed with the JS
through the roundup. When it tallied short, they threw in."

Frank was a long time building the smoke. "You certain the Gradens filled that contract?"

"With a hundred and fifty choice head. I seen them
makin' the drive."

"That don't prove nothin'." His tongue curled slowly
along the upturned edge of the rice-paper shuck.

"Maybe it don't . . ."

"Night drive?"

"And quiet."

Frank nodded. "There wouldn't be a hundred and fifty slick ears they could pick up in the time they've been in the Basin." He held the match until it burned his fingers. "You see the brand on any of them?"

"Nope. I was told though."

"How so?"

Jim looked at him. "You figure I'd let them walk a hundred and fifty head across the old man's graze without callin' them on it?"

Frank edged the return look with a fleeting grin. "Likely not. What did they say?"

"That they was drivin' for a new outfit, seein's how the old man was goin' under."

"That all?"

"That and a little matter of business."

"Yeah?"

"Yeah. They'd tend theirs and I'd better tend my own."

"They called the brand for you though."

"JT on left hip."

"Earmark?"

"Smooth crop, left ear. Crop and half underbit, right ear."

"A JT brand don't run worth a damn over a JS."

"I said I was told. I didn't see the goddam thing."

"Maybe the Agent'll catch it on them over to Fort Apache."

"The hell!"

"Yeah, I reckon. Where's the brand book for this Basin stuff?"

"Prescott mostly."

"Nice town?"

"Nicer than most."

"Purty country along the way?"

"As any."

Frank paused, looking idly across the far level of the bench grass. "Red Boy's full of oats," he said at last.

"So's his old man," grunted his companion. "What you thinkin', Rachel?"

The half-breed never called him "Frank." Always that last little touch of Indian reserve. By equal practice and because in any event he felt it that way, Frank never called him "Fewkes."

"Just this, Jim. You ever see a finer day for a ride?"

"Can't remember one. Where to?"

"How about you?" The hard grin flickered and was gone.

"Prescott, likely."

"Great minds . . ." nodded Frank and turned for the stud corral.

"Hold up now." The half-breed's words checked him in midstride. "Prescott's a three-day ride, comin' and goin'. No use the both of us makin' it, I'm thinkin'."

Frank continued toward the bay stud's box as Jim joined him.

"How so, Jim?" he asked. He hadn't missed what he took to be an undue urgency in the lean breed's dissent. A man couldn't figure it and it put him on the alert. "You ain't rightly needed at the JS for a spell."

"It ain't that. Ed and John have gone to Globe, checkin' to see has any new outfit hit in there lately. The Gradens left me to think their new owner was a Globe man."

"What's that to do with us? What's Ed and John bein' gone to do with you and me ridin' to Prescott?" As they talked, Frank was throwing the blanket on Red Boy.

"It don't leave nobody but our old man at our place. There's women and kids there and I don't cotton to leavin' them alone just now. I smell trouble comin' in the Basin, Rachel. Best leave me make the Prescott ride."

Frank eyed him, still not figuring it. What was the half-breed afraid of? Somebody botherin' his womenfolks? Or of somebody riding with him to Prescott? The thought no sooner hit him than he was ashamed of it. Jim was his friend. The only real one he had ever had. A man didn't handle a friend that way, not even in his mind.

"All right, Jim. What you figure me to do? I owe old Stanton one, anyway. If somebody's liftin' his beef, I don't aim to sit up here and leave them lift it by their lonesomes."

Jim nodded, gesturing Basinward with his answer. "You

go down to our place and stay. Tell the old man I'll be gone three days. Tell him," he underlined it, "that Jim said you was to hang around till he got back."

"Now just a damn minute!" Genuine alarm took hold of his tall companion. "I ain't goin' down there and be around them women for three days. You listen here, Jim . . ."

"You listen." The half-breed's voice dropped. "There's somethin' stirrin' in the Basin, Rachel. You can spend them three days lookin' under the dust it's raisin'. You know what I mean?"

"The Graden place."

"Yeah. They'll be the rest of the week gettin' back from Fort Apache. Likely you'll have plenty of time."

Seeing the way it was going, Frank broke the conversation abruptly. "Speakin' of time, we're wastin' it. I'll see you at your place Wednesday night."

"Good enough." The breed swung the roan. "And Rachel"—his parting words came as the big man legged up on Red Boy—"you tell the girl what we're up to. Not the old man, mind you. Just tell him what I told you. But tell the girl the rest of it. Otherwise, keep your mouth quiet."

"I ain't based my long career on makin' noise, my friend." The narrow stare matched his companion's. "And let me tell you one thing, Jim Fewkes . . ."

"Tell it," grunted the half-breed.

"It goes this way," nodded Frank. "I'll ride down and talk to your folks. That's for you. And I'll maybe mosey around the Graden place. That's for the old man. But past that and past what you find in them brand books at Prescott, I'm done. Washed. Cashed out. You hear me?"

"In the words of my mother's people, 'my ears are uncovered,'" said Jim Fewkes. It was his first reference to his Indian blood. He made it with a flicking smile. But the eyes didn't move with the wide lips. "What you meanin', Rachel?"

Frank let it out softly.

"That you ain't the only one born with a big nose for trouble. And I've stuck mine in the last backhouse I mean to. You tail my drift, pardner?"

"You ain't buyin' no chips if us and the Gradens comes to a call. That it?"

"That's it," Frank said.

"It suits us." The turquoise eyes were dark and slitted, staring across the sunlit basin. "Us Fewkes takes care of our own. We was first in the Basin ahead of the Gradens. Likely we'll be last behind them."

"It figures." The dry grin came as Frank reined the bay stud for the canyon head. "Say, Jim"—the question called after the already cantering Fewkes, sounded like innocent afterthought—"what's the girl's name anyhow?"

The breed spun the roan, apparently not buying any innocence that morning. "Libby." The one word carried short and unqualified across the mesa between them.

"Libby what?" Frank was still grinning.

"Fewkes," called the breed, his voice monotone-flat. "She's a blood sister. *Remember it.*"

Frank sat staring after him until the roan disappeared past the ranchhouse rise.

It had been a warning. A man couldn't take it otherwise. But how meant? Was Jim telling him to look after the girl, or out for her? Or had it been just the way it sounded? To look neither out nor after her, but not even *at her.*

He shrugged. Play them the way they fell. Only tin-horns picked them up before they were all down. "Stretch it," he said grimly to the haunch-swinging stud. Then, grunting it, "You got a woman, you got trouble. You don't spell them no different."

Sure as signal smoke

He passed the first of the Fewkes' cabins at sunset. He knew it for young John's place, standing a short distance up the valley from that of the elder Fewkes. Jim had told him Ed ordinarily stayed here with John. So far the breed's story was tallying. At any rate Ed and John weren't home, and from the sign they hadn't been for a couple of days.

Minutes later he was checking the bay stud in a heavy stand of scrub uptrail of the main Fewkes' place. The Fewkes were not the ones to encourage callers. His friendship with Jim had not yet broadened to bring in the rest of the family. Accordingly, he hadn't been this close to the clan's headquarters before. He studied it now, frowningly.

The ranch lay in a crescent of low ridges, the open side of the crescent to the southeast and downvalley. There were three buildings: a one-room ranchhouse, a cook shack of equal size standing a scant ten yards from the main house, and a hogshed better built than either of the other structures and standing as close to the cook shack as that building did to the ranchhouse. One thing was sure, the Fewkes were "hog poor."

The beaked ridge of Frank's nose wrinkled ever so slightly. It was a big, patrician, stockman's nose. A cowman's nose and a horseman's. If there was one thing a real hand hated to see more than he did sheep, it was pigs. And Frank was seeing pigs. Twenty of them at least. Big black and spotted sows, pink-teated and grossly fat, their jaws champing strings of ropey slaver as they swung their snouts against the evening breeze seeking the whereabouts of the new man smell; and little oil-shiny porkers, squealing a nervous echo to their slobbering dams' unrest; and a razorbacked, coarse-haired herd boar, honing his tushes with quick blubberly chops as he moved forward ahead of the grunting sows.

They had him spotted now. He shook off his disgust of them. Deliberately, he jumped the bay stud into them, cursing their ugly, squealing resentment of him and the bay. He had time, in the second before the cabin door slid open, to see the rest of the spread.

Two ancient valley oaks stood in front of the main cabin and cook shack; another beside the hogshed. Backing the oaks, a snaggled necklace of half-dead cottonwoods hung in desolate silence. A spider web of broken equipment, broken-wheeled wagonbeds, rust-caked moldboard plows, staggering hayricks and bladeless mowers, lay over the whole place.

"You'll be wantin' somethin', Mister?"

It had to be Old Man Fewkes. You couldn't miss that. Tall, rail-thin, gaunt-shouldered, he was as handsome in his leathery, aged way as any of the boys. And if you couldn't see the blood tie in the way he looked at you, you could easily tell it in the way he handled his old-model Winchester.

"I'm Rachel . . ." he began.

"We know that," Old John Fewkes interrupted him. "What you want?"

"Jim sent me. Said to tell you he'd be gone three days. Said maybe you'd have me around till he gets back. Seein's Ed and John are away."

"They're always figurin' their old man needs a wet nurse. Get down." There was nothing of peevishness in the old man's observation. Watching him, Frank saw the little wrinkle at the eye corners when he said it, and nodded quietly to himself. He and Old Man Fewkes would likely get on.

He dropped the bay's reins, following Fewkes toward the cabin. At the door, the old man stood aside, holding it for him. Frank hesitated, glancing at him.

"Age before beauty," he said soberly.

"It's a fact." The older man let it come slowly behind another eye-corner wrinkle. He went in ahead of him.

The Fewkes womenfolk were no different from their men, gaunt, watchful-eyed, slow with their words.

"It's all right, Lyd," the old man said to the eldest of the three. "It's Rachel. The boy as rode for old Stanton last year. Jim's friend."

Lydia Fewkes was tall, fair-skinned, gray-haired. When she spoke, Frank remembered Old Man Stanton telling him she was an Englishwoman, married to the senior Fewkes only the year before.

"This is Mary, John's wife," said the old man. "Lyd's girl." The second woman, a pale-haired replica of her mother, smiled nervously.

"And Bess, she's Ed's woman." Bess Fewkes looked at

him. There was no smile and no nod. She was a dark woman, looking more like a man would expect, more like a Fewkes. And acting like one.

The supper was put on the table: fried fatback, heavy corn pone, home-jarred turnip greens, stale backstove coffee. They ate in silence, Frank shortly following the old man back out into the dusk of the ranchyard. They built their smokes and sat in continued silence over the first, deep lungfuls.

Presently the old man hawked and spit.

"Likely Jim told you about the girl."

"He give me a message for her."

"None for me, eh?"

"He said you wouldn't need one," lied Frank. "Where is she?"

"Be along directly, I allow."

"It don't match up," said the big rider, watching him.

"It don't?" He was being watched back.

"Her not bein' in. Jim said there was some trouble here in the Basin. Or the smell of it anyway."

"Jim smells further than most. We ain't got any trouble. Lib's upvalley to Stanton's, buyin' a mare. She's horse-crazy, that girl. Some plain crazy besides, I reckon."

"How you mean?" He asked the question idly, his main thought on the girl's interest in horses.

"She don't like it here. Hates the loneliness, she says. Don't see the rest of it. She's a bit-tosser. Pulls natural agin any steady hand. Don't curb worth a damn and never did. Course, she's just only comin' seventeen. Might settle down later on. I doubt it. Anyhow, I'd say anybody that wouldn't call this Basin God's front yard is a little crazy. Wouldn't you, Mister?"

"I reckon I would." His companion looked past the cottonwoods to where the coming moon was tipping the Mazatzals. "How about you, old man?"

"Comin' to me, I see it this way. What more could a man want? Or a woman either? I been thirty years on bed-cozy terms with trouble and I'm heartsick of it. Here we got peace and we got quiet. A man can stretch his elbows and not punch nobody in the ribs doin' it. We got our hams and bacon and a few head of cattle. You can shoot fresh meat, deer or antelope, from the backdoor of the cook shack. The boys are growed and they got their own families comin' nice. We all got wood and water and grass. The 'Paches ain't been in the Basin since '79 and it ain't likely they'll come again."

The old man paused like a man will when he's taken with the thought he's already said too much.

"Now where's your trouble in all that?" he asked defiantly. "Goddammit, Jim's as crazy as the girl."

"Maybe," nodded Frank. "How about the Gradens?"

"What about the Gradens?" He asked it too quickly.

"Nothin'," Frank covered. "Nothin' at all. Just wondered how you got on with them, seein's they're new and all."

"There's no trouble with the Gradens," said the old man. "They're both good boys, hard workers too. Don't talk much neither. Not as much as some . . ."

"I hear you, old man." He grinned the acknowledgment. "A man gets lonely up on the bench."

"Talk brings trouble. It brings it quicker than anything else. I'm goin' in." Frank sensed the quick resentment, wondered at it even as the old man was turning for the door. "You can set out here. The girl will be along directly."

The door had scarcely closed on the yellow lamplight when the soft voice hit him from behind. He came off the bench, turning and crouching.

"Jumpy, aren't you, stranger?"

He loosened his muscles, feeling the thrill of the satiny voice, trying to make out the shadowy form behind it. "I didn't hear you comin'. You don't make much noise, girl."

"Oh hell, Mister," her easy naturalness slid over the word pleasantly, "an Indian never makes any noise. You ought to know that by now."

"I ought," he said, the continuing nerve tingle of the low voice racing up his spine. "You *sound* enough like Jim. Move out and let's see how you look."

That was the first time he heard the laugh. The throaty melody of it was enough to put the short hairs of a man's neck straight on end. And back of the laugh came the girl, stepping into the patch of light from the cabin window.

Then if the laugh hadn't already done it for you, that first look did. If a man's breath wasn't coming short now, it never would.

"My God . . ." was all Frank Rachel could manage.

For the rest of it he just stood there, the hard squeeze of his belly pushing the held breath between his teeth.

In the unflowered parlance of the range, Libby Fewkes would have been called "a looker." In the stricter sense of dramatic fact, she would have to have been called savagely beautiful.

A tall girl, she was as dark of skin and hair as her brothers. A man couldn't see her eye color there in the lampwash, but from the slant and flash of them he could guess they were as brilliantly turquoise as Jim's. Her features, too, were softened by the lamplight, but even so you could make out the straight, short line of the nose, the full cut of the curving mouth, the clean angularity of the high cheekbones and the bold tilt of the provocative chin.

She laughed again now, the wide lips dark and glistening over the flash of the white teeth.

"You're doing your share of the looking, Mister. Just let me know when you're done."

"I'm done," he said, letting his muscles ease with the last of the held breath. "Your turn, I reckon." With the grin, he moved forward, facing her in the lamplight.

She didn't answer, just looked. He held still for it, cursing inwardly. Damn it to hell, the way she ran those slant eyes up a man made him feel he was standing there naked as a G-string reservation buck. And about as nervous.

"Well? Seen enough?" He tried putting an ease into it he didn't feel.

"Too much, Mister." There was that heat-lightning smile again. "I don't like them so big. I want a man more of a piece."

Smile or no smile, it set a man back. It was said in a level way that made it sound like it wasn't meant to come with a smile in the first place.

"You always get what you want?" He couldn't keep the belligerence out of it.

"I aim to mostly, Mister. How about you?"

He hadn't meant anything except did she always get her

way about everything. Not about anything special. He had
been thinking for the most part about what her old man
had said about her being headstrong. But her return question hadn't meant but one thing. Him and her. She was
calling him straight out. No man could miss it.

"I don't want much," he said flatly. Her boldness rattled a man. Made him bristle where he hadn't wanted to.
"I ain't lost no women, if that's what you mean. Leastways, no little kids."

He meant it nasty and he said it that way. It had just occurred to him that Old Man Fewkes had said she was only
coming seventeen.

She stepped close into him then, the wash of the lamplight limning the wanton mold of her body and the wicked
upturn of her lips. Even in the warm half dark there was
no mistaking the invitation. No misreading the snaky
weave of those hips as she moved toward him, nor of the
deliberate backflinging of the shoulders which brought
the big, firm tilt of the breasts suddenly hard forward and
upward beneath the thin cling of the cotton shirt.

He came into her, one long arm sweeping behind her to
pull the weave of the hips into his, his free hand sliding
up and across the thrusting breasts to bury itself in the
tumbled blackness of her hair.

She let herself come into the embrace like a hungry
flame into long-dry wood, her dark head turning to seek
the eagerness of his lips. Then, as his wide mouth met
hers, she twisted away from him with a low animal cry.

He saw the flash of the clean teeth and felt the quick
pain of them against his neck. He saw, and felt too, the
ringing slap of her open hand slashing across his cheek.
Then he was hearing the throaty laugh across the lamplit
stillness between them.

"You shouldn't play with little kids, Mister. You're too
big!"

With that she was gone, the soft closing of the cabin
door leaving him standing dumbstruck and alone in the
Arizona night.

The lamp in the window faded quickly and went out.
He stood a moment more, then turned away with an angry curse.

A man could not yet know what kind of trouble was
building in the Basin for the rest of them. But he already
knew the cut and color of his own.

Just as sure as Chiricahua signal smoke, he had been
right in the first place.

Trouble for Frank Rachel was spelled Libby Fewkes.

The iron in the fire

He rode slowly, following the main trail up
Cherry Creek toward Parker's Store, his thoughts far from
Tom and Judd Graden and Old Jim Stanton's disappear-
ing cattle. His mouth still burned from the half kiss Libby
Fewkes had torn away from it. The lean pinch was still in
his belly and the feel of trouble lay heavily upon him.

He scowled, the twist of the expression runnning short
and ugly across his lips.

If a man truly meant to ride wide around the bad water
in this well he had better begin by laying his trail as far
and fast away from that girl as his horse could carry him.
He grunted with the nod which cemented the thought.

He would scout the Graden place and that would be
the end of it. He would wait and have his talk with Jim
when the latter got back from Prescott and then ride for
Apache Bench and stay there. A man needn't have ridden
close herd on trouble as long as he had, to know the near
feel of it.

The store was just ahead now. He threw the stud off
the trail, kicking him up the low ridge which flanked the
Graden place to the south. At the top of the rise, he
checked the bay, his scowl deepening. Yonder there in the
moonlight, not a quarter-mile from the crossroads and
the store, lay Judd and Tom's spread.

It wasn't much, even for a two-bit homestead: a one-
room ranchhouse, open-faced hayshed, bare pole corral,

water tank and cook shack. There was no stock in the corral and none wandering loose. The cabin stood dark.

He clucked to the stud, sending him down the ridge. Swinging past the cabin he brought him up at the hayshed. If there was anything to be found, it wouldn't be in the house. From the size of the firebed centering the corral, a man knew where to look. Considerable hide had been burnt here, and not too long ago. If he was to find anything to go with that fire spot, it would be in or around the shed. Likely they'd used a running iron. But if they hadn't . . .

They hadn't.

He found the iron in the saddle corner of the shed, thrown in among a pile of old wire and corral poles. His finger ran the cold rim of the brand, quickly tracing the crude turns of the home-forged metal. The scowl faded under the frost of the grin.

Well, they hadn't lied to Jim about one part of it anyway. A man could at least hand them that. What he couldn't get, though, was how come they had left it laying around in the wide open? Either they were powerful dumb, which didn't figure, or they didn't give a damn, which might. Still, it left a man wondering if maybe they didn't have another, better reason; like thinking they didn't have anything in particular to hide, or nobody in particular to hide it from.

He had come up figuring to check if they had been doing any recent branding, and hoping perhaps to find some sign that they had. He sure hadn't thought to find the iron though—not, at least, a regular brand iron like this one.

He shrugged, swinging up on Red Boy.

"Hike it, hoss. Beginner's luck, old son. We got the one-spot to an ace-high straight workin' here. Just wait'll we play it on friend Jim."

Ed and John rode in late Tuesday afternoon; Jim, at dusk, Wednesday. Frank hadn't seen the girl in the meantime and hadn't said more than six civil words to Ed and John. He had talked with Old John Fewkes a little, enough to convince him that if his boys were in any way tied in with the Graden outfit, the old man knew nothing about it. Nevertheless, the suspicion grew in Frank's mind. The two places were only ten miles apart. The half-Indian brothers weren't the breed not to keep a slant eye on neighbors that close. And all of them, Fewkes and Gradens alike, had ridden for Old Jim Stanton at the same time. There was a dead calf somewhere in this deal and a man didn't like the stink of it.

He hadn't mentioned the iron or his midnight trip to the Graden ranch to any of them. Nor had he given Jim's message for Libby to any of them. But with Jim's return, the pot opened fast.

After the silent supper had been wolfed down, the half-breed motioned to him and Ed and John, and went outside. With the Durham spilling carefully into the cupped rice papers, the game got under way.

"What'd you find in Globe?" Jim struck his match, holding it while his answer came from Ed.

"Nothin', not a damn thing." The elder brother made his light, put it to his shuck. Frank watched him, wondering if there hadn't been a touch of defiance in the reply. If Jim caught it, he didn't play to it.

"It figures," he grunted. "I done a little better."

"How so, Jim?" Where Ed's answer had been touchy, young John's seemed more on the apprehensive side. The boy worshipped Jim though he sided more with Ed. Frank had noticed the paradox but had figured he understood it. Jim wasn't the one you got cozy with, not even if you were his favorite kid brother.

"This so," said Jim, his answer ignoring John and going to Ed. "There's a JT registered in Prescott all right. And not to no Globe man. *It's to Judd and Tom Graden.*"

"That's a damn lie!" Ed's denial broke heatedly.

Jim moved into him in the dark. "I said it. Don't call me."

"Nobody's callin' you, goddam it!" Ed's voice was still high. "It just ain't possible."

"I reckon you know better than that, Ed." His words were still flat and soft. "You too, boy," he added to John.

"What the hell you sayin', Jim?" A man couldn't miss

the anxiety in the youngster's voice now. "It ain't addin' up."

"It's addin' up all right, and I don't like what it's addin' up to."

"Meanin' what?" Ed's demand was blunt.

"You tell me," said Jim softly. "I come in past Old Man Stanton's this afternoon. He told me a thing or three."

"Such as what?"

"Such as you never went to Globe, neither one of you."

"Oh, for Christ's sake, Jim . . ."

"Don't 'Jim' me, Ed." The interruption was still low. "Stanton tailed that bunch of beeves the Gradens was drivin' for Fort Apache. He seen you and John ride in to side their fire, Monday noon."

"All right, we didn't go to Globe." Ed's voice cooled out and dropped with the shrug. "What the hell was the use of it? You know there ain't nobody in Globe ownin' for them. Me and John wanted to see that brand for ourselves —in the daylight. After all, you never seen it and was only told."

"You're lyin', Ed."

"By God!"

"You're lyin' and I'm callin' you." Again the interruption held its monotone flatness. "I wasn't the one that knowed there wasn't nobody in Globe ownin' for Judd and Tom. You was."

"You'll eat that, by God!" Ed's crouch and set were quick, but not quick enough. Frank was between them, the move too swift to follow.

"Wait up, Ed. I got cards in this deal too. Jim's called and I'm standin' pat. You can kick over the table or throw your hand in. You too, youngster." The dark nod went to John. "Lay them down or make your plays. Just don't neither one of you try to draw out on me, you hear?"

"I pass," said Ed, stepping back slowly. "Jim's bluffin' and you're holdin' deuces."

"John?"

Young Fewkes stood silent.

"Last chance, boy. Either we lay them straight up or it's no shuffle. You boys are all the friends I've got, but I ain't backin' no play to sandbag Old Man Stanton. How many you want?"

"I'm out, Frank." John dropped his eyes with the low admission.

"By God, boy!" Ed moved menacingly toward him.

"Don't crowd me, Ed." The youngster's resolve held, his voice steadying. "I said I'm throwin' in. If what Jim says is true, the bastards have crossed us. We ain't got no move left but to side with our own blood. Jim's a right to know anyways. I always said it."

"Jim's a right to know what?" demanded the brother in question. "What's goin' on here, Ed? Talk out."

"Yeah, Ed," Frank's drawl eased. "We got our ears uncovered."

Ed eyed him a minute, then turned to his brother, his questions open and steady.

"Jim, you certain that JT was recorded to Judd and Tom? Not nobody else with them?"

"Not nobody. Who was you expectin'?" asked Jim acidly. "Old Man Stanton?"

"Nope. Me and John."

The answer came as easy and uncovered as though he were admitting he had forgotten to close the backhouse door. Jim and Frank looked at him a long three drags. It was the latter, finally, who flipped his cigarette away.

"You was in it with them. Liftin' the old man's stuff on a deal to register it four ways in the brand book."

"More or less," shrugged Ed. "The registerin' part of it anyways. We wasn't liftin' just the old man's stuff though. We wasn't choosy. Anybody's would do, so long as it wasn't deep-burnt. Me and John run the stuff in. Judd and Tom done the blottin' over to their home place."

"I might have knowed it"—it was Jim Fewkes' soft voice —"you was cozy with them all summer long. I never liked the bastards. They ain't cattlemen."

"They will be," said Ed easily. "That Judd, he's slick enough. But Tom's the cute one. Give time, they'll hog the Basin, you see. Me and John figured to throw in with them and hog right along on equal shares. What the hell would you have done, if you had got onto their game?"

Jim shook his head. "I wouldn't have took no cut off of

the old man. He's treated us white where half the ranchers
in this valley wouldn't ask us to get down and come in for
coffee."

"You're breakin' my heart, Jim."

Jim didn't call the irony. Cattle-stealing, just as such,
wasn't the point. They had, all of them—Frank Rachel no
doubt included—at one time or another swung the wide
loop. It was Old Jim Stanton that made the difference. He
went on thinking out loud.

"He's been good to Libby, givin' her those mares for
half what they're worth. He's kept us on and paid us where
there wasn't work enough for a green-belly dude, let alone
three full hands. It don't add, Ed. Not even for you, let
alone John."

"It don't add for John, not no more, Jim." The youngster meant it, Frank decided. "We figured we could pay
him back one way or another after we got started. There
would be ways to do that without him ever catchin' on.
Now it looks like we ain't even goin' to be able to do that,
and I'm done with it."

"Ed?" Jim said to the older brother.

"All right. Me, too. Anyways on the old man's stuff.
That make you happy?"

"Don't get smart with me, Ed."

"I ain't. Look here, Jim, it's different with you than it
is with John and me. We got kids comin' along where you
ain't. We thought we could take the cream off this Fort
Apache bunch and buy in a few head of good she-stuff of
our own. A man don't like to stay hog-poor when he's got
young ones comin' up."

"I'll talk to the old man," said Jim dully. "It won't
make it right, but leastways he'll know it ain't us Fewkes
if he keeps on missin' stuff."

"Yeah," nodded Ed slowly, "and I'll talk to Judd and
Tom. The old man's stuff or not, I'm aimin' to get my cut
on that Fort Apache bunch."

"We'll talk to them," amended John. "I'm real curious
about that JT over to Prescott."

"Don't forget what happened to the cat," grunted
Frank, moving through the dark toward the saddled form
of Red Boy.

"What cat?" Young John's query showed idle interest, along with a backwoods lack of knowledge anent nosey felines.

"The curious one," nodded the big rider, heeling the stud around. "He got kilt."

"Go to hell," grinned the younger man. "I've shot my share of cats, Mister. Them Graden toms don't scare me none."

Frank pulled the stud in. His offside hand slid down and under his knee, easing the slender branding iron free. "Think it over," he advised softly. "And here's something to think it over on."

With the words, he tossed the iron toward them. He saw it arc and turn in the moonlight, and heard the muffled, metal ring of it as it struck the thick dust of the yard. He waited only until Jim reached to pick it up, and lit the match to examine it. Then he turned the stud away.

Passing the ragged cottonwoods fronting the darkened cabin, he looked back.

The guttering light of the match still lit the three lean faces peering above it, still lingered harshly along the crude twist of the iron's handwrought JT.

The silence of Dry Canyon

The following Sunday brought no blue quail whistles from Dry Canyon. Another week passed, and another. Still the canyon was silent and Frank waited no more for the familiar signal. It was clear now that the split over the lifting of the JS cattle was going to cut between him and Jim as surely as it did between Ed and John and the Gradens.

The more he thought about it, the deeper he got mired. And the more positive he became that he wanted no further part of any of it.

He had ridden with a running iron under his own stir-

rup fenders too many times to feel any lasting upset over
the way Ed and John had treated Stanton. He had been
pleased enough to find out Jim was in the clear, for tough
and hard as he was the half-breed wasn't the kind you'd
expect to bite your hand while he was eating out of it. But
the rest of it had figured normal enough. Half the cattle
spreads in the West were started just that way, by the
hands stealing the owner blind and taking his pay for the
privilege of robbing him. Likely in his day Old Jim Stanton
himself had slapped a brand on one or two beeves that
had never sucked his own she-stock. It was the way things
went, that was all. And with he and Jim having called Ed
and John on the deal, and then backed them down to
where they had agreed to leave the old man's stuff alone
in the future, he had done what he could short of calling
for more cards.

And he had no intention of calling for any more. He
had meant what he said about keeping out of the Basin
and away from the girl.

As far as his part of that resolve went, it was good
enough. But men do not deal with women like Libby
Fewkes on their own terms. With a lady in the game, the
deal passes. The fourth Sunday following his showdown
with her brothers, Frank Rachel found that out.

He was cleaning Red Boy's box and the big stud was
running free in the corral. Suddenly the stallion's whistle
shrilled fiercely. Hayfork in hand, Frank stepped to the
box door.

His eyes swept to the head of Dry Canyon, following the
point of Red Boy's curious muzzle. Shortly, three mares
hazed by a single rider on a classy sockfoot sorrel stumbled
out of the rocky defile and headed in across the bench. But
it wasn't the mares nor the class of the rider's mount which
narrowed Frank's eyes.

He had a long time to look while the little string trotted
forward. He didn't waste any of it.

If a man had thought that girl looked like something in
the Fewkes' cabin lamplight, he had learned far better by
the time she had brought her mares across an open mile
of Apache Bench daylight.

She looked like Jim all right, just as he had thought she

would. She was dark and tall like him, had his turquoise
eyes and sat a horse the same Indian-straight way. After
that, you forgot all about Jim Fewkes or her blood kinship
with him or anything else. You were just looking at her
and not believing what you saw.

She was dressed in faded Levis, Apache boots and a cotton workshirt. Clear across the bench you could see the
boldness of her body. But at that distance you still had a
little time to mark the flashing beauty of the dark-skinned,
light-eyed face. When she got to the ranchhouse and turned
past it to head for you and the corrals, your time for the
face suddenly ran out. Watching her drop the reins and
swing down off her pony, a man could only step back into
the shadows of the box, hoping she hadn't seen him yet,
and then just stand there and watch that body.

She walked slowly toward the stud corral, her eyes on
the nervous pacing and head-flinging of the bay stallion.
Frank felt the warning pull-in of his belly, tried to clamp
off the quick tremor of his jaw muscles. It was no use. A
man saw what he saw and his belly went right on pulling
in.

She had the shirt open three buttons down and far less
knowing eyes than Frank's would have widened to the
revelation thus afforded. Except for the laundered-thin
fray of the shirt, she was naked under there. There was no
mistaking the firmness of those breasts, nor the rising
points of them where they pressed their fullness outward
against the soft cloth.

Under the skin-tight cling of the Levis she was narrow-
waisted and, a man could guess, slim-legged. But those
hips were a full woman's. Big, deep-curved, cleanly carved,
sleek as new satin. Yet bold and saucy and sharp-cut as
statue bronze. The shift and play of them put more hell
to work inside a man that he could hope to handle.

Frank fought down the dark impulse, broke his gaze
from the girl. He put his broad back to the box wall and
closed his eyes. He knotted his big hands on the smooth
hickory of the hayfork handle, the cordings of his face
muscles twitching and running to the fierce set of his jaw.
A man should be ashamed, even a man like him. She was
only a kid for all the wanton face and body of her, and

she was Jim's sister, his *little* sister. Where in God's name was a man's pride that he could be peep-tomming like this! Sure, he was woman hungry. Any man in his place would be. But not this woman. Not her, by God. Not ever . . .

When he stepped from the box, the dark blood had ebbed away and the set of the jaw eased. The peculiar amber lightness of his eyes had cooled and the brief grin was lifting the wide mouth corners.

"Hello, Libby." He hadn't meant to call her that. It had just slipped out.

She turned, smiling and leaning easily back against the fence. When she replied in kind, it wasn't any slip.

"Hello, Frank. You ease around pretty quiet yourself."

He knew she was talking about the way he had jumped when she'd come up on him in the dark outside the Fewkes' cabin. Somehow, it nettled him.

"You'd best come clear of that fence, girl. The stud'll bite."

"So will I." She didn't move and again he knew what she meant. His hand went involuntarily to the side of his neck where she had bitten him that night. But now he was grinning.

"Yeah, I know. All the same, move out from there. He don't like women."

"He'll like me."

"You're a woman, ain't you?"

"He's a male, isn't he?"

"Meanin' what?"

"Man or studhorse, where's the difference? He's a male."

"Meanin' he'll kitten down for you, is that it?" Frank asked sarcastically.

"Likely," she shrugged. "Let's see . . ."

"Get the hell down from that fence!" His warning was too late. She was up and over the top pole and dropping into Red Boy's jealous domain before he could move to stop her.

He leapt for the fence, yelling and waving his hat at the advancing stud. He got as far as the top rail and there he sat, dropping his jaw along with his useless hat. That damn horse, that would likely kill any human other than himself who came up to him afoot, was nuzzling and head-bunting

Libby Fewkes as though she had handfed him off his dam's
bag. He followed her back to the fence as meek and mince-
footed as any bottle-raised bell mare.

In spite of his disgust, a man had to admit this girl had
more to her than a fair face and a fancy body. She had, for
one damn sure thing, more guts than a Government mule.
And for another, a rarely wonderful way with horses. His
grin broadened as he handed her up onto the fence beside
him.

"I taught him better, honest to God. You got to believe
that, girl."

"I believe it all right," she said coolly, "but there isn't
anything you could teach him that I couldn't handle with
my eyes shut."

"I'll buy that too," he nodded, returning her level stare.
"What brings you up here, girl? It ain't like you, seein's
you're after all a Fewkes."

"What the hell's that got to do with it?" As with the
previous time at the cabin, the profanity slipped out with
easy naturalness. "With you and me, I mean."

"Nothin', I reckon. Only that I had allowed the boys
wouldn't set still for you mixin' with me after the other
night."

"Ed and John and me aren't close. It's Jim that counts
with me, and he thinks more of you than any man alive.
Though why he should, beats me."

"Me, too." Frank's voice was thoughtful. "I ain't never
had a friend before, a man I mean. I sure do miss Jim."

"Why don't you go down and see him then? You afraid
of Ed and John? Or maybe so, the Gradens?"

He looked at her. She caught the sudden chill in the
pale eyes. "Yeah, scared to death," he said slowly. Then,
the eyes warming, he added, "He ain't been to see me,
that's why. I figured he was done with me for callin' Ed
and John on liftin' Old Man Stanton's cattle."

"You figured crazy. Jim's half-Indian, remember that.
If you're his friend, you're his friend for life. It's that
way with Indians. But he's proud too, that's more of the
Indian part of it. Blind-proud, Mister. He'd die sooner
than come up here as long as he thought you mightn't
want him."

He was glad to hear about Jim, mighty glad. Right now though, a man couldn't get his mind off of Jim's sister.

"How's about half-Indian women?" he grinned. "They the same as the men? About their friends?"

"I don't know," said the girl, a sudden intensity shooting the turquoise eyes. "I'm like you. I never had a friend."

The way she said it and the look she sent with it started the dark blood into his face again. He swung down off the fence.

"You didn't come up here to tell me Jim still wants to be friends. What brung you? Them mares?"

"Likely . . ."

She had slipped off the fence and stood facing him, her face turned up to his, her lips curving to the slow smile.

He stepped back and turned for the box. He was getting angry now. Every look and word she gave him seemed to mean just one thing. If she didn't get the hell out of there . . .

"I don't want your mares," he said thickly. "Get them and yourself out of here, you hear me, girl?"

He was at the box with the order, pausing in the opened door, still fighting his anger and the other, uglier feeling that was rising in him.

"I said you hear me, girl? Get out of here. Get away from me. And stay away!"

She moved up to him, still smiling.

"The mares are for Red Boy. I want to leave them. I'll come back for them or you can bring them down. That's all right, isn't it?"

"It's all right," he said. "I'll bring them down. Now you fork that sorrel and ride. Ride fast."

With the warning, he swung his back to her and stepped into the box. Seizing the hayfork, he thrust it savagely into the opened bale, shoved the fragrant hay in a spreading tumble over the clean floor. Shouldering another bale from the low loft, he broke its wire and dumped it upon the first, working it around with the fork. He gave her time to be well started, then cursed and dropped the fork.

A man couldn't blame himself for taking one more look at her. It would be safe now. She'd be well across the bench, maybe almost to the canyon—the thought broke in midstride as he came around. She was still standing there.

His eyes widened and he stepped back, lips twisting, heart pounding wildly.

She moved toward him through the open door, out of the glare of the sun and into the gloom of the box. She stopped, standing so close to him that the perfumed tumble of the black hair grazed the hard angle of his jaw, so close that the heated, fresh, woman smell of her came up and around him and over him, smothering him with its thick excitement.

"Frank . . ."

"Damn you, girl, what do you want of a man?" His voice sounded muffled and strange. It wasn't his, yet he knew it was coming from him. "I can't have you, you know that. Get away from me! You hear me, girl!"

"Frank . . ." The slender softness of the hands slid up his chest. The moving hips came forward with the reach of the arms. "Frank . . . finish that kiss!"

"Oh, goddam you, Libby . . ."

"You want the rest of it, don't you, Frank? All of it?"

He seized her, pulling her into him, his clean teeth driving into the curving turn of her shoulder. She writhed savagely with the embrace, her own teeth finding his neck. The deep hay came up and around them, her body twisting as it did, her voice whispering thickly.

"Frank, oh Frank! God . . . God . . ."

He twisted with her, pinning the frantic surge of her hips with his, smashing her gasping lips apart, hungering for her mouth, cruel hands buried in the tumble of her loosened hair. She writhed away, crying now, the hot tears flooding silently. The movement broke the last tenuous cling of the shirt buttons. His hands slid down, ripping the rest of the flimsy garment back and away. Her own hands, rough with haste, leapt past his, easing the tight prison of the Levis, freeing herself from them.

He heard the throaty cry of the muffled voice. "Now, Frank! Oh, now, now . . ."

His answer was a wordless growl, deep, brutal, primitive; and ugly with a savage hunger, two long years in the fasting.

And many a similar puncher

   He bred the mares in the stud corral to make
sure of them, putting the first of them in the day following
Libby's visit. She took the stud at once and he turned her
loose to run with his own mares.

Two days later he put the second mare to Red Boy and
got another good coupling. The third mare turned fractious
and a man could see she had quit horsing. He tried her
again the next day, Saturday, but she was going out fast
and nearly kicked the stud's head off when he went nosing
around her. Unless a man wanted to sit around waiting
for her to come in again, he was done with her right then.
Frank had better ideas on what he wanted to do with his
next thirty days.

Sunday, sunrise, found him hazing the two bred mares
for the canyon head, riding one of his own mares and
leaving the third of Libby's mounts behind in the bench
pasture with the stud and the Apache Ranch mares. Red
Boy could get her on his own sweet time. That was his
problem and his pleasure, not Frank Rachel's.

He pulled Stanton's JS by noon. There he watered the
mares and had coffee and a short talk with the old man.

Apparently, things had been moving fast in the Basin,
particularly as of the week just past.

First off, about a month ago—that would put it right
after he had gone back to the bench—Ed and John had
gone to the Gradens for their showdown. What the old
man knew, he had gotten from the close-mouthed Jim,
who still rode up to help him out week-ends. The other
brothers had come back from the Graden place to report a
stand-off. Judd and Tom had refused outright to split on
the Fort Apache sale, backing their play with four new
hands.

The hands were new only as hands. As Basin residents, they were something else again.

They were the four Bivins brothers who, with their father, "Old Mark" Bivins, had for three years been running a big loop spread in the upper box of Canyon Creek. The Bivins boys were Texas gunmen and open rustlers. They had never worked a solitary day for any of the honest ranchers in the Basin and their appearance as Graden hands simply pointed up the rumor that Judd and Tom were intending to take in the valley grass from wall to wall.

Remembering Ed Fewkes' hard-eyed prediction of just this intent, Frank nodded to himself.

From what little he had seen of the Graden boys at the JS last fall, he couldn't figure them for big ranchers. Or you could spell that "rustlers" if you had a mind to. Either way, they didn't figure. But a man could be wrong, and sometimes almighty bad wrong. He would take a second look at Judd and Tom Graden.

All thoughts of Judd and Tom went quickly under as the old man's continuing words picked up the track of another Graden, one Frank had never heard of, let alone seen.

"Name's Garth," scowled Stanton. "Big devil and a slick dresser. He ain't a cowman, you can lay. Rides a blood horse and wears his guns tied down."

"Where's he been all this time? I thought there was just Judd and Tom and that kid brother of theirs." He was referring to young Billy Graden, a nineteen-year-old boy lately arrived in the Basin.

"So did everybody else," grunted the old man. "This new one ain't a brother, it seems. Some kind of a cousin or somethin'. Anyways, he don't look like the other two, nor like young Billy neither."

"They're sure gatherin' the clan," nodded Frank. "What's this one look like? Just in case I should ever run onto him in a dark trail."

"Big, like I said. Not as big as you, but beefier. Not fat now, boy. Just beef big and bone hard. Looks to be maybe a gambler or well-off cattle buyer. The kind of fresh-scrubbed buzzard you'd expect to see up to Dodge or Abilene in the old days. The ones that was always waitin' for the boys to come in off the trail so's they could clean them of their pay or fleece them out of their cows, either way they wanted it. You know the kind."

"I've seen a few," said Frank. "What's this one done that he's gettin' talked about so much? Shot up Charley Parker's store or run off with somebody's best girl?"

The old man didn't return the short grin.

"He ain't shot up the store," he said slowly.

"Meanin' what?" Frank was eyeing him.

"Meanin' somebody's best gal maybe. I dunno." He eyed the big rider back with the slow statement.

"By God, not Libby!"

"Who else, son?" He frowned, seeing the quick, bad light shooting the pale eyes. "There ain't no other best gal in the Basin, is there?"

Frank stood up. "Where's he at?" he asked softly. "Right now, I mean."

"How the hell should I know?" Stanton let it come as though he were riled-up at its unimportance, hoping thus to throw the Apache Bench rancher off the track. "He ain't in my tally book. And besides, boy, you lemme tell you somethin', you hear?"

"Tell it, old man. I got a Graden to look up."

"Just what I mean," nodded Stanton. "Now you look here, boy. You stay clear of them Gradens and them Fewkeses, both. There's only one good one in the whole bunch of them, and that's Jim."

"Meanin'?"

"Meanin' just what I said."

"What about Libby?"

"I didn't say nothin' about Libby."

"You said Jim was the only good one. Don't put off on me, old man. Where's that leave Libby?"

Stanton didn't miss the menace in the soft question, and he didn't want to say what he had to. He liked this big pale-eyed boy. He liked him a lot. But sometimes a man is called to talk. This was one of those times.

"It leaves her out," he said quietly, and having said it he stood up.

He saw the muscles twitch and run along the lean jaw,

saw the sudden clenching of the big fists, watched the pale
eyes flare and then go dead.

"Don't you say that to me, old man, you hear?"

"I hear, boy, but I ain't listenin'."

"By God, you'd better listen!"

"No," Stanton nodded slowly, the faded blue of his
eyes holding the big rider's. "You're the one that better
listen, boy. I'm an old man and I'm soon done with this
Basin. There's hell-to-pay comin' due here. I'm not goin' to
be around to settle with the devil. But, boy," he paused,
"you will be, if you don't listen to what I've got to say."

Frank dropped his eyes, feeling the quick shame of
having threatened the old man. "You mean about Libby?"
he asked quietly.

"About her and her kind. Will you listen, son?"

"I'll listen. I know she ain't right for me."

"She ain't right for any man, Frank, you hear me?"

It was the first time he had called him by the name since
he had come into the Basin. Frank knew by its use that he
was deadly serious. By the same token he knew what he was
going to say before he said it.

"I hear you, old salt. Get on with it."

"I ain't never married," Old Man Stanton began, his
eyes slowly running down the valley, and so, back through
the long years. "It's her kind is the reason I ain't."

He paused, letting his gaze find the top of the rim and
hold there.

"I was twenty-eight, the gal no more'n eighteen or so,
maybe younger. I never found out. Never had time to. I
met her and had her and got her weddin' promise all in
the same thirty days. I was so hot in love I couldn't think
nor work nor eat. All I could get my mind on was that
hellcat face of hers and all I wanted to get my hands on
was that twistin', white young body."

He paused again, hawked and spit into the dust, his
eyes coming back to the tall rider.

"The date was set and the ring bought, but the bells
never got around to ringin'. A gamblin' man come up the
river from the Gulf towns—this was in Texas, better'n
forty years gone . . ."

His voice trailed off with the shrug, leaving Frank to

ask irritably, "What the hell you gettin' at, old hoss? I don't foller you."

"See that you don't," he growled. "I know that kind, boy. They're all alike. They can be sixteen or twenty-six or thirty or forty. But they're of a kind and you can tell them. They've eyes that look at a man like he was naked. Every time they move it's with their butts and their breasts and their mouths in a way the average woman couldn't learn in a million years of tryin'. It's somethin' born in them and that they can't help. But it's somethin' that's poison to me and to you and to all men like us, and we can't help takin' it even though we know it's going to kill us.

"Boy," his voice slowed as the gnarled hand found the broad shoulder, "that Libby Fewkes is pure poison. If you get a good enough dose of her, you're dead."

Frank Rachel looked at him a long, slow breath. Then he swung his eyes downvalley toward the Fewkes place, letting another long silence grow.

"I'm already dead," he said at last, and turned away, not looking back and not returning the old man's hesitant wave of good-bye.

He was never to come again to the JS and was to see Old Jim Stanton only once more. The occasion of that final meeting was to be more grim than either had at the moment any reason to imagine.

The pureness of the poison

There was no one around John's cabin when he rode up. Knowing Libby ran her pet stock in the younger brother's pasture, he turned the girl's mares in with John's saddlestring and swung his own mount back up Cherry Creek toward Parker's Store. He cut away from the creek below the store, turning west.

The Graden place had changed. He checked the mare on the ridge and eased himself in the saddle.

Two big haysheds were under construction. A twenty-foot bunkhouse had been added to the main cabin and a ten-acre pasture fenced in beyond the branding corral. Clearly the rumors weren't rumors. The Gradens were spreading out.

He had just time to wonder where all the money was coming from when a man came out of the cabin below, saw him silhouetted on the ridge and ducked back through the door.

He clucked to his mount, putting her down the ridge and across the meadow toward the cabin. Outside the door he pulled up and sat waiting. Presently, Judd came out. He made no show of the Winchester, just cradled it thoughtfully.

"Howdy, Rachel. What you want?"

"One or two things. Where's Tom?"

"Maybe I'll do, try me."

"Always preferred Tom. Where's he at?"

Judd Graden looked at him. Judd was medium-sized, about Frank's age, thinly brown-haired and plain-faced homely. His broad chin receded beneath the straggle of his mustache and his eyes, peculiarly wide-set, were a pale china blue, heavily browed. He was, like Tom, a quiet, self-possessed man and sizing him now Frank saw that it was this quietness which at first fooled you about the two of them.

"Right behind you, Frank . . ."

He hadn't heard the older brother come around the ranchhouse. The latter's voice, answering the question he had put to Judd, unsettled him. He turned slowly so as not to show the fact.

"Howdy, Tom. I want to talk to you."

"Sure. Get down and come in. Where's your Western hospitality, Judd?"

"You never know about him." Judd hunched his shoulder toward Frank. "A man can't rightly tell if he's aimin' to shake hands or shoot."

"He ain't aimin' to do neither," said Frank.

Both brothers looked at him. Neither missed his meaning. "Get on down and come in," repeated Tom. "We got coffee on. I been wantin' to talk to you, too."

They went inside and pulled up chairs, Judd pouring the coffee, Frank and Tom doing the talking.

"What's on your mind, Frank?"

"Trouble."

"Well, we got plenty of that," said Tom bluntly. "You want some of it?"

Frank eyed him, not knowing just how he had meant it.

Tom was different from Judd. He was a fairly big man and roughly handsome. His hair was thick and curly and he wore it that way. He had the same bushy brows as his brother but his shadowed a pair of lake-blue eyes as cold as snow water. He was broad-jawed, big-nosed, wide-mouthed. He always looked at a man smooth-faced and quiet. Like he was looking at Frank now, waiting for his answer. Ed Fewkes had been right. Brother Tom was the one.

"I don't want none that ain't rightly mine. That's why I'm here."

"Fair enough. What's your deal?"

Tom kept it short, and a man had to like that about him. As a matter of fact, a man had to like several things about Tom Graden. It was easy to see how Ed and John had come to throw in with him. You had to watch Tom's kind. They were born to make friends and to keep them, and beyond that to use them. You didn't line up with Tom's kind unless you were ready to line up *behind* them.

"There's a big trouble buildin' in the Basin. I figure it's mainly between you and the Fewkes. I don't want no part of it. You ain't neither you nor them clean in the matter and I got my own dirt to worry about. I'm sayin' you Gradens stay shut of me, you hear?"

"What about the Fewkes, Frank?"

"They're already shut of me."

"You're sayin' you won't side with them? How about Jim? You're pretty thick, you two."

"We was," nodded Frank, "and maybe we still are. That ain't nothin' to do with you and me. I'm tellin' you to give me and my place a wide ride. You do it and I don't take sides. You don't, and you ain't begun to learn what trouble is."

"Sounds like a threat, Frank. Is that the way you mean
it?"

"It's the way."

They eyed each other. Tom Graden broke first, pushing
back his chair, gesturing in agreement.

"It's a deal, we'll leave you alone."

"You will, all right," grunted Frank. "But that ain't the
whole of my deal."

Tom said nothing, just stood waiting. Frank let him
wait, making him break again.

"What else you want?" he said finally.

"Garth Graden . . ."

He tailed it off, coming to his feet with it. Tom held
and again the silence took over. At last the latter shrugged.

"He's not here, Frank."

"Where's he at then?"

"Out ridin', I reckon."

"Alone?"

"Not likely."

"Who's he with?"

"That would be his business, wouldn't it?"

Frank moved around the table. Tom caught the slight
forward hunch of the shoulders and the way the flexing
hands dropped unconsciously toward the holsterless seams
of the Levis.

"I said who's he with?"

"I heard you."

"Well . . ."

"Make it a 'female friend.' "

"You mean a *lady*, don't you, Mister?"

Again Tom held. "If I'd have meant it, I'd have said it,"
he nodded quietly. "He's with Libby Fewkes."

Frank hit him in the belly, doubling him over. As he
came forward, he smashed at his jaw. Missing the chin
point, the blow glanced across the cheek. The big man
went into and over the rickety table. Coming back up onto
one knee, he shook his head dazedly. Frank moved in on
him, and with the move he heard the forgotten Judd's
slow voice.

"I wouldn't, Rachel . . ."

Frank came around, stepping carefully away from the

steady point of the Winchester. Stopping, he faced them both.

"That's two men have said that about the girl," he grated. "The next one gets killed. You hear me?"

"We hear you," said Judd. "Now get on your hoss and ride."

"Wait a minute." It was Tom, moving around the broken table, his hand slowly wiping the blood from his face. Frank saw the sickly white of the exposed bone beneath the slashed cheek. "We made a deal, Frank. You shouldn't have hit me but that's between you and me. The deal covers others and it still holds."

"Not for me, it don't. You see me again, either of you, and you'd better ride around. You hear?"

"I don't give a damn about you." Tom's voice was steady. "I've handled your kind before. But I don't want no more trouble in the Basin. Jim Fewkes feels the same way. We've talked, Jim and me, and we've made our deal the same as you and me just made. He keeps his bunch shut of the JT and we stay clear of them. The best you can do is get back to your ranch and stay there. Don't mess with Garth. I can handle him but I wouldn't advise you to try. There's no more certain way to turn hell loose in this valley than crossing Garth Graden. He'll be gone next week and I'm askin' you to leave him be and let him go. We don't want him here and we mean to see that he gets out."

"Is that all?"

"That's all. Take it or leave it, but think it over."

He was thinking it over. He had made a fool move and he knew it now. The kind of a move that had had him in trouble all his life. If he had had his gunbelt on, Tom Graden would have still been on the floor and staring wide. Instead, he was standing there with his face half torn off and offering him a second chance to hold on to what he had finally made for himself here in the Basin.

"I'll take some and leave some," he said at last. "Our deal stands—for you and me."

"How about Garth?"

"Garth goes," he said slowly. "And not next week."

"Frank, don't mess with him."

"Libby and me is goin' to be married." He didn't hear Tom's interruption. "Anybody thinks different, savin' her own self, has got a short hour to saddle."

"Don't push it, Frank. Garth's just horsin' around with the girl. He's not the marryin' kind, he's not after her that way. Leave him to me, I'll talk to him."

"Talk takes time. Time's what I ain't got. You see him before I do, you tell him to get goin'. Happen I see him first, you won't need to tell him."

"By damn, Rachel," it was the slow-talking Judd, "don't you do it. We can handle him, me and Tom. You just leave us do it."

"Save it." Frank was through the door. He stepped up on the mare, jerked her around, pulling her soft mouth cruelly. He growled the word, gravel-deep. "If that bastard has got to Libby, he's a'ready dead."

They stood in the doorway, watching until the mare had topped the ridge and was gone. Then Tom Graden turned. "Frank Rachel's the one to watch out for, Judd. We've got to remember that from now on."

"I've said so from the beginnin'."

"Yeah, I know. He'll side-up with the Fewkes when and if the trouble comes, that's certain."

"He will, and the trouble's comin'. That's certain too. We ain't no chance to avoid a showdown with the Fewkes sooner or later. Rachel and that Injun, Jim, are thicker'n two sheepdogs in a strange town. Comes that showdown, he'll side with the Fewkes like you say."

"I'm sorry about that, in a way," said Tom Graden thoughtfully. "I always sorta liked Frank."

"Not me," growled Judd. "I can't stand a killer, and Rachel's one for certain sure. His kind gives me the creeps."

Tom returned his brother's uneasy look. He thought a moment, then nodded. "Likely you're right about Frank, at that. Fetch Harp Bivins up here."

"Now hold on, Tom. You ain't goin' to sic Harp on him."

"Fetch him, I said. Nobody, Frank Rachel included, is startin' my war before I'm ready for it."

"Well, it's a cinch Harp Bivins ain't startin' it for you. Not right now anyways."

At Judd's slow words, Tom wheeled on him.

"What you mean by that?"

Judd shrugged. "Harp and the rest of the Bivins, Clint, Jake, Simm, the lot of them, they all rode off with Garth early this mornin'. They ain't none of them come back yet."

"That goddam Garth!"

Any profanity was rare with Tom Graden. The use he now made of the heavy oath put its own doubtful value on the missing Garth. "We got to find him, Judd. Before he gets to that girl. You shouldn't have told him about her bein' Frank's best girl, damn it all! You know how Garth is with women. It's like wavin' a red flag in front of a proddy bull, to let on to him some other man's beatin' him to a flossy dish like Libby Fewkes."

"He'd of found out anyways. If he's aimin' to take a cut at the girl, we couldn't have held him no matter if he knew about Frank or not." He paused, eyeing his older brother.

"And if he is, Tom, you already got your war, ready or not!"

It was coming dusk when he rode down on the first Fewkes' place. John's cabin stood dark but down at the main ranch the lamps were turned high. The door stood open, flooding the yard with the yellow light. Three saddled horses stood, reins trailing, just outside the lamp's glow. He recognized them for Ed's and John's and Jim's, even as the latter's familiar voice was hailing him from the darkness near the woodpile. He rode over and got down.

"What's up, Jim?"

"Choose your partners," it was the hard-voiced Ed answering him, "the dance is on."

"Don't riddle me none. What's happened?"

"Lib's gone," said Jim.

It hit him back of the knees, put the sink in his belly clear to his toes. Still, when his words came they were as quiet as Jim's.

"That Graden bastard . . ."

"Likely. She's been seein' him."

"You sure she's took out? Maybe they're just late gettin' in. Let's ride."

"Rachel," Jim's answer slowed, "you know me better than that. I ain't settin' here over no twilight pasear. She's gone. Took her best dress and what few pretties she had."

"She'll be back!" It came out of him defiantly, without thought.

"I know Lib," said Jim. "She won't be back."

"She'd better not be," added Ed harshly. "Not to our place anyways."

"Meanin'?" Frank stepped toward him.

"Meanin' she's no good, Frank." It was young John, bitterly soft. "She never was. Pap always said she'd end up runnin' off with the first son of a bitch showed her a twenty-dollar gold piece."

"Goddam you, boy."

"Hold up." Jim moved forward. "There's no call for a show. John's right, Rachel, and I allow you know how I feel about Lib. But she's gone and she's gone of her own free will. Bracin' John ain't goin' to bring her back."

"I'll kill him!" snarled the big rider, his thoughts already far from Jim or any of the Fewkes.

"You'll have to catch him first," grunted Ed cynically. "They're fast mounted and there's no moon tonight."

"Yeah," John sided his older brother soberly, "they could have been gone for hours, Frank. She left here early this mornin'. We didn't see her pull out and thought nothin' of it till Pap checked her room after we'd ate just now."

"They could have rode four ways at least," Jim calculated thoughtfully. "No tellin' if they hit for Prescott, Holbrook, Globe or Phoenix. You can't ride four ways, Rachel."

"How about you? And Ed and John?" The question was deep with anger. "You three makes it four. You all just goin' to set by and see your sister took to hell?"

"She wasn't took," said Jim softly.

"You don't know that, goddam it!"

"I know Lib."

It was all he said, but the way he said it, slow and without the bitterness of the others, heavy and tired and hurt maybe, too, took the fight out of Frank. And it held him quiet long enough to think.

"Will you look after the mares up on the bench, Jim?" he said finally. "And see to Red Boy? The mares would get along likely, but he needs handlin'."

"All right. You goin' after them?"

"As far as the trail reads."

"You can read that trail without ridin' it." The half-breed's words were still heavy. "She don't want you, Rachel. You ain't her kind. She can't stand loneliness, she never could. She never liked it here and she never wanted to live here. She's gone now. Maybe she'll be happy where she's went. Leave her go. Leave her find out."

"It ain't her I want right now. And I don't never want her, Jim, if she don't really want me."

"You don't want Garth Graden neither. Leave him be, too."

"Either way," said Frank bitterly, "whether she'll have me or not, I got to see Libby. I got to know she don't want me. We was goin' to be married, Jim! I got to know she's all right and wants to be where she is, even if she don't want me. My God, I know she's wild, Jim, but I love her. I can't help that and I got to know she's all right."

"What if she ain't all right?" The other's short question fell harshly, the big rider's answer coming the same way.

"If he's done her any dirt, I'll kill him."

"What about her?"

"I'll bring her back. I will if she'll have me and will come. A man ain't got no pride left when it comes to that. I said I loved her."

"I reckon I do, too," said Jim Fewkes quietly. "But you'll not bring her back here to our place. She's made her bed and she's got into it with muddy boots. She's old enough to know what she's done, Rachel. She wasn't weaned yesterday."

Frank Rachel nodded. "I'll not bring her back to your place, Jim." His words were as soft as the half-breed's but they seethed with bitterness in them. "I'll take her up to Apache Bench, with me, where she belongs and where she's wanted. And every night I'll get down in the dark on my goddam knees and thank God he was good enough to give her back to me."

He paused, his flat-staring, pale eyes sweeping the three brothers. "And I'll not come here again myself," he added softly. "Not so long as Libby's alive, I won't. You hear me, you bastards?"

"Yeah? And what about when she ain't alive?"

It was Ed Fewkes again, still angry, still caustic. There was no humor in his hard remark, and none intended.

"When Lib ain't alive," said Frank Rachel slowly, "and if there's a Graden mixed up in it to the fartherest cousin they got, this Basin will bury the last, livin' one of them— with *his* goddam muddy boots on!"

A long and lonely road

The spring of 1884 came, and the early golden fall. The first year passed and with it passed Jim Fewkes' somber prophecy. Libby had not returned to the Basin and Frank Rachel had not found her. He had been close behind her again and again, but each time he was an hour or a day or a month too late. He rode on. Santa Fe, Taos, Las Vegas, Silver City; it was always the same. Yet, no, after Silver City not quite the same. After that there was no more track of Garth, only of Libby.

He heard of her again in Albuquerque and months later, in Tularosa. He lost her there and it was almost fall before he picked up the trail in Tucson. From Tucson the track led to Tombstone, and there it ran out.

Everywhere in Tombstone the questions and answers were the same: dark girl? queer blue eyes? tall, mean-built, quiet? Yes, she had worked the Oriental for a spell. Then the Crystal Palace and the Bird Cage. Where was she now? Still in town? Who would know, or care? A man forgets that kind as soon as he's done with them.

But she was gone from Tombstone, as she had been from every town before it. Frank had gotten that from Big Minnie Bignon. Yes, she had worked for Big Minnie. Called herself Lib Garten, or Grayton, something like that. Hell no, she hadn't worked as a chippie. In her condition, Mister? Sick? Of course not, you damn fool. Sure, I kept her here till the kid came. Yeah, it was a boy. Born dead too, better luck for her. Gone? Sure she's gone! That was in August. This is September, sport! Say, Mister, was that girl a damn breed of some sort? Me and the girls often wondered. She never talked. . . .

Tombstone beat him, broke him down, whipped him back into the corner of the cage. If old Jim Stanton could have seen his lion now, he would not have known him for the pale-eyed, soft-walking, dangerous predator he had let into his ranch cabin those long months before. Frank Rachel slunk back to Apache Bench like an ageing big cat who had found in his freedom too much of the harsh lash, the prodding chair and the powder-burning blankgun, and who wanted nothing better than to get back behind the shielding bars and stay there.

The winter of '86 passed and spring ran into summer. He went to the Basin only for supplies. At first the ranchers spoke to him, but a man who will not answer back is soon enough let alone. Jim came occasionally to the bench, or sometimes rode part way with him from Parker's Store. But by late summer the big rider's moroseness began to wear even on the loyal half-breed. It was clear Frank did not want to see or talk to anybody, not even him. Jim took him at his own weight and word, came no more to the Apache Bench Ranch.

With October wearing away into November and November following swiftly into the first crisp snows of December, Frank Rachel began his fourth lonely winter on the bench.

He knew now that Jim was done with him, and the deep hurt already in him grew uglier.

He had ridden the complete loop again. He was right where he had been when he had first checked Red Boy on the rim to gaze down into Peaceful Basin. It was a lonesome road stretching away down Dry Canyon and into the silent valley now. A man did not have to look very far down it to see where it was it was leading him. Maybe another year, a month, a day, maybe even another hour. It made no difference. There it was and a man could see it: stark and hard and lonely as always. Lying there. Watching him. And waiting for him to come to it.

The end of the trail again.

A week before Christmas—Frank never forgot the day, a Sunday like always—a mountain quail whistled from Dry Canyon. He ran from the hayshed, waving the pitchfork and yelling. He threw the fork away, grabbed off his hat and waved that. Then he just stood there waiting for Jim to ride up.

As he rounded the lee of the ranchhouse knoll, Jim saw him and swallowed hard.

Hair grown shoulder-long, driving in the heavy wind, him standing there bareheaded in the whipping snows of the ranchyard, twisting the old black hat in his hands—well, it did something inside of you when you looked at him like that. It made you feel sudden-lonely in a way that hurt you bad, way down below your heart. And it made you slide off your pony and plow toward him through the snow, hardly able to wait to get his hand in yours.

"Hello, Frank. Merry Christmas!"

It was the only time the half-breed had ever called him by his first name, or ever would again. It came out strange and awkward, stumbling a little on the way. But it came out, and it came backed with his lean brown hand.

"Jim! By God it's you, Jim!"

"Yeah," the thin rider grinned bashfully. "Now lay off poundin' me and help me get these hosses into the shed. They'll chill standin' in this wind."

Frank looked more closely at the spare mount Jim had led in across the bench. "Why, that's Libby's sockfoot sorrel, pardner! What's the idea?"

"Little Christmas present," grinned his companion. "Forget it for now. You got a couple of hoss blankets handy?" They were in the shed now and Frank got the blankets as the half-breed added fervently, "I hope to Christ you got a pot of coffee on."

"Sure, pardner. Fresh made this week." His own grin was working now. "God Amighty but it's good to hear a man's voice again. Even yours!"

In the ranchhouse they shucked out their wolfskin coats, kicked the snow out of their boot-arches, bellied up to the pine table. Indianlike, Jim Fewkes came straight to the point.

"Sorrel mare or no sorrel mare, I ain't playin' Santy Claus, Rachel. It's more trouble in the Basin. The Gradens have swore out warrants for rustlin' against Ed and John. Ever since them and Ed and John split up over that first bunch they stole off Old Jim Stanton, the Gradens been spreadin' it around that Ed and John are the ones keepin' up the rustlin' that's been goin' on since that time. Now they got out these damn warrants and that ain't all. They got Billy Mulvehey to serve them. Billy's a good friend of mine but he's also sheriff of Yavapai County. He's a tough bird, and four-square. You add most of the Basin ranchers swallowin' that Graden story about Ed and John doin' the rustlin', to Billy Mulvehey settin' out from Prescott with them warrants for their arrest, you got real trouble. And, Mister," he paused scowlingly, "it's started a'ready!"

"How so?" grunted Frank, returning the scowl.

"There's been gunplay."

"I'm still listenin'."

"Old Jim Stanton's got a new foreman, feller named John Gilliom. He's roundin' up Old Jim's stuff for final sale. Like you know, the old man's pullin' out of the Basin. They've rustled him blind, the bastards."

"Still the Bivins boys workin' on the q.t. for Judd and Tom, you figure?" Frank knew what the half-breed's answer would be.

Almost from the beginning, the Fewkes had claimed the Bivins were behind the Basin rustling. A man didn't actually know, but maybe they were. Maybe they were working at it with the backing of the Gradens, maybe without them and just on their own personal hooks. Either way Jim was likely right when he allowed Judd and Tom had the biggest part of the other stockmen in the valley convinced the Fewkes were the main rustlers.

The half-breeds were sullen, hard-eyed men, never having mixed with the valley people nor made more than a half dozen friends among the little squatter-ranchers like themselves. Such close-keeping made enemies of other men, even honest ones, without you did a damn thing crooked to earn the enmity. God knew, Frank Rachel knew that. And knew what it led to, what Jim had just said—gunplay.

But by now the whole thing between the Gradens and Fewkes had gotten so snarled up that about the only law the half-breeds *could* fall back on was the last-court jury of seven lead slugs—with one in the chamber making eight —sitting under old saddleworn Chief Justice '73 Winchester.

"Yeah," said Jim, breaking the little pause, "it's still the Bivins. But I'm talkin' about this bird Gilliom."

"So you're talkin' . . ." said Frank softly.

"Well," grunted the half-breed, "Gilliom was out huntin' a bunch of fresh-stole JS beef. He run acrost Ed on the trail and accused him of havin' lifted the missin' bunch. Naturally, Ed downed him. That was clear back in August."

"Kill him?"

"Just broke his leg. Ed held wide a'purpose. I reckon you know he wouldn't miss, accidental. Anyhow, it was all the excuse them Graden bastards needed. They got out a bench warrant for Ed's arrest, and the war was on. I couldn't hold Ed and John back no longer, and I allow I didn't try too hard. There's been plenty of hell since," concluded the half-breed bluntly, "all of it addin' up to what's brung me up here to see you."

Frank, sensing he was getting to it now, asked slowly and with eyes hardening. "And just what *has* brung you up to see me, amigo?"

Jim matched his hard stare. "Ed's made a deal that will knock them lousy Gradens clean back to Ioway or wherever the hell they originally come from. It's a long shot but will pay off in high numbers if she hits."

"How long a shot, Jim?"

"Long as they come."

"I'm listenin'."

"Sheep!" rasped the half-breed.

"Jesus Christ! You gone crazy, Jim? You can't mean it serious. Not bringin' sheep into the Basin, you can't!"

"All the same, I do. Me and Ed and John. And right now we're askin' you in on the play."

"You're askin' the wind. I don't hear you."

"You're either in or out, Rachel. Nobody stays neutral, not with woolies comin' over the rim. You know what that means."

"I've been there," grunted Frank, and fell silent. Presently, he asked. "Who's puttin' up the sheep?"

"Skaggs Brothers, up to Flagstaff."

"They're big boys. They'll play rough."

"I'm growed now. We ain't meanin' to be playin' for chalkies."

"When you aim to start bringin' them in?" He asked it easily and quietly; Jim's answer, just as easy and quiet, pulling him clear off his chair.

"We shoved the first bunch over the rim in September."

"God A'mighty, three months ago!"

"More or less."

"Anybody we know killed yet?"

"Nope, nary a one. The Bivins and some of the Hash Knife cowboys from up on the rim have run a couple of big bunches over the canyon edge on us. Another bunch was clubbed and shot while they held the Navajo herder under a gun. We still got better than two thousand head on graze and nobody on our side hurt serious yet. We managed to sandbag one bunch of their hired sheep-butchers in a night camp. Couldn't see how we done, for the dark. But we hear there's three of them won't set a easy saddle for quite a spell. It was enough to quieten Judd and Tom down for a bit, I reckon. Leastways, we ain't heard a shot out of them since."

"A man never hears the slug that hits him," said Frank grimly. Then, acidly, "What are you Fewkes gettin' out of the Skaggs deal? The sheep crap?"

In answer to the bitter question, Jim quickly told him

of the Fewkes' historic deal with the Skaggs Brothers to bring sheep into Peaceful Basin.

The sheepmen had long had hungry eyes for the lush ranges of the mild-wintered valley. They were being crowded off their old grasslands along the main rim by the swift, gunfighter-guarded growth of the Aztec Land & Cattle Company, that destined-to-be-fabulous "cow empire" of the '80s already known to the local ranchers by the more colorful, familiar name of the brand by which history has chosen to remember it—the "Hash Knife Outfit."

Driven to it by their ever-multiplying flocks and shrinking ranges, the sheepmen had banded together under the Skaggs Brothers, biggest herders in the southwest, to seek a means, and any means, of forcing a way for their woolies into the grass paradise of Peaceful Basin.

The Skaggs, old at the game, and tough at it as all their persecuted breed, had thought long and thought hard, and in the end had hit upon the obvious opportunity of exploiting the bad blood known to exist between the Fewkes and Gradens. Jim Fewkes, naturally, did not see it that way nor put it in those words to Frank Rachel. But the big rider was an old, old hand at reading between sheep and cattle lines, and what was apparently being missed by Jim was clear as summer creekwater to Frank. He only nodded scowlingly as the half-breed continued.

The Skaggs had contacted Ed right after the Gilliom shooting. Ed had savagely relayed the offer to Jim. And the latter had snarled in angry turn, and snapped it up.

The Skaggs' position was out in the open, Jim insisted, as Frank queried him sharply on the point.

They wanted into the Basin. They knew getting into it would mean a first-class war. All they wanted were first-class troops to fight it for them. The Fewkes and their few disgruntled friends were cattlemen, as indeed were all the other ranchers, large and small, in Peaceful Basin. The Skaggs knew that as well as did any of Arizona's hated sheepmen. They also knew the Fewkes and their handful of allies were dirt-poor men. Dirt-poor and fighting a losing battle to hold onto their little pieces of the Basin grass, against the encroachment of the Gradens and the three or four other large spreads which were, between them, running 90 per cent of the cattle in the Basin.

It had occurred to the wealthy and ruthless Skaggs Brothers that these starving little ranchers, properly induced, might be just the hard-tail recruits they were looking for.

The inducement was equally out in the open, the half-breed claimed: a share of the profits from any sheep run successfully in the Basin; the chance to win back their own and take over the other, even more coveted, grazing lands, now held by the larger cattlemen of Graden complexion.

The deal, finally, was simply this, Jim scowled: the Skaggs to supply the sheep and the money, the Fewkes and their friends to put up the guts and the gunplay.

"So," grunted the half-breed, winding up the longest continuous speech of his close-mouthed life, "that's what we're gettin' out of it. Fifty-fifty down the line on all sheep profits, plus the chance to get back some of our grass and get a goddam knee into Tom and Judd's guts."

"It don't hardly sound like enough to go to war over," said Frank thoughtfully.

"By God, don't it!" rasped Jim. "Rachel, if we get by with it, we'll make more honest money in two years than the Gradens have made crooked in five! And there'll be an end to rustlin' and we'll get some of our grass back."

"I'll bury you nice," grunted Frank, coming to his feet. "Under that hog wallow back of the big oak. You'll make tough acorns."

"Soft ones make bad bacon. You ain't answered me, Rachel. What cards you playin'?"

"The draw's down to me, eh? And you're callin'?"

"It is, and I am."

"So what you think I'll do?"

"Throw in with us."

"You figure I ain't got no choice?"

"I figure you ain't."

"You figure crazy. I ain't changed my mind none."

The coffee cups were on the table now, the black pot empty, the talk pulling swiftly to its close.

"You'll change it."

"Don't crowd me, Jim." The pale eyes began to ice over. "There ain't nothin' left in this world would take me back into the Basin."

"There is, Rachel. You're forgettin' somethin'." Jim's eyes caught his and held them. "Somebody, I mean . . ."

Frank was on his feet, leaning across the table, eyes wild. His voice came hoarse and hollow and deep. His hands gripped the pine planks until the knuckles cracked. "Jesus God, Jim, you don't mean *Libby!*"

Jim Fewkes nodded, his slant blue eyes warm for once. A man couldn't miss the pain and loneliness and sudden wild hope his words had put into the big rancher's hoarse cry. Not even if he was half Indian and hard as a dry-oak wheelhub. He knew now that he hadn't before begun to guess what the girl had meant to Frank Rachel. But he wasn't guessing any more. Now he knew. And he knew what his next words would mean to his friend.

"I found her," was all he said. "I know where she is."

Of birds and cages

"Where?"

The single word dropped into the silence as Frank, the wild light fading from his eyes, let go of the table and sank back into his chair.

"Back at the Bird Cage."

"How come you to find her, Jim?" His mind was clearing now, his voice steadying.

"I never did quit lookin'," said the half-breed simply. "When I knowed from you she had been in Tombstone, I figured she'd come back sooner or later. It's the biggest camp short of San Francisco and when a girl's down like that she either works or dies hungry. Lib ain't the dyin' kind."

Frank stood up, facing him across the table. Jim took the big hand, clearly embarrassed. "For hell's sake, Rachel, it ain't nothin'." He dropped the hand quickly. "Just go and get her. It's why I brung her mare. Pack and get, I'll watch your spread. If you rustle your butt, you can be home by Christmas."

"Christmas . . ." Frank let the word fade, his hand taking the half-breed's arm, his pale eyes holding on the dark face. "*God bless you, Jim!*"

He was gone then, the door sucking shut behind him, the building howl of the blizzard smothering his tall form before he was halfway to Red Boy's box stall.

He pushed the horses hard, raising the twenty-four hour lights of Tombstone about 11 P.M. the second night, that of the 18th. Shortly before midnight he was riding down Allen Street. Just past the corner of Third he turned in at the O. K. Corral stable. Putting the horses up, he told the boy to strip them, rub them down, throw a feed of hot bran and rolled oats into them, have them ready to go in an hour.

The Bird Cage was three blocks up Allen, cornering it at Sixth Street. He had never been in it and now the hurdy-gurdy of it nearly stampeded him. He downed three straight bourbons at the outer bar, signaled the houseman. The latter sidled up, disdainful of his rough, out-country, rancher's clothes.

"How'll you have it, friend? Plain or fancy?"

"Fancy and pronto. I ain't spendin' the winter here."

"Box Five, inside, friend. Anybody in there will show you the stairs up to the boxes. Any preference in girls?"

"Yeah. Lib Graden."

The houseman looked at him. "She ain't the best, friend. I could send you something a mite fancier!"

The big hand slid to him, seizing the tight roll of the cutaway lapel. "You send Lib Graden, friend."

"Lib Graden coming up. Box Five . . ." The houseman backed off hurriedly, not liking what he saw in the pale eyes. These damn cowmen were all alike, hell on whiskey and women, and wanting both before they were five minutes out of the saddle.

Frank squeezed into the main auditorium of the ill-famed Bird Cage and looked around. The huge room was jammed with drunks and with half-naked women. It was crowding midnight now and the place was going full blast. On the stage down in front, a chorus row of six girls, all black silk legs and pink-skinned breasts was kicking and yelling and poking its collective behinds into the customers' admiring faces. Somewhere a tinpan piano and a Mexican cornet were murdering a bastard musical offspring sired by "Camptown Races" out of "Oh, Susannah." He spotted the staircase leading up to the boxes and pushed toward it. Inside Box Five he trimmed the gaslamp, turning it far down, and stood back by the entrance curtains to wait.

She came in soundlessly, not seeing him, sank to the red plush settee and sat staring at the floor. Frank's belly pulled in, his heart settling in him like a thrown stone in deep, cold water.

She was not yet twenty, but the work of ten years had been done in the last three. About her whole person was an aura of sickness and despair. And more. Of lostness and desolation and abandonment. And of misery which would have broken the heart of a rock. As he watched her, his chest tight with the ache of his held breath and headlong memory, she coughed hollowly.

The cough, built rackingly behind the crumpled soil of her handkerchief, became a spasm, then subsided. The dark stain of the flush spots over the gaunt cheekbones spread with telltale swiftness, carrying ominously even in the gloom of the gas lamp. Frank, his face as white as hers, moved away from the wall. The one word, deep and soft beneath the muffled, brassy intrusions of the Bird Cage's revelry, broke the stillness of the box.

"Libby . . ."

She stiffened, then turned, the turquoise blaze of the slant eyes fierce and wild as ever. She arose slowly, hands pressed to the bareness above her dress-top, as though she sought, subconsciously, to shield it from him.

"Lib, it's Frank. I've come to take you home, girl."

"Frank—oh God—Frank Rachel!" He saw the tight quiver break across the compressed line of the lower lip, and saw the quick welling glitter of the tears before she turned half savagely away.

He stood, not daring to touch her, the ache in his throat swelling unbearably. "Did you hear me, Lib? I said we're goin' home. Don't put off on me now, girl!"

The shoulders straightened but she did not turn. Her voice came haltingly and tear-thick, all the old magic of it building in him, tearing at him, taking his heart back across the lonely years. "Frank—oh God, Frank, you don't want me any more. Go away, go away!" The cough came again, breaking her plea, racking the thin shoulders.

He took her then, gently and tenderly as a child, holding her to him until the spasm died and the labored breathing grew still. The big hands ran beneath the black hair, smoothing it back, lifting the tear-stained wetness of the face. He kissed her on the forehead, awkwardly, almost shyly. His arm came around her and he turned, with her, toward the curtains. For a brief moment the old grin softened the edges of his wide mouth.

"Come on, Lib girl. You shouldn't play with these big kids. You're too little . . ."

It was the 24th of December, a black night and with the wind rising again, when they cleared the junipers below the ranchhouse knoll and got their first sight of the Apache Bench cabin. They pulled in their horses, sitting them in wordless wonderment.

Through the starlit stillness of the Arizona night, the candles winked and glittered behind the frost-trimmed casement of the single, tiny window. Their lights danced gaily along the awkward dangle of the tinfoil strips, peered flickeringly among the clumsy puffs of cotton batting, festooning the little cedar's limbs. Even the lopsided Star of Bethlehem, tin-snipped from the rolled-out side of a tomato can and girded onto the topmost twig with a rusty cinch of baling wire, managed to respond to the struggling spirit of the occasion by assuming a dignity not bequeathed it by Jim's talents with the tin shears.

"My God," Frank breathed. "It's a Christmas tree! Old Jim's gone and put up a tree for us! First one I ever seen on Apache Bench," he concluded happily.

"It's the first one I've ever seen any place," said Libby Fewkes quietly.

He looked at her then, seeing the swift glitter of the tears against the frost-rime of the wolfskin collar. Kneeing Red Boy, he moved to her side. He leaned over and kissed the wet cheek, circled the fur-clad shoulder, pulled her to him.

"Now don't cry, honey. We're home, girl, you hear me? There's no more trouble in this whole world for you and me, Lib."

She nodded, snuggling to him, and he paused, tightening the circle of his arm. His voice dropped softly, with his lips and the tender kiss.

"Merry Christmas, Libby . . ."

The winter of 1887 was the happiest time of Frank Rachel's life. Libby seemed to mend rapidly in the high air and clear sun of the bench and Jim came regularly from the Basin to make their Sundays perfect.

By hard-eyed agreement, the girl's presence on the bench was kept a secret, and by equal agreement Frank and Jim rarely discussed the situation in the Basin. The trouble there was growing but insofar as Frank knew or cared, only sheep had so far died in the Peaceful Basin War. Jim, declared an equal partner in the Apache Bench horse ranch by Frank's insistence, was their only contact with the valley and he never talked unless asked. And he was seldom asked.

In March the half-breed took Red Boy's first crop of three-year-olds to the spring sale in Phoenix, realizing a record price for green colts. The big stud's fame was growing swiftly and that growth should have bid fair to predict a safe and certain future for Frank Rachel and his hard-earned hopes. That it did not and was in opposite fact to guarantee the beginning of the end of the bloodiest range war the West was ever to know, could scarcely have been foreseen those early, happy months.

No, Red Boy's part in the Peaceful Basin War was not yet to be, but another, more sinister part of that war, the part which in the end must be held to have really decided the course and termination of the bitter feud, was growing unseen and swiftly in the wasted lungs of Libby Fewkes.

With the raw, cold winds of March the cough, nearly

gone the past months, began again. By April the racking
convulsions had become constant and the torn squares of
bed-sheeting, pressed fiercely to her tortured mouth by the
feverish girl and always hidden by her from the hovering
Frank, had begun to show the angry, bright stains of the
thin blood.

But May and the first, soft breath of the Tonto spring,
brought a seeming hopeful rally to her weary flesh and
spirit. She was shortly able to be outside and sit in the
warmth of the ranchhouse porch, watching Frank work
the green colts. During this time the sucking foals, in-
variably fronted by their arch-necked sire and backed by
their concerned dams, made a play yard of the area around
the porch. Libby never tired of handfeeding them the lump
sugar and dried apples which Frank grinningly supplied.
By month's end the bay stud had become such a pet and
pest that Frank mock-seriously sought Libby's permission
to build a box-stall wing on the main cabin, that she might
pass him his sugar during the night, "Happen the silly
bastard should get lonesome in the dark!"

Libby had laughed at that, her first time in weeks. The
throaty happiness of the sound put the quick hope springing again in the big rancher's breast. With the spring of '87
safely passed and summer running smoothly along, a man
could begin to feel he was going to win, was going to lick
that damn cough and everything which lay behind it.

It was the first week in August, a Sunday with Jim due
to whistle any minute from Dry Canyon, that it happened.

He had gone out late, after fixing Libby a holiday
breakfast of fried venison. As he started across to the corrals, his grin was as light as the lift of the morning breeze
in the new grass. But the lightness died aborning and the
breeze failed short as his glance leaped across the yard to
the swinging door of Red Boy's box stall.

He ran, awkward in his haste and the pinch of the Texas
boots, to the deserted box; scrambled from there to the
top rail of the corral fence, eyes sweeping the bench north
and south.

It was as empty as the box.

No need to whistle the stud in. Nor to ride down and
scout for him in the junipers toward Diamond Butte. A

man knew his horse, and he knew the heavy sink of his heart within him.

Red Boy was gone.

They sat at the pine table, he and Jim, stirring the sugar into their coffee, talking low and quick and dry-lipped like men will when they are too angry for loud words. By the open porch door, Libby rocked silently in her chair, not hearing them, not knowing they were there, her eyes finding the deserted run of Red Boy's corral, her ears alert only for the shrilling whistle of the stallion's neigh.

Jim Fewkes cursed again, growling his answer to the man across the table. "Whoever it was took him, Rachel, they'll spread it in the Basin that it was us Fewkes did it. That's sure as hot hoss apples smokes!"

"They'll have to spread it pretty thick for me," grated Frank. "I reckon you know that."

"Thanks." The nod was short. "But that ain't gettin' us your hoss back. And from the looks of the way Lib's carryin' on about him bein' gone, we'd better get him back! She was sure crazy about that hoss, Rachel."

"She ain't talked since I told her he was gone." Frank said it out loud, as though alone in the room.

"It's what I mean," said Jim quickly. "Folks sick with that damn lung fever can't take no bad setbacks like this."

"Lib will do. She's been gettin' better right along." Frank was still talking to the room.

"She won't, and she ain't been." Jim dropped his voice. "You're so close you can't see her fadin'. She don't weigh ninety pounds. I seen our mother die of it. She got better too . . ."

"Lib will do, I said!" The anger of fear was in the outburst. Jim sensed it for what it was.

"Sure," he shrugged, watching him. "Leave it go at that. Likely she will. Happen we get the hoss back in time."

Frank looked at him, voice suddenly steady again, cornered lion's eyes flaring wickedly. "I'll get him back!" he snarled.

"We'll get him back," amended Jim softly. "But not settin' here on our dead butts."

"Let's ride," said Frank Rachel.

"In the words of my mother's people," murmured the half-breed, getting up, "my ears are uncovered. I hear you talkin'."

"After you, Chief . . ." Frank reached his hat off its wall peg, swept it sardonically toward the door.

He followed Jim out, neither man speaking again or looking back. At the corral Frank said, "You got any spare .44 Winchester? I'm low."

"Enough," grunted the half-breed. "It only takes one in the right place."

The tracks that failed

They cut the stud's sign south of the home pasture, following it down over the south rim of the bench past Diamond Butte. On good ground where they could read it clearly, they made out five sets of shod prints overlaying the familiar twisted right rear hoofmark of the bay stallion.

"It figures," said Jim shortly. "Four Bivins and Anse Canaday."

"Who the hell's Anse Canaday?" He hadn't heard the name in the Basin before but it struck a memory bell somewhere.

"New foreman for the Gradens. Texan and a gun fighter like the rest of them. Some say he's a half brother to the Bivins. He don't look it to me. Different cut entirely. Not big enough and too spare. Weasel-faced bastard, laughs like a girl. Likely he . . ."

"Hold up." Frank checked his mare. "Strawberry blond? Skinny, gopher-jawed, buck teeth, bad cast in his right eye?"

"Where'd you know him?" Jim grunted.

"Texas. Before I done my time in Colorado. They say right. Real name's Anse Bivins. He went out of Fort Worth ahead of me and for the same reason."

"Man dyin' of unnatural causes?"

"Yeah. But mine saw it comin'."

"Anse's didn't, eh?"

"No. Shot in the back. Hole in his belly was three times the size of the one in his back."

"I figured him for a bushwhacker. And a bad one."

"Go to the head of the class, Jimmy boy. You get a hundred on both counts."

Jim Fewkes did not return the mouth twist that was supposed to be a grin. They rode on quickly.

For several miles after they got down off the south wall the track lay plain and easy, giving Frank the idea and opportunity to catch up on his local history lessons, by this time pretty far in arrears. Jim had not talked of the Skaggs Brothers' Basin invasion for the past three months or more and he hadn't pushed him, allowing the sheep venture must be going along fairly well.

He soon learned how fairly and how well.

"Say, Jim, how's the war comin'? Made your million yet? Seems like I ought to get a cut on your share, seein's how I'm splittin' with you on our hoss ranch."

"It's a deal," said his companion, his expression not altering. "You got a shovel with you?"

Frank, not getting the meaning of the cryptic remark, asked puzzled. "Meanin' I'll need a shovel?"

The half-breed nodded. "You will," he said, "to scoop up your share of what I've made off them goddam sheep. It's like you said, Rachel. All I got comin' from my gamble with them woollies is six months of piled-up sheepcrap. Them damn Skaggs backed out on us and pulled their flocks out of the Basin weeks ago."

"Naw! The hell they did! Why, last I heard of the deal you'd only lost a few hundred head. That and the Navajo herder that got plugged back in February. Don't tell me losin' a Injun sheep nurse and havin' two, three flocks stampeded by the Gradens and their Hash Knife friends scared you Fewkes off!"

"Not likely. We give them Graden riders a shade more hell than they give us. And Navajo herders is a nickel a dozen. Sheep is somethin' else again, though. They cost money."

"So?" said Frank, watching him. "How much money?"

"Month before last," growled the half-breed, "them god-dam Hash Knife cowhands ganged up with the Graden outfit again, after layin' cute and quiet a long time to get us let-down and careless.

"They picked a good night for killin' sheep too. Nice moon and all. Plenty of light to catch white wool through a Winchester backsight. It was the biggest bunch the Skaggs had had us bring in. We had five Navajos watchin' them. The Injuns later told us there was anyways twenty riders in the bunch that jumped the flock .They got the drop on our Navajos and tied them up. Laced them to some scrub pines where they could get a good look at the butcherin'. Them cowboys of Graden's shot and clubbed among them sheep for two hours."

"Sounds sweet," grunted Frank acidly.

"Sweet enough. We rough-counted better than twelve hundred dead sheep next mornin'. I reckon you can't blame the Skaggs for pullin' out on us after that. They could see, I allow, that us Fewkes wasn't goin' to be able to handle the Gradens, and they could feel it when Tom and Judd had shoved it into them up to their ears. So they just pulled out."

"For good you figure?"

"Bad or good, they won't be back. They lost upwards of two thousand head, all told. That's a lot of dollars, wool-backed or otherwise."

"That leaves the Gradens settin' a better saddle than ever, don't it? How did Ed and John take it?"

"They didn't," the half-breed grunted, his eyes leaving the line of shod hoofprints they were following to sweep ahead. "Yonder's Cherry Crick. Likely we'll lose the trail now."

"Likely," grunted Frank in return.

But the far side of the creek told a different story. The rustlers had made no attempt to hide their trail by riding up or down water. They had come straight out the far bank and swung due north along it.

"Damn white of them to stick to the soft ground like this," nodded Frank. "They couldn't have left us a better set of prints if they'd tried."

"Which they did," scowled Jim.

"Could be. What you thinkin'?"

"What I already told you. Them easy prints will lead smack to our place. After that we'll have to look for them."

The tracks lay exactly as the half-breed had predicted, straight and clean into the Fewkes' main pasture. Also, as he had forecast, from there it got tougher.

It had been a dry summer after a wet spring. The grass lay everywhere thick and heavy over hard ground. It would have been difficult trailing a two-ton circus elephant, let alone four or five range ponies with rockworn, half-smooth shoes.

"They figured you would never look past the pasture," glowered Jim. "Countin' on you bein' none too warm with Ed and John, and jumpin' to conclusions. The Basin still mainly thinks that's the way it sets between you and them. I always figured to leave them think so."

"You always figure pretty good," said Frank. "Where do we go from here?"

"Canyon Crick, ten gets you one."

"We can't run no trail between your place and there. It's solid rock from the back of your pasture on."

"I don't aim to run no trail. If I'm wrong, we've wasted a long ride. If I'm right all we got to do is follow up Canyon Crick till we spot their sign comin' in off the rocks from this side. Let's go."

"We're gone," the big rider shrugged.

The two horses swung out of the pasture, loping due east along its straggling fence line.

As Frank has said, Jim always figured pretty good.

Ten miles below the Bivins' place on Canyon Creek, Red Boy's twisted hoofprint, overlain by those of his abductors' mounts, came down out of the canyon rocks and turned north up the creek bank.

They followed the sign, pushing fast before the light gave out. Dusk caught them a mile from the Bivins' ranch, the tracks still leading straight on. The last light failed five minutes later, lasting only long enough to bring them within three hundred yards of the house and corral, the tracks still holding.

They reins-tied their horses in some juniper scrub behind a knife-edge of granite, topped the ridge and lay on their bellies, watching the house. There were no lamps going in the cabin and no supper fire smoke lipping the chimney pipe. They gave it half an hour more, then moved in.

The cabin was empty. The greasy dishes on the lone table, together with the coffee pot sitting on back of the stove and still faintly warm, brought their grim nods. In the corral were five used-up ponies, saddle-marked and blanket-lathered and not yet sweat-cooled.

"They've been rode today," said Frank sarcastically.

"And half of last night," added his companion. "They ain't been out from under leather an hour and a half."

"What you think, Jim?" The question came only after a long pause.

"I don't like what I think. Your hoss is gone."

"Likely it'll go bad with Libby," was all the big rancher said.

The half-breed looked at him through the dark. Nobody had to tell Jim Fewkes what this big devil thought of that stud horse. The fact he could look losing him squarely in the face and still think only of the girl put the final brand on the kind of love he felt for Lib.

"Likely it will, Rachel," he answered softly. "What you want to do?"

"Kill a man." The reply came just as softly.

"It figures," nodded Jim. "Anse?"

"Anse," said Frank.

"Who'll look after Lib meanwhile?"

"Who else?"

"All right, Rachel, I'll do it. I'll go home, get a fresh hoss and head up to the bench. If you don't show by tomorrow night, I'll bring her back down to the Basin."

"I'll show. Get goin'."

"I'll tell her you're still runnin' the hoss. On a good, fresh track."

"Yeah, thanks. That'd help to keep her quiet. See you downtrail."

"Look sharp," said the half-breed. "Them Bivins is bad medicine."

"I'm scared to death," grunted Frank. "Hop your butt."

Seconds later he was alone. Jim's disappearance from the corral was as soft and soundless as the Apache moccasins which carried it out. One moment he was there, hand-close and solid in the starlight. The next breath he was gone as completely and instantly as though the dirt of the ranchyard had opened up and swallowed him.

Frank rigged a lead-line for the five horses in the corral, got his own mare out of the brush, rode back to the ranch and picked them up.

He was careful to keep to the soft ground of the creek bank, leaving a clear trail. Two miles downstream, he cut into the rocks east of the creek, tied the horses and bellied down to wait. If things worked out, he would have his man for breakfast. If there was one thing a horse thief couldn't stand, it was another horse thief. Bivins would come after those saddle mounts, and he would come never figuring who it was had lifted them.

About midnight he ate some of the cold beef he had brought in the mare's saddlebag, snuck down to the creek and filled his belly with cold water. After that he pulled the saddle off the mare, borrowed her blanket and made the best of it. Dawn came early, crowding four o'clock.

And crowding four-thirty, with the light still murky and bad, came something else.

He heard his man coming before he saw him, the slow clip-clop of the ridden horse muffling up from the creek bank gloom. Then he could make him out, head down and watching the ground and holding the horse in. As he swung away from the creek and headed toward the rocks, following the tracks of the missing horses, Frank could make out something else: the Winchester out of the scabbard and held across the horn.

He could begin to see him pretty well now, coming closer. Not the face yet, but the cut of the body build; thin, high-shouldered, Texas-straight in the saddle. It was Frank's hand, queens full.

And Anse Bivins was holding aces and eights.

He let him get just past the rocks, then shadowed out on him.

"Bivins!"

The horseman fired from the horn into the sound of the voice. The reaction was so fast that his glance, held down on the horse tracks he was following, was still coming up to tail his snap shot, when Frank killed him.

The big .44 slug took him under the breastbone, ruptured out his back, knocked him off the far side of his horse. The mount neighed wildly and plunged back toward the creek, his rider's boot hanging up in the stirrup for the first three jumps. Then the body smashed into a trailside boulder, broke loose, slid down into a pile of granite chips and lay still.

Frank waited in the rocks five minutes. Hearing no sound of riders coming from the ranch in answer to the gunfire, he moved down to the body. Turning it over on its back, his eyes widened.

It was the old man, Mark Bivins.

He studied him a minute, mind racing. This was a cayuse of an off color. Since he had come alone after the horses it wasn't likely he had been with the bunch that stole them. Probably the poor old coot had come home late last night, seen the horses missing, waited for first light and set out after them.

Well, it made no real difference. He was dead. There was no use leaving him there to brag about it. The light was coming fast now. A man could figure it was high time to get the hell shut of the Bivins' backyard.

Working swiftly, he caught up the old man's horse, laced the body across the saddle, shoved his fallen rifle into his own mare's scabbard. Keeping his own Winchester out and handy, he climbed aboard the mare and drifted.

An hour later he paused to let the horses blow on the main ridge. Far below he could see the flyspeck dots of the Bivins' cabin and corral. The corral was still empty. No smoke showed above the cabin chimney. Nodding, he swung off the mare, pulling the old man's rifle out of the scabbard and looking around. He saw the lightning-riven cedar close off the trail, stepped over to it and dropped the gun into its waiting trunk-hollow. Next, he unfastened the lead-rope of the pack horse, his glance searching swiftly again. The second nod was as grim and quick as the first.

Yonder crack in the granite caprock would do fine. It looked to be deep enough and to have no way for a horse to get down to it. Coming to its edge, the third nod flicked briefly. If they looked for their old man, they would be a long, lonesome time finding him now.

He watched as the slack body bounded and twisted off the sides of the cleft, crashed and disappeared into the thick brush choking its narrow bottom. He looked down for a moment, then grunted with the fourth and farewell nod.

"Like father, like son. You should have raised Anse better, old man."

A high and wild and lonely place

It was midday when he topped out on the bench and rode toward the Apache Ranch buildings. Jim came out of the cabin as he was putting the mare up, crossing the yard hurriedly and joining him at the corral. Frank turned to meet him, took one look at the half-breed's face.

"Lib?" he asked shortly.

"Yeah, she's bad." He gave it to him tersely. "Hadn't been to bed when I got back last night. Still sittin' in that damn rocker. Tiltin' back and forth and starin' out the window. Wouldn't say five words. I got her in bed and got some coffee down her. She ain't ate a damn thing though and she ain't let up coughin' long enough to get her breath."

"Pull the saddle on the mare." Frank was turning for the cabin, his face white. "Stay shut of the house for a spell, you hear, Jim?"

"Sure. I wouldn't tell her we figure the stud's clean gone. I told her we'd got Ed and John on the job."

If Frank heard him, he gave no sign. Outside the cabin door he paused a moment, head down, hand on the latch. Then he opened it and went in.

She lay motionless, eyes closed. He watched her a long time, then said softly, "Libby . . ."

"Frank," the eyes remained closed, "don't put off on me. Red Boy's gone."

"Lib, he ain't," he lied awkwardly. "Ed and John's still trailin' him. We figure it's some 'Paches lifted him. Sign is barefoot and points over toward the White Mountain Reservation. Ed and John'll get him back."

"You're lying, Frank. You would never have left off trailing him."

He sat on the bed, his hand finding the thin shoulder. "Lib, honey, they're trailin' him. I come back to see you, that's all."

"It isn't . . ." The wrack of the cough broke her words. "I was out by the box and followed his prints to below the corral where they had their ponies tied. Whoever took him was riding shod horses, Frank."

"Damn it, girl, you shouldn't have! Out on the open bench like that, windy-cold and all. You got to watch yourself, Lib. You're all I got, honey."

"You haven't got much to begin with then . . ." she paused, her eyes opening and turning out the window toward the empty box stall. "And nothing at all to end with, now that Red Boy's gone."

"Don't talk like that no more, Lib. We'll get him back. You'll see, girl."

"I won't." She shook her head, the pause building again. "Frank . . ."

"Yeah, honey?" He caught the sudden change in the voice. It put the frost in his belly, hard and deep.

She turned to him, taking his hand and holding it crushed against her cheek. The sharp fright in her voice twisted in him like a knife. "Frank, I'm sick. Awful sick. And scared, scared to death! I'm going to die, Frank . . ."

He felt the parched heat of the cheek burning his hand, and then the quick scald of the silent tears. He took her to him, holding the frail body close, his big hand patting

and smoothing the black hair. "Libby, Libby, don't talk no
more. No more at all now. Hush, girl, you hear me? You
ain't goin' to die, honey. You ain't now, you hear?" His
whisper rose savagely, then fell.

"You can't, baby girl, you just can't . . ."

He felt the thin arm tighten around his neck, and let
the final words come with fierce softness, his eyes looking
past the dark nestle of her head and across the lonely sweep
of the bench.

"It's like Jim said, Lib baby. You ain't the dyin' kind!"

Frank's grim defiance bore bitter and sudden fruit.
Libby Fewkes died in the early morning of August 9, 1887,
five days almost to the hour following the disappearance
of the stallion, Red Boy.

She went quickly and without Frank's knowing it, in
her sleep and peacefully. She was asleep when he went
out to fed the weanlings. When he returned, minutes
later, she was still asleep. He called her name three times
before he realized she would never waken again.

For an hour, and until the insistent whickerings of the
weanling colts demanding their release from the feed corral
and return to their pasturing dams cut through the stone
silence of his grief, he sat with her in his arms, holding
the still form close, softly and repeatedly stroking the
tumbled black hair, wide lips moving soundlessly, the slow
run of the tears moving unheeded down his face.

He stood up, finally, putting her gently down.

He didn't look at her and didn't cover her face. Outside,
he released the weanlings, went to the shed and got her
saddle. He caught up her favorite mare, the little sockfoot
sorrel, threw the saddle on her and cinched it tight for
the double carry. Then he was ready.

He rode with her in his arms, light and easy as a child.
He had dressed her in her old clothes—in the worn fray of
the cotton shirt, the faded blue of the denims, the soft
tanned cling of the Apache moccasins—the way he wanted
to remember her.

In the whole of the long ride down the bench and up
the steep trail of the backing wall—the trail which led to
the lookout spot where he had taken her those sunny

winter days to look out over their bench and the grazing
dots of her beloved mares—his eyes never looked down.

On the outer jut of the lookout, under the shelter of the
lone, twisted juniper, he halted the mare.

Two thousand feet below, Peaceful Basin lay in brooding, uneasy quiet, the broken tumble of its floor rolling
southward mile upon lonely mile until lost in the distant
haze of the Sierra Anchas. Immediately below, another
sheer and jagged thousand feet, spread the thick-grassed,
pine-dotted level of the bench. And beyond the bench, far
across the timbered reach of the Basin itself, breathtakingly
defiant in its naked granite might, rose the rearing, mile-
high bastion of the main Mogollon Rim.

Frank Rachel nodded. It was the place. High and wild
and lonely, like herself.

No visitor would pass here but the wind. No caller
would come but the winter snow. No night would fall but
the blessed one of the Basin. No light would shine but that
of the mesa stars and the Mogollon moon. No warmth
would come but that of the pine-clean mountain sun. No
sound would break but the friendly chatter of the piñon
squirrels and the cheery, long, clear call of the blue
Mexican quail.

He worked quickly, lifting and shouldering the big
granite boulders each into its reverent and careful place.
When he had done, he stepped back looking down upon
their rough pile.

He bared his head, the big hands twisting at the stained
brim of the black hat as he held it awkwardly to his shirt-
front. He stood a full minute before he could say it. But
he said it quickly then.

"Good-bye, Libby girl. I reckon you know I loved you.
God bless you and God help me. I can't say it no better."

He turned away, his head swinging up to let his eyes
sweep across the bench below and out into the timbered
silences of the big valley beneath it. The last words came
so low the wind scarcely caught them.

"And God help every Graden in that Basin . . .

"You killed her!" the savage whisper raced. "You killed
her sure as you'd done it with a knife. You hear me, Tom?
You hear me, Judd?"

The short laugh was ugly, chilling. It was unsteadily deep, profaning the stillness of the time and place. "You hear me, Garth Graden, wherever you are?

"*Get your goddam muddy boots on!* I'm comin' down there now . . ."

Back at the ranch, he worked silently. The green colts in the hayshed corral were hazed out and sent galloping down the bench to join the mares in the open pasture. He pulled the bottom poles on both hayricks, wedged the corral gates open so the stored hay could be gotten to when needed. Then he checked the stock tank back of Red Boy's box, making sure the piped spring which fed it was clean and running free.

What he could do, was soon done. Beyond that, it was up to the horses.

There was still plenty of standing summer hay out on the bench. Little Tonto Creek ran some kind of a trickle even through August and September. The spring foals were rising three- and four-months old and could move fast enough to stay clear of prowling bear and lion. The grown stock were all grass-fat and the whole works could go on and winter through if it came to that.

He took Red Boy's bit and bridle and his old low-horned roping saddle and rigged them on the sorrel mare. Libby's tack and all the rest of his own was left in place, hanging in the harness shed. All else of Libby or of Red Boy that he would take with him, would be the little sockfoot mare and the bay stallion's last foal, now six-months heavy in the little mare's rounding barrel.

He was not long in the cabin. The floorboards behind the Buck's range came complainingly away to the pry of the rusted crowbar. The heavy bundle, carefully swathed in its thin oilskins, was lifted quickly out.

His fingers, steady now, pulled the buckskin thongs, unrolled the greasy wrappings.

He looked at them, his first sight of them in four years bringing the old pull to his belly and the unconscious, talonlike set to the big hands.

The blunt, woodsmoke blue of the four-inch barrels, the gape and cold-empty stare of the huge boreholes, the wicked sweep and curve of the scarred walnut handles, the hawk's beak hook of the case-hardened hammerspurs, God! A man forgot how beautiful they were!

He belted the double leathers on, feeling the buckletongue hit and slide into the old, worn hole. He picked the Colts up, sliding them deep into the oil-soaked holster pockets, his hands coming into the cold touch of their butts like those of a lover long hungry for the touch of his beloved.

The rest of it was soon done.

It was perhaps two minutes later when he smashed the glass well of the table lamp over the firebox of the range. The released coal oil splashed over the kindling box and the rumpled pile of soiled bedding he had wadded between it and the wall. When he turned away, the first racing lick of the flame had run the side of the box, leapt through the bedding pile and flared up along the tinder dryness of the cedar logs.

Half an hour after the sorrel mare had braced her forefeet for the first steep pitch down the head of Dry Canyon, all that remained of the Apache Bench Ranch was what had been there before Frank Rachel: the stark, standing emptiness of the abandoned sheds and corrals; the ashblackened stone of the cabin chimney and the gaunt ribs of its granite sills.

The only differing traces were the lingering deep glow of the cedar coals and the sullen slow drift of hanging smoke. And these too, were cold and gone before the night wind failed and the morning star winked out over the eastern rim of the Mogollons.

Gone, too, before that wind failed and that star winked out, was all lingering doubt from the mind of Frank Rachel.

The rustling of Old Jim Stanton's cattle suspected of the Bivins brothers, the invasion of the Basin with the Skaggs Brothers' sheep by the Fewkes, the defeat and destruction of that invasion by the Gradens; all these factors in the valley feud had briefly flowered, harshly withered, bitterly fallen away. Now the Basin had been quiet for many months. The victorious cattlemen of the Graden faction were beginning to think, and to say, that the war

was over. That the Gradens had won and the Fewkes had
lost. And that honest men could soon once more walk
abroad in the daylight and unafraid.

Through all of this, Frank Rachel had kept his promise
to Tom Graden and Jim Fewkes and to himself, had kept
aloof and aided neither one side nor the other.

So much, any man in the Basin would have thought
he knew, that starlit summer night in 1887.

One man, alone, knew more. But he was not yet in
the Basin. He was only then riding down upon it from the
smoking ruins of Apache Bench.

If it were the final act of his harsh life, Frank Rachel
would bring his vengeance down upon the house of Garth
Graden, and upon the houses of the last of Garth Graden's
kin. He would bring his guns and his hatred into the beaten
camp of the little cattlemen and to the dark-skinned side
of the three half-breed brothers who were their defeated
leaders. And he would not rest, nor lay aside those guns,
until Garth Graden was found, and cornered, and called
out for the last time.

The war, over! It had not started yet. And the Gradens
had not won it. They had lost it. Lost it the day and the
hour and the minute, just past, when Libby Fewkes had
closed her tired, frightened eyes forever.

As Frank Rachel guided the sorrel mare out of the
mouth of Dry Canyon, onto the spreading floor of the valley, the look of the lion was once more in the vacant,
faraway stare of his pale eyes; in the hunch and crouch
of his lean, tense body, in the dark-lined set of his wide,
dry lips.

The lion was loose. And circling for the kill across the
moon-dark night winds of Peaceful Basin.

How to belly-sneak in tall grass

The five men riding down the ridge toward the Graden cabin in the early moonlight of August 9th, even softened by Luna's mellow glow, would have required the west's favorite generic term for such descriptions. They were, beyond all argument, bona-fide hardcases.

Harp, Clint, Simm and Jake Bivins rated the label with little argument; Anse without any at all.

The four full brothers were big men, cut on the standard cattle land pattern for all-wool, grade-A, imported Texas gun hawks: high Texas-booted, wide black hatted, double gun-belted, ramrod straight and tall in the saddle. The fifth brother, the half-blood Anse, was of the same pattern but cut on the bias.

The others were honest rustlers and hard-working hired gun hands by professional choice. Anse was neither honest nor hard-working. He was, of course, a professional. But he came by his particular calling through birth and not by choice.

It would take a knowing man no second look to call Anse Canaday a born killer.

In front of the cabin they halted their ponies, legged off of them, left them reins trailing. There was no knock at the door and they filed in, hard-eyed and without formal greeting, to face Tom Graden.

"It's been a week, Tom. We're done fooling around." Harp did the talking but it was Anse whom Tom Graden watched. "We've covered the country south to Globe and north to Holbrook. Nobody's seen the Old Man."

Tom remained seated at the table, only moving to shove the kerosene lamp aside to get it from between him and his visitors. "Give it time, Harp. He's been gone a week before."

95

"Time's up, Graden." It was Anse now, his thin voice flat. "Old Charley Cooper found Pap's hoss in Rock House Canyon this mornin'. Saddle still on and cinched up to ride."

Tom gestured easily. "That's no call to start shootin', Anse. Like I said before, he could have been throwed off or hurt by accident. It happens every day."

"Not this way, it don't." The reedy voice rose angrily. "The bit was pulled and the reins tied up so's the hoss could graze!"

"That so, Harp?" Tom put the confirming question calmly, still not moving from the table.

"Goddam you, Graden!" Anse stepped around the table. "You callin' my word?"

Tom did not move. "Your name Harp?" he asked quietly.

"You son of a . . ." The big rancher caught the reflex shift of the dropping hand as the thin gunman stepped back.

"I wouldn't, Anse." He stood up with the words, stepping away from the table and around it toward the snarling Canaday. "Somebody might call it murder."

Tom Graden never wore a gun. Every man in the Basin knew it. The big JT owner had just the naked kind of nerve necessary to such a social deviation in a land where every boy's first investment in leather goods was a gunbelt, not a razorstrap. Anse Canaday was well aware of both conditions. The hovering hand fell away from the holster. Tom eyed him a minute, turned to Harp.

"Harp?"

"It's so, Tom." The elder Bivins nodded uneasily. "The hoss was found the way Anse said."

"All right," Tom Graden's voice was suddenly far from soft, "so somebody shot the Old Man. We don't know they did, but we'll say it. And on top of sayin' that, we'll say this . . ."

He paused, letting them get set for it.

"We don't know who done it, nor if they done it, and we don't care. I'm still not havin' any open war in this Basin. We've licked the Fewkes and drove the Skaggs' sheep back up on the rim. We've done it without one white man we know of gettin' killed. You know my orders. They haven't changed none—no *killin'*. That goes if you find your old man tomorrow and with six slugs in his back and Jim Fewkes' name carved in his belly. You understand that, Anse?"

The latter turned for the door, saying nothing. Tom slid around him, barring his way. "I ask a question, Anse, I generally aim to get an answer."

"All right," the other's scarred mouth twisted to the empty grin, "so I understand. Anything else, *Mister* Graden?"

"There is. See that you remember it." There was no grin. "Judd tells me somebody run off that bay stud of Frank Rachel's. I ain't namin' no names. But Rachel's the last man I want pulled into this Basin trouble. Happen you put off on me once more, Anse, you're done here. You got that?"

"I got it," said Anse Canaday, the empty grin fading. "Now you get somethin', Graden. Your nose ain't exactly drippin' honey in this mess. There's those of us can wipe it for you, come the need. You got these Basin farmers stunk up with the idea you smell like a rose. That don't hang with me nor with Harp nor the boys. We know where you are and we know how you got there. You remember *that*."

"I'll remember it, Anse." Tom moved for the door, standing clear to give him passing room. "Just see you don't forget, none of you," the wide-set eyes went to the other riders, "what I said. You stay clear of the Fewkes and double clear of Frank Rachel."

"Why sure, Mister Graden, clear as the skin on a schoolmarm's leg." The woman-high laugh broke jarringly. "What do we care if the half-breed bastards murdered our old man? Or if that slob, Rachel, spreads it around the Basin we stole his studhoss? It don't mean nothin' to us, does it boys? We're just simple cowhands."

"We are, and it don't." Harp Bivins added his hard grin to his half brother's laugh. "Let's ride, Anse. Tempus, as the book fellers say, is fidgetin'!"

"So am I," grunted Clint. And, "Double it for me," said Simm.

"It's close in here," observed Jake. "Smells a little high. I need air."

The five riders filed out, climbed on their ponies and kicked them into a hammering gallop up and over the ridge.

Tom Graden watched them go, his face expressionless.

"Live by the sword . . ." he finally said to himself, and turned and went into the cabin.

The horses swung south of Parker's Store, moving closely bunched in the moonlight. At Cherry Creek their riders pulled them up. Anse broke the silence which had been thickening since the parting with Tom Graden.

"You don't suppose Mister Graden would mind if we took one more look for Pap, do you?" he asked pleasantly.

The big-shouldered Harp took the matter under sober consideration. "Why, now that you mention it, I don't suppose he would. What do you say, boys?"

"Suits me fine," said Clint.

"Where'll we look?" queried the unimaginative Jake, his wonderment seconded by the even slower Simm.

"Yeah, we done been every place in the Basin."

"Well, almost." Anse had the twisted grin working. Harp was right behind him, his mind moving faster than those of the other brothers.

"It ain't hardly likely he'd be visitin' *them*. But we can't overlook nobody, it ain't polite."

"You're right, it ain't." Clint had caught up with the drift. "Course, it's a little late in the evenin' for a social call."

"Well, that's so," said Anse thoughtfully. "I reckon we'd best ride on down all the same. Dark's the finest time to call on their kind. Happen it was daylight they might see us comin' and go to some trouble. We wouldn't want that."

"Naw," Harp grinned. "No point in puttin' them out. We can just hole up here and there around their place so's we can let them know we're there, first thing in the mornin'."

"Yeah, that's better," agreed Clint. "They ain't got the room to put us up anyways. Let's get along."

By this time even the literal Jake and Simm had worked up to the dust of the drag.

"By God," smiled the latter, happy with the speed and brilliance of his deductive powers, "you're aimin' to visit the damn Injuns! How did you figure that, Anse?"

"It's like he said, you dimwit!" Jake, proudly filling in for Anse, explained it for his less gifted brother. "It's the only place we ain't looked!"

"Let's get along," repeated Clint, unsmilingly. "I could use a little sleep before the shootin' starts."

"Me likewise," echoed Harp. "It ain't healthy to be heavy-eyed when you got your sights full of half-breed bucks."

"It ain't," nodded Anse succinctly. "Nor to be heavy-footed neither. We'd best leave the hosses at John's place, happen he's not home, and work on down afoot."

"You ain't just whistlin' Dixie," drawled Harp. "Let's ride."

"We're gone," said Anse. "Hold the hosses to a walk once we're clear of the crick. That damn Jim could hear a cinch buckle squeak in a six-foot snowstorm."

"Upwind," amended Clint dourly.

"And with ear muffs on," concluded Harp.

The horses splashed across the shallow stream, cut sharply right along its east bank. The faint jingle of the spade bits and the rhythmic creak and pop of the stirrup leathers gave the only sounds to mark their moonlight passage. Even these were soon lost beneath the friendly southward accompaniment of Cherry Creek's rush and bubble.

Frank crossed below Parker's Store and took the east bank trail about nine o'clock. He kept to the pine stands and juniper clumps where he could, riding slowly, continually casting the trail ahead.

Back home on the Texas border, at least when he had been a boy there, they had called this a "Comanche Moon." A man had been taught early to keep his eyes and ears open when it was lighting up the country.

Half a mile above John's place, the little sorrel mare

began to wind eagerly. He threw her off the trail, into the brush, sat listening intently. But there was nothing to be picked up above the noisy rush of the creek. After a minute of trying, he gave it up.

His next moves were a part and parcel of the conditioning a man came by after enough years of staying healthy on the highline. He got down off the mare, nose-wrapped her, tied her hard and fast to a post-thick piñon. When he came out of the pines, he was just another shadow joining those already strung along the brawling course of Cherry Creek. Only the occasional dull glint of the moon on the short barrel of the Winchester would have told a trained eye any differently.

At John's place, he held up for five minutes watching the silent cabin and the open moonlight of the corral. At the end of the time he went in, satisfied the place was deserted save for the little clump of saddled horses in the corral.

It was the way these horses were standing, all in a bunch nosed into the fence, that a man wanted to get a closer look at.

When he had had his look, he knew where his work lay.

He never forgot a man or the horse he rode. In that bunch of ponies were some he remembered. Harp's roan, Clint's buckskin, Jake's and Simm's two raunchy bays . . .

Where the creek trail opened into the main clearing of old John Fewkes' place, he held up again. A minute's swift study showed him nothing. The cabin lay dark and quiet, with only an occasional sleepy grunt from the hogpen to give the silence any life at all. Still, a man knew better. Somewhere out ahead of him were five men and as many rifles. It was just a hunch they were bedded-in waiting for daylight. But it was all a man had to go on. If he meant to help the Fewkes, he would have to ride that hunch.

He had one easy choice. The only way up to the cabin was along the pasture fence and upwind of the hogpen.

That would bring him to the water tank and the two big oaks. From there in, it was nothing. But getting that far was another matter. If one of the Bivins wasn't spotted

under the old juniper at the corner of the pasture fence,
they had missed a prime bet. Old hands like they were,
didn't pass up any such good spots as that fence corner.
One of them would be there.

Minutes later, easing up to the juniper through the
waist-high hay of the fenceline, he grinned.

The thicker shadow at the base of the old tree looked
to be nothing more than a field boulder. But field boulders
did not often wear wide hats. And even less often did they
snore in their sleep.

Simm Bivins never knew what hit him. For the historical
record, it was Frank Rachel's '73 Winchester butt, lovingly
planted behind his left ear. Frank watched him a minute
to make sure he would not wake up. He wouldn't, the
big rider decided, and moved on. An old sow winded him
and put up a short complaint, but her penmates did not
get the passing scent and she quieted quickly. Twenty
crouching steps later, he slid around the cook shack and in
past the hanging cowskin which served it as a door.

If the sleeping arrangements at the Fewkes' menage had
not altered, he should find Jim bunked in here by his
lonesome. They hadn't, and he did.

"Lost your way, stranger?"

The polite inquiry came backed by the welcoming shove
of the gun barrel's crown impacting the area between his
left and right kidneys. He had sense enough to stand hard
and fast and to talk the same way.

"Yes sir, I'm lookin' for little Jimmy Fewkes. My name's
Frank Rachel and I'm a good friend of his."

"Why you goddam fool, I could have killed you . . ."

"You pays your money and you takes your chances,"
grinned Frank. "I figured you'd be out here. Where's Ed
and John?"

"In the front cabin. Why?"

"Get them. The war's back on, boy. Anse Canaday and
the four Bivins is ambushed out yonder."

"How'd you get through?"

"Down the fence and past the hogpen. Simm is out
there at the pasture corner. I cooled him but he won't keep
all night. Rustle your butt."

Jim cursed, his mind moving swiftly around the perimeter of the trap. "We'll have to go afoot. Up the fenceline and into the rocks . . ."

"No we won't," interrupted Frank. "Hump it and get the boys like I said. We'll go in style. The Bivins left their hosses up to John's corral."

"You should have been an Injun," grunted Jim admiringly.

"I just joined the tribe," said Frank Rachel. "Get goin'."

The half-breed's eyes narrowed at the implication of the short phrase but he said nothing. He was back in three minutes, Ed and John shadowing him. "Lead off, Rachel," he growled quickly. "It's your war party."

The four men drifted past the hogpen, slid silently along the pasture fence. At its corner Frank paused, checking Simm. The big man had not moved and he hit him again to guarantee he wouldn't.

"I ought to scalp the son of a bitch!" rasped Ed, half meaning it literally.

"Save it for Anse," said Frank, meaning it all the way. "He's the prime pelt in that pack."

"I'll skin Harp for mine," muttered Jim. "He's the biggest cub in the litter."

"It don't leave me much," complained John. "Jake's half bald and Clint's mangey. Howsomever," his grin picked up, "beggers can't be choosers."

"They can't," grunted Frank. "See you stay to the high stuff along the fence, and keep your butts down."

"Look who's tellin' us Injuns how to belly-sneak tall grass!"

Nobody answered the youngster's mock indignation. His grin fell away as he turned to follow the others down the moon-black fenceline.

Whether it's beans or lead

They got safely away from the cabin clearing and headed up the Cherry Creek trail, Jim Fewkes coming last and covering the rear.

At John's place each man picked his horse. Frank cut the spare pony loose, knowing he would drift upcreek for the Graden spread, be of no use to the Bivins. Jim was the last mounted, the last out of the corral. Riding up to side Frank in the moonlight in front of John's cabin, he got his first good look at him. His slant eyes narrowed as they fell on the crossbelted Colts.

He and Frank Rachel had few secrets. In the long, lonely talks of their early friendship on the bench the big rider had sketched in much of his former life. Enough of it at any rate, to let a man know his face was on file with half the county sheriffs west of Fort Worth, and that the name under the picture on those filed flybills, wasn't Frank Rachel.

Jim had never seen the short barreled peacemakers but he had known about them. And known about the hard promise which had put them under the floor boards behind the Buck's range. He knew now, before he spoke, what had brought them out. Knew, too, what that bringing out would mean.

"Lib's gone." He broke his eyes from the guns, seeking Frank's face, voice held guardedly down.

"This mornin', Jim . . ."

"Quiet?"

"And peaceful. She never woke up."

"It was the studhoss done it." The half-breed's words were bitter. "Most of it, anyways."

"It was Garth Graden done it—*all of it!*" A flat, ugly deepness underlay the slow rise of the denial. Jim's nod and shoulder hunch came as he reined Harp's roan around.

"Likely we're both right. We'll collect double."

"Double or nothin'," was all Frank said. "Let's ride."

"Hold up a minute." Jim's wave checked him. "Ed, John . . ." The low call brought the two crowding up. "There's been a little change of plan."

His brothers looked at him, saying nothing.

"Likely you was figurin', like me," he went on, "that we'd hole up in the old hideout."

"Likely," nodded Ed. "Who says we ain't?"

"Lib does."

"Lib?"

"Ed. She's dead."

"Naw! How come you to know that? Where at?"

"We ain't told you," Jim replied. "It's the way she wanted it. But I spotted her down to Tombstone last winter. Frank rode down and brung her back for Christmas. She's been up on the bench ever since, just about happy enough to break your heart. She had the lung fever though. This mornin' she died of it." He paused, voice dropping. "She was doin' pretty good up till the studhoss disappeared."

"I ain't never said it," Ed said simply, "but I sure missed her."

"And me," nodded John softly. "Where did Graden leave her?"

"She never said. Frank found out she'd had a baby, born dead. He missed her in a dozen camps before then. No word of Graden in any of them past the first two or three."

"I reckon all of us are owin' him one," Ed concluded quietly.

"You're none of you owin' him nothin'!"

Frank heeled his mount around.

"If he ever shows in the Basin again, I'll kill the first man that touches him!"

"He's all yours, Frank. No need to get touchy over it." It was young John, keeping the peace. "Where do we ride now, Jim?"

"We'll head for Will Mittelson's. He's away to Globe and he won't mind us usin' his place. Not for what I got in mind."

"He sure won't," said Ed quickly. "He's lost his share of beef to the Bivins. I reckon you're aimin' to leave them a clear trail, that it, Jim?"

"Clear as the crick bottom. They'll smell Frank's rat along about daylight. Time they get hosses out'n our pasture, they should be along to Will's place for noon dinner. Any objections?"

"Suits me."

"And me."

"How about you, Frank? You mind shuckin' out a free feed for the Bivins boys?"

The big rider shook his head. "Not me," he said thoughtfully. "I'm thinkin' about somethin' Old Jim Stanton told me, the first handout he give me when I rode into the Basin."

"How's that?" Jim asked quietly.

"He said a man does better with his belly full, dependin' on whether it's beans or lead it's full of."

Ed Fewkes' grin spread wolfishly. "Somethin' tells me," he turned his pony with the slit-mouthed opinion, "Anse and his big brothers ain't goin' to like our brand of beans."

Frank swung his own pony to follow Ed's. Jim and John kneed their mounts in behind his.

"A man never likes it in the belly," Frank said unsmilingly.

It was twenty minutes past noon, Saturday, August 10th, when Harp Bivins pulled his borrowed horse off the Mittelson Ranch road a half mile below the house. With him were Anse, Clint, Jake and Simm, and three newcomers, John Payton, Tom Tuckman and Bob Gillespie.

The latter were all Hash Knife cowboys, former allies of the Gradens in the clash over the Skaggs Brothers' sheep. Payton was a Texas gunman with a considerable reputation, having headed the Hash Knife forces in the sheep fights. The three of them had met the Bivins group by accident, had joined up to "see the fun."

It was a day and time when no self-respecting gunhand ducked the chance to hear lead fly. When known "sheepmen" were involved, what was an ordinary pleasure became a happily anticipated duty. None of the group had

any idea Frank Rachel was with the Fewkes, all of them
having assumed the fourth horse to be ridden by old John
Fewkes. What historical difference this may have made
had they known it, must remain among the Peaceful Basin
imponderables, for it is a clear-cut certainty that no one
in the valley at that time knew Rachel had come down
from Apache Bench.

"You boys hold up here, back of the ridge," Harp
ordered. "Me and Anse will ride up and look around."

"Don't be all day," grinned Payton. "We're supposed to
be huntin' strays for the Hash Knife, not shootin' sheep-
herders for the Gradens."

"The Aztec Land and Cattle Company can afford the
delay." Anse's high laugh jarred the stillness.

"Yeah, besides," nodded Harp grimly, "this won't take
long." With the words, he wheeled his horse quickly up
the ridge, Anse swinging his mount to follow him.

Topping the ridge to look down on the Mittelson cabin,
his eyes narrowed. Anse returned the triumphant look and
they slid their horses back down the incline.

"Boys, we're in big luck!" Harp could not hold his
eagerness. "There's only one hoss tied out front, Clint's
buckskin. Otherwise the place is bare as the back of Jake's
head."

"Yeah," smirked Anse, breaking out the high laugh
again. "And guess who goes with that one hoss!"

"One's as good as another," grunted Payton.

"Which one of them, Anse?" Simm, the dullwitted one,
rubbed the big blue lump behind his left ear. "By God,
I hope it's Jim. He'd be the one that snuck out and
slugged me, sure as hell."

"You hope right," said Harp quickly. "We seen him
throwin' out the coffee grounds. It's *him!*"

"If we get Jim, Ed and John'll come easy. Jim's the
he-coon in that family tree." Payton was turning his horse.
"I'm hungry," he grinned. "Let's ride up and ask for some
noon dinner."

"It's as good a way as any," said Harp. "I'll do the
talkin'."

They rode up, halting their horses in front of the low

yard fence which surrounded the cabin, Harp centering the group.

Flanking him right and left, sat John Payton and Anse Canaday. The others, a little nervous even at eight-to-one where that one was Jim Fewkes, unconsciously edged their mounts back, giving their three leaders gracious working room. The cabin remained silent, no sign of life showing in or around it.

Harp shifted uncertainly, looking at the others. Anse laughed nervously. Payton scowled. The others looked away.

"Hello! Anybody home?"

Harp's inquiry echoed an understandable trace of nerve-edge.

The cabin remained silent.

"It's me, Harp Bivins. We seen you, Jim. Answer up in there."

The cabin door swung inward. He lounged against the jam, his strange blue eyes quiet and still, his guttural voice soft. In his slender hands the short-barreled Winchester did not move.

"I'm answerin', Harp. What you want?"

Again Harp shifted, again looked at his companions.

It had seemed like a Sunday school picnic five minutes ago. Now, and suddenly, it no longer felt so funny. The silence built and still Harp could not find his words.

John Payton, dark-faced and tense, kneed his horse forward a step.

"We was wonderin' could we get some noon dinner . . ."

"No sir," the answer was flat and short, "we don't keep no hotel here."

Once more the silence held, Tom Tuckman, the second of the Hash Knife cowboys breaking it uncertainly.

"Is Mr. Mittelson here?" The inquiry sounded inane, awkward, and simply like what it was, a pure stall.

"No sir," the monotone of Jim Fewkes' voice did not shift but the worn barrel of the Winchester did, "he done rode off somewheres."

Nobody spoke. Not a man moved.

Tuckman, not stalling now and patently wanting to

break it off, laughed nervously. "Well, boys, what say we
drift? We can go on down to Voseman's and get our dinner . . ."

"You'll get it here, you bastards!"

The interruption fell, deadly soft.

None of them had seen the big man move around the
east corner of the cabin. They saw him now. And they
heard him now.

"You come for it here, and you'll get it here. Make your
move."

With the words, he stopped moving forward, stood waiting, long arms loose, big hands brushing the tied-down
holster tops.

"*Frank Rachel!*"

Anse let it out as though it had been driven from him
by a fist in the belly. No laugh came with it and the
crazy, twisted grin was long gone. He held a moment,
white-faced, then suddenly jerked his horse back and
around. In the same instant John Payton, the Texas gunman, flashed his draw.

Frank cursed, in the last second cheated by Anse's rearing mount. With the curse and with incredible speed he
threw down instead on Payton. The leap and roar of his
right-hand gun shaded the Texan's, but the smash of the
.44 slug missed the Hash Knife gunman to quarter through
the barrel of his mount. The horse went back and up,
crashing to the ground, its deadweight pinning Payton's
leg. The latter's shot whined off the cabin corner, show-
ering the splintered wood a foot from Frank's face.

Harp had not moved for his guns when Jim Fewkes'
Winchester bellowed in echo to Frank's Colt. The tremen-
dous weight of the rifle's long bullet smashed into Harp's
face, shattering the nose, ranging upward and blowing out
the base of his skull. He was in the dust and sprawled
lifelessly at the same moment Payton's mount was going
down.

Blending the reverberations of Frank's and Jim's fire,
the other Winchesters crashed from the cabin windows,
Ed and John calmly levering their shots into the rearing,
side-plunging tangle of the cattlemens' horses.

Tuckman was hit, the big slug ripping broadside through

both lungs, knocking him half off his horse. Bob Gillespie drove his mount free of the tangle, shot through both arms and the right thigh. Payton, freeing himself of the pinning weight of his dead mount, came to his feet.

Jim snapped one at him, the bullet taking an ear away, ploughing on across the jaw. The Texan stumbled over his horse, shaking his head to free it of the blood. Frank shot him in the belly, four times. He twisted, staggered two steps, fell over Harp Bivins' torn body.

Anse Canaday had never been in it.

The thin gunman's first wild turn on recognizing Rachel had put his horse on the far sides of those of his companions, making it impossible for Frank or the men in the cabin to throw down on him. As his mount raced now for the shelter of the ridge, those of the other survivors followed frantically after.

Clint and Jake were unwounded, Simm had a clean hole through the flesh of his left side. Bob Gillespie, last away, riding side-and-side with Tuckman to keep the lung-shot Hash Knife cowboy in the saddle, was bleeding from three flesh wounds.

Ten seconds after the opening crash of John Payton's shot at Frank Rachel, the fight at Mittelson's Ranch was history, obscured then as now by the slow drift of the black powder gun smoke.

Two men were dead. One, Tuckman, clearly done for. Two others, Gillespie and Simm Bivins, were badly shot up. Anse and the dead Harp had never gotten into action. And their companions had thrown only scattered, wild revolver shots as they fled the deadly fire from the cabin.

Payton's opening shot at Frank had chipped the cabin corner. One of the general, wild shots had splintered the door jamb alongside Jim Fewkes. Those two foot-wide misses provided the sole degree to which the avenging Bivins' forces had made good their lethal intent that long-gone August day.

The entire affair, from Harp's call to the silent cabin to the echo of the final shot fading against the towering face of the rim, had taken less than a full minute.

Of such grimly brief duration were the hopes and ha-

treds of Harp Bivins. He was the first white man officiallly
to die in the Peaceful Basin War.

His death bloodstamped the beginning of the ugliest
vendetta in the remembered history of the frontier.

Just hold a pebble in your mouth

The killing of Payton and Harp Bivins was the
torch. The flame it set spread through the Basin like wild-
fire.

What had been a desultory sheep and cattle war burst
into a deadly outbreak of personal violence in which all
logical range-rights beginnings were quickly lost. Water
and grass and sheep and cattle were forgotten. It was man
against man and the battle cry on both sides was a life
for a life. A Navajo herder was nothing. Two thousand
shot and bludgeoned sheep were less. The stolen beef, the
reckless charges and counter-charges of rustling which
had set the sordid stage, vanished alike with the gunsmoke drifting away from the Mittelson cabin.

It was to the death now, not of stampeded sheep, missing cow, or even stolen horse, but of any man named
Fewkes and of any man named Graden, and of all of
those of any name who followed either cause.

The meaning of quarter was not mentioned nor thought
of. Every scarred boulder and twisted piñon in Peaceful
Basin hid a man of one side from the trail rider of the
other. To remain neutral was beyond the courage and
sanity of most of the valley's ranchers. To do so was only
to invite the lead of both feud factions. Every man rode
armed, when he could not avoid riding at all, and the
order of the day was to shoot first and turn the body over
for identification afterward. Many of the newcomers left
the Basin at once, a few of the old-timers slipping out un-
noticed under the dust of their departures.

Among these latter, Old Jim Stanton was the first and most notable.

But even in thus bowing from the stage he had helped set by granting Frank Rachel his original asylum four years before, the old pioneer paused long enough to pay one last respect to the lonely rider whose destiny he had from the beginning so grimly foreseen.

It was the early morning of August 13th when Ed Fewkes, lounging outside John's cabin, saw the old man's gelding swing in off the Cherry Creek trail.

"Mornin', Ed. Didn't rightly expect to see any of you boys around." He pulled the gelding up, eyeing the silent cabin. "Where's Frank?"

"Mornin', Jim. He's around. Why for you want to see Frank?"

"I'm leavin' the Basin. Dropped by on my way out. Aim to tell the boy good-bye. Where's he at?"

"Down at the old man's cabin."

"Jim and John with him?"

"Jim is. John's up coverin' the Mittelson spread. We had some trouble up there. Seems to me you're pretty full of questions, old hoss."

"Ed. Get your pony." Stanton ignored him, his glance going uneasily over his shoulder, upcreek.

Ed looked at him a minute, nodded quickly. He was back around the cabin in seconds, astride a mount which had obviously been saddled, waiting. They rode at a sharp trot, neither one talking.

Frank saw them coming and called into the cabin.

"Old Man, fetch Jim. Yonder comes Ed Fewkes and Jim Stanton."

Old John Fewkes came out, peered at the advancing horsemen, went without argument toward the cook shack. He was back at once, his middle son trailing him, the omnipresent Winchester in his brown hand.

Stanton rode up, staying on his horse while Ed slid off to join the dismounted group. "Hello, John." The JS owner's greeting went to the elder Fewkes. "It's been a spell."

"Yes, Stanton, I allow it has. We ain't seen you since Lib went off. What brings you downvalley?" Old John watched him, his built-in feel for trouble rising swiftly within him.

"Come by to see Frank mostly. I bid him into the Basin, he can bid me out of it."

"What you meanin', old man?" Frank moved forward with his question.

"I'm leavin' the valley, son."

"I had heard you was some time ago. What's got you started so sudden?"

"I reckon you know most of it. I come by to give you some of it you likely don't know, boy."

"Such as?"

"I just come from a meetin' at the Gradens' place. Every cattleman in the Basin that's on their side is up there. Tom is still tryin' to hold them back from comin' after you boys, but he ain't goin' to make it this time. That cussed Anse Canaday is talkin' wild and wantin' to lead a posse out after you right now, Tom Graden or no Tom Graden. And I'd say the majority of the Graden riders is backin' Anse and will ride with him. I come down to give you boys fair warnin' so's you'd have a halfway start at runnin' for it, if you want to. Way it is, I think maybe you got a few minutes to the good, happen you use them fast enough."

"Meanin' what, percisely?"

"Way they were talkin' when I left, they wasn't figurin' you'd be holed-up here. I wouldn't have, myself. I just figured to tip Old John off and let him get the word to you. They're aimin' to head for Mittelson's Ranch and trail out what tracks you left gettin' away from there the other day. That ought to give you a little time, like I said."

"We're beholden, old hoss." Frank eyed him, frowning. "Why'd you do it?"

Stanton shrugged uncomfortably, looking away. "Just say I never felt I'd paid you off in full for tryin' to help Johnny Fallon out of that train robbin' mess when that posse was after him. Happen you hadn't sided the boy, you wouldn't never have come to Peaceful Basin in the fust place, and wouldn't be in no trouble now. Like I say, figure it that way, son."

Frank stepped up to his stirrup, his heart telling him

why the old rancher had come. Telling him it had nothing to do with the old man's dead nephew or that long-
ago train robbery posse that Frank had tried to help the
kid away from. And telling him, too, that when Old Jim
Stanton left, one of the two real friends Frank Rachel had
ever made would be gone.

He looked at the grizzled rancher, shook his head. "It
don't figure that way," he said simply. "Gimme your hand,
old man."

Their hands met, the older man very clearly embarrassed. He broke the clasp quickly, not wanting to admit
there was any meaning in it. Picking up his reins, he
wheeled the gelding abruptly.

"Be careful, boy," he nodded. And then, softly. "I wish
you was ridin' along with me, Frank . . ."

He went out of sight around the creek bend as they
watched, not looking back nor turning to wave. It was
the last Peaceful Basin or Frank Rachel ever saw of "Old
Jim" Stanton.

Minutes after the old man had left and while they were
still arguing the best trail to lay as a result of his warning, John Fewkes raced his horse into the clearing. The
time Stanton has estimated they would have to make
their getaway, shortened uncomfortably with the youngster's first words.

"They're right behind me, headin' this way, followin'
our tracks from Mittelson's. Anse and about ten of the
Basin boys, along with four or five Hash Knife hands."

"How far they behind you?" snapped Ed.

"Ten, maybe twenty minutes. They was holdin' a stiff
lope. I run my mare all the way."

"She's blowed all right," said Jim quickly. "What happened up there?"

"Daybreak this mornin' Charley Parker showed up. He
had Jack Maddows with him. I reckon the Gradens sent
for Maddows, figgerin' they could sic him on us for them
killin's up yonder. They heaped some rocks over Harp
and Payton, and Maddows snooped around the place over
an hour. Him and Charley was just leavin' when Anse
and his bunch showed up."

"Maddows comin' with them now?"

"No, him and Charley headed back toward the store. Reckon Maddows means to go on back to Payson and wire Billy Mulvehey at Prescott."

"Well, that helps." He turned to Frank. "Maddows is the justice of the peace over to Payson. He's a square officer and ain't on either side. He'll go after either a Graden or a Fewkes, happen he thinks they're guilty. Right now, it's likely the way John says. He's left the Basin to get in touch with Billy Mulvehey and report what he found up yonder to Mittelson's. What you figger we'd ought to do, Rachel?"

"Best hit for your hideout, and fast. They ever pin us down in this hedged-in clearin' here at your old man's place, we're dead and done."

"Ed, John, get the canteens. Throw some beef in a bag." As the brothers ran to carry out the orders he turned to Frank.

"We can't make the regular hideout. It's clean up yonder back of Mittelson's. The kid's hoss won't hold up that far. The old man's been lookin' for our hosses the Bivins run out of the pasture, but he ain't got them rounded up yet."

"I know. Where can we head?"

"Second best bet is Rock House Canyon. That's the one you used comin' back from lookin' for Red Boy. There's an old Hopi pueblo up there built on a rock shelf forty feet high. It's what the canyon takes its name from."

"All right." Ed and John were coming from the cook shack. He swung up on his horse, holding theirs. "Any water up there?"

"Spring at the foot of the shelf," nodded Jim.

"At the foot!"

"Yeah. It ain't perfect."

"Any way out for us? Say, come dark tonight maybe?"

"Down the shelf. That's it."

Frank grabbed the canteen Ed handed him, pulled his horse aside as the latter and John legged up.

"I know a canyon that's goin' to have a new name before we're done with it," he grinned at Jim.

"Like what?" suggested the half-breed, guiding his pony in to side him.

"Like 'Rock Hearse,'" said Frank evenly.

"You still should have been an Injun," grunted the other rider. "You got a great sense of humor!"

Five minutes later, topping the hogback behind the Fewkes' pasture, they had a last view of the clearing below. At the same time the clearing had a final look at them.

"Last one over the ridge is a hind tit pig!" hissed Ed, eyes slitted toward the distant cabin.

"Yeah. They seen us," added Frank noncommittally.

"One of them things," shrugged Jim. "They sure brung enough 'friends' along this time, I'd say."

"By God, didn't I tell you!" Young John showed the only excitement.

"You did, boy," grinned Frank. "Let's go."

"And fast." Jim wasn't grinning. "We ain't goin' to have more than just time with that damn mare of John's done-in the way she is."

The half-breed's words were prophetic enough even for Frank Rachel's tough association with trouble. They slid off their horses and clawed their ways up the face of the cliff dwelling's shelf perhaps three minutes ahead of the pursuing cattlemen. It was a close shave by any barber's standards.

Short as the time was, it was sufficient for Frank to size up the Hopi redoubt.

Like Jim had said, the shelf stood up about forty or fifty feet above the canyon floor. The floor itself was at this point some two hundred yards wide, badly broken up with wash boulders, water cuts, mesquite and piñon scrub. Upcanyon, the throat of the gorge narrowed so swiftly a fair-sized man on a big horse could just about squeeze it. Downcanyon, it flared wide. Up and down and cross-canyon, there was cover enough to hide all the cowmen in Yavapai County. And the kind of cover which would let them swing a sight on anything bigger than a pine mouse that might try getting back down the face of that shelf.

The bench itself was well laid out. It was about fifty

feet deep, and ran back under the overhang of the wall so
that no one could get above you. Its outer edge was
lipped with waist-high rocks heavy enough to turn a three-
inch shell. Across the canyon the wall was just as precipitous, guaranteeing that no one could shoot down on you
from that side either. As far as firing back, it was all your
way. You could keep them pinned down in that canyon
bottom until hell not only froze, but thawed.

Frank shrugged, the quick grin bitter as alkali dust.
Rock House Canyon was a perfect hole-up.

The Graden forces could not get in at them in a million years, and in maybe twice that time they might figure some way to get out on the cattlemen!

Their pursuers camped six hundred yards down the
canyon. They were in clear view but well out of rifle
range. Four or five of them crept past the shelf, using the
ample cover of the house-sized boulders along the far
wall. These set up a guard in the upper gorge. The others
made themselves as comfortable as they could in the
lower camp. After a short while, Anse and two Hash
Knife hands worked up the canyon floor a ways and lobbed
a few long shots at the shelf. Ed and Jim promptly
sprayed them with lead and rock dust, nicking one of the
Hash Knife men in the shoulder. Things quieted down.

Noon came and was sweated under. The heat under
the cliff house wall was intolerable, that on the canyon
floor little less. The men on the shelf panted and cursed
and watched the naked shimmer of the rocks below.

By four o'clock the water in the last canteen was gone
and by six their suffering from thirst became unbearable.
Then, just before dusk, they observed some movement in
the downcanyon camp.

It became shortly apparent that the bulk of the cattlemen were returning to the Basin for siege supplies, their
main need no doubt the same as that of the thirst-crazed
defenders—water. The tiny rock pool of the spring at the
base of the shelf was the only supply for either camp, and
it lay under the guns of both.

By full dark the men on the cliff knew they were finished. It was get water or die, and get it before the moon

came up. They had an hour, perhaps an hour and a half.

"I'm goin' down," croaked Ed. "We're dead anyways."

"Goddammit, we can shoot through them!" John's water had gone first. The youngster was talking wild. "There ain't no more than five, six of them left down there!"

"There's eight, countin' the one at the spring." Frank corrected him, thinking out loud, his own tired mind forcing itself to the problem.

"Yeah, you're talkin' crazy, boy." Jim put his hand on his brother's shoulder. "What we got to have is water, you hear? We get water, we can hang on another day. We hang on another day, somethin's bound to break. I'm goin' down now. You and Ed cover me from the lip. Gimme them canteens, Frank. You cover too."

"Hold up, *paisano*." The big rider retained the canteens. "I got a better idea."

"I'm listenin'. Make it good."

"You don't bull me none with that tomorrow talk. Ed's right. We don't get out of here tonight, we ain't goin' to get out. There ain't nobody comin' up that canyon in the mornin' with a reprieve from the Governor."

"Keep talkin', you ain't said nothin' yet."

"You go down like you say, totin' the canteens." Frank pushed his words, knowing the need for hurry. "Ed and John stay up here, coverin'. I follow you ten, maybe twenty feet back. They got that one hombre coverin' the spring like I said. Back of that yucca clump yonder. Am I right?"

"You're right. What else?"

"You get down there to the water without you're heard. You fill them canteens. When they're full and you're ready to take off, you bang one of them on a rock, deliberate."

"You crazy for Christ's sake?" Ed's hard voice cut in.

"Nope. Feller down by that yucca is."

Quickly he sketched the rest of it for them, Jim nodding as he went along, Ed scowling, John blank-faced. It was a desperate proposition but they were desperate men. Even so, when he had finished Ed's query was immediate and acid.

"Yeah? Then what? The whole gang of them down

there opens up on you two. And me and the kid sets up here all day tomorrow suckin' pebbles and watchin' the bottleflies blowin' you and Jim!"

"I said it ain't guaranteed," shrugged Frank. "But neither is God." Then, after a significant pause, "Anybody thirsty?"

Jim spat out the smooth pebble which he, like the others, had been sucking most of the long afternoon. He stood up, taking the canteen from Frank.

"It'll be like Rachel says, Ed. You and John stay up here and cover us for the first part. When you see Rachel's gunflash, follow down fast. Now remember, no shootin' unless they open up on us goin' down, or until Rachel opens up on them. You got it?"

Ed picked up his Winchester, his scowl easing.

"Like the proud-cut stud said to the flirt-tail filly, leave us at least give it a try."

Frank grinned. Easing off his boots, he handed them to Ed. "If we don't make it, pardner," he promised soberly, "you can have them."

"Oh, goody!" grimaced the other. "Just what I've always wanted. A real pair of cowboy boots!"

"Aw shucks, it ain't nothin'," said Frank magnanimously.

"You're right it ain't," said Ed. "Hop your butts!"

Jim went first, sliding over the lip of the shelf and down the foot-wide trail which slashed its face diagonally toward the spring below, his Apache moccasins soundless on the naked rock. Behind him, stocking-footed and cat-gingery, moved Frank, his own passage a shadow of the half-breed's.

Two endless minutes later Jim was at the spring, filling the canteens. Twenty feet above him, Frank crouched against the face of the shelf, Winchester cheeked tightly, the invisible swing of the weapon's muzzle trained toward the spiked silhouette of the yucca plant.

He waited for what seemed an eternity for the signal from Jim. At last it came, the jarring, hollow clank of a metal canteen "accidentally" banging against a trailside rock.

The orange flame spat at once from the base of the

yucca, the lead ricocheting harmlessly off the granite above the spring. Frank held, pulling the butt stock closer. The yucca shadow moved, grew more solid, took on the blurred shape of a crouching rifleman. Twice more in rapid succession the orange flames spurted toward the spring.

Frank fired then, holding low on the shadow and levering four shots into it.

He saw the shadow straighten up, twist violently, fall back behind the yucca. He heard the strangled cry and the dry rattle of the rocks as the body bounced in among them. He was up then, and running, hearing the slide and scramble of Ed and John behind him on the shelf trail and seeing now, ahead of him, the looming blur of Jim's form.

The four shadows drew into one, moving swiftly along the base of the north wall. As they went, the alarmed voices of the downcanyon camp began to call back and forth across the darkness, working up the south wall toward the agonized groans of the wounded sentry. Jim led his shadows past theirs, the confusion of the sudden firing compounded by the outcries of the injured man covering the split-second timing of the escape.

Shortly, he passed out the refilled canteens, along with some cogent advice.

"We'll go on out, afoot. They'll never follow in the dark. We'll likely make it now, and we can get hosses later."

As he talked, the others drained their canteens with sucking, dragging gulps, Frank holding half of his for the half-breed. He handed it to him and Jim drained it. When he had, he sailed it across the canyon. It hit bangingly on the far wall, bounced and rattled to the granite floor. "It'll give them somethin' to stalk," he grunted. "Let's drift."

Ten minutes more and they were at the canyon's mouth.

Jim turned north, skirting the piled boulders and deep brush of the main ridge. He moved fast, knowing they would need the rest of the night to reach the hideout north of Mittelson's on foot. The others followed, single file, wordless, all their breath required to hold the half-breed's swinging dogtrot.

Within the hour the moon rose white and glaring, spilling its clear wash into the narrow gorge of Rock House Canyon. By its light, the seven Graden horsemen picked their careful ways through the boulder litter choking its mouth, their progress as grimly silent as had been the flight of their intended quarry.

Silent, too, was the eighth horseman, his body sagging across the saddle of his led-mount, the awkward flop of the shattered thighbone which had bled him to death before his companions could move him, bumping and jolting the flank of his nervous horse.

History has not left the name of the cowboy who guarded Rock House Spring that night. He was the third recorded white man to die in the Peaceful Basin War.

The unmarked headstone of that simple fact has remained his only epitaph these sixty-odd, forgotten years.

The Devil's deputy

On the third day following the Rock House fight, Frank, on guard above the cliff path leading to the hideout, saw two horsemen far below. One of them stick-straight and familiar, was Old Man Fewkes. The other was a stranger. He sent the quail whistle up the mountainside and shortly Jim came down to join him in the lookout. Studying the horsemen below, his eyes narrowed.

"It looks like Jim Hook," he growled.

"Who the hell's Jim Hook?" Frank matched his frown.

"Deputy for Sheriff Perry Odens over in Apache County. *Es hombre malo . . .*" he tailed off in the patois Spanish of the territory, scowl deepening.

"So he's a bad one. Where's he sit in our game?"

"With us, somewhat. I never liked the bastard but he bought-in with the Skaggs on them sheep. On the q.t., naturally. Anyways, he's run more or less with us since then."

"Live and learn," shrugged Frank. "Seems I ought to have heard about him before now."

"How so?" scowled Jim.

Frank looked at him, returned the scowl. "It strikes me we're gettin' powerful messed up with sheriffs around here. First we got Mulvehey, then Maddows. Now, this Hook bastard shows up. Mulvehey and Maddows I can figger. They're both Yavapai County boys and like you and John say, I can see where they would work together. But I don't get this Hook. Where's he figger in a Yavapai County play like this here Basin fracas?"

"I don't rightly know, no more than I've a'ready told you. All I know is he lets on to be for us and agin the Gradens. I allow he's got some ax of his own to grind but we ain't none of us found out what it is. He don't bother me none, though. I reckon we can handle him and his shifty kind. It's the straight ones like Maddows and Mulvehey you got to worry about. You can't buy off neither of them and they're both out to clean up this Basin mess if it means gettin' all of us, Gradens and Fewkes alike."

"Still seems to me," said Frank, hard-voiced, "that I ought to have heard about this Hook before. One way and another, he bothers me."

"His idea. He don't want no speeches made about the fact he's backin' us. Says he figgers he can help us more if it ain't too generally knowed whose side he's on."

"Well then, dammit, what you got against him?"

"Too fast with the *pistoles*. He's a natural killer like Anse. Just rightly likes to see a man grabbin' his guts and goin' into the dirt."

"Birds of a feather," muttered Frank bitterly. "He's on the right side."

"We ain't killed yet that we didn't have to," retorted Jim sullenly.

"I don't know." The big rider shook his head, thinking out loud again. "It's somethin' gets into a man once he's buckled on a gun and knows how to use it." He paused as the riders below headed into the rocks and began to climb. "You goin' to let the old man bring him up here?"

"No, I'll ride down. See what he wants and then ride back out with him. He might try doublin' around, I never

trusted him. Meantime, you stay here and arrange with
the old man to have them hosses and provisions at the
ranch next week." He turned to go, adding quickly, "And
don't forget the ammunition."

"I'm likely to," said Frank. "Get goin'."

He watched Jim slip down the mountainside and halt
the horsemen. Old John Fewkes at once dismounted, giving Jim his horse. He began the precipitous climb up the
hideout foot trail as his son talked swiftly and earnestly
with the Apache County deputy.

It was a short talk, Jim riding off with Hook before the
old man reached Frank.

The latter's questions to the elder Fewkes brought immediate and acid answers.

The deputy had given old John a long yarn about having an Apache County warrant for Judd Graden, sworn
out against him by a Fewkes partisan Hook refused to
name, and based on a counter-charge that it was the
Gradens themselves, not Ed and John Fewkes, who had
been doing the Basin rustling.

Hook had claimed that Sheriff Odens had arranged
with the Yavapai authorities to issue the warrant, since as
sheriff of Apache County Odens was more or less a neutral in the Basin trouble and might hope to get a peaceful
surrender where Billy Mulvehey, as sheriff of Yavapai
County, couldn't begin to. He had refused to show old
John the warrant, insisting on being taken to Jim.

It developed that the old man had no more use for the
Apache deputy than did his slant-eyed son.

Hook claimed to have been in the Basin over a week,
waiting to jump Judd when and if he could catch him
alone. The whole deal smelled as high as a ten-day dead
horse to Old Man Fewkes, and trouble was as bound to
come of it, he grumbled, as the sun was due to sink in
the west.

When he had finished, Frank gave him Jim's orders
about the horses, food supplies and ammunition. He
promised to have everything at the cabin by week's end
and after a short talk with Ed and John, slipped back
down the mountain and headed south on foot.

The hours seemed to drag on without end, the sun to

hang motionless over the Mazatzals, as though it were never going to sit down. Dark came at last. A nervous hour later Jim Fewkes followed it in.

His report was as short as it was sinister.

"Where the hell you been?" demanded Ed querulously. "We thought for sure Hook had double-crossed you."

"He for sure did," snapped Jim. "Me and you and John and Frank and everybody in the Basin that's sided us. *He's killed Billy Graden!*"

The silence held while in the minds of each of the listening men, the bleak implications of Jim's final words raced swiftly.

Billy Graden was just past twenty-one, the barrel-choice apple of Tom Graden's proud eye. The boy had had little to do with the war. Frank had not seen him more than two or three times since the youngster had arrived from the Iowa homestead of the Gradens' parents sometime during the late fall of '83. He was a big, blond, curly-headed kid, hard worked and making rapidly into a top hand. He had never in the least way been mixed into the Basin trouble, Tom having succeeded in keeping him free of Anse and the Bivins and the whole Parker's Store crowd of feuding cattlemen.

None of the silent men, Frank, Ed or John, had the slightest doubt what his killing would be called, nor what its occurence would bring about. It would be called murder. And it would bring Tom Graden raging out into the open at last.

Frank was first to break the growing stillness.

"How'd it happen?" was all he said.

"It ain't sweet so I'll make it short," grated Jim. "The Old Man has told you about the warrant?" The others bobbed their heads and he went on.

"Well, Hook give me the same line. I called him on it and he folded. Wouldn't show me the damn thing. Maybe he had it, maybe he didn't. But when he wouldn't leave me see it I told him to ride. He argued some, sayin' Odens had ordered him not to show it around. I held. He said, 'All right, Jim, I'll have to serve it alone. I thought maybe you boys could help me locate Judd.' I didn't say nothin' and he rode off."

"Sure smells fishy," grumbled Ed. Frank and John muttered low agreement and Jim continued.

"Did to me, too. I let him get started then cut out and tailed him down the Basin. He stopped at Haggler's Ranch for noon dinner. Haggler was evidently scared stiff of him, likely on account of him being thought to side with us Fewkes. He fed him fast and got him off the place inside of fifteen minutes.

"Hook swung a wide circle and hid out in some brush alongside the Payson trail where it crosses north of the Graden meadow. I hid out on a ridge higher up and waited along with him.

"Along late in the afternoon I seen a horseman comin' from the direction of the Graden Ranch. I thought he was alone and apparently Hook did too. It looked like Judd at first, a big man and wide-set. The trail was pretty well shadowed by then, you see. But by the time he had rode past me and headed on toward Hook, I seen it wasn't Judd but young Billy.

"I let down some then, figurin' it was all over and never dreamin' Hook would make a show against the boy."

He paused, growling the rest of it savagely.

"I was that close above them I heard every word of it. Hook kicked his hoss out in the trail as the kid rode up. He had his gun out. He said, 'I want you, Graden. I got a warrant.' I reckon the kid didn't know Hook. But he knew a gun. He went for his own and not hesitatin' none. He never got it out, naturally."

"That all?" asked Frank, after waiting for Ed or John to say something.

"I wish it was, but it ain't. The kid hung onto the saddle and his hoss got him out of there, gallopin' wild back toward the ranch. Hook dusted on west and I started east. I told you I thought the kid was alone. He wasn't. One of the JT hands had been ridin' behind him. I was just crossin' the ridge when he galloped up and grabbed the kid's hoss. I reckon he seen me, for I was in the open when he broke around the trail."

"Who was it?" Ed put the terse question.

"Looked like Joe Ellensburg. Light was bad by then. Couldn't be sure."

"Did he see Hook, Jim?" Young John put the big question, waiting nervously.

"No. He just heard the firin', rode up fast, and seen me leavin' the same way."

"Well, that's just dandy," Frank drawled. "Now what the hell do we do?"

"We get out of here right now!" snarled Ed.

"How come? They don't know this place." Frank was very uneasy now, knowing the hell the killing of young Billy Graden would let loose in the Basin.

"They *didn't*," said Jim meaningfully. "But Ed's right. What with Hook and the Old Man both having been in here today, we can't chance it. They could have spotted them comin' in, or me and Hook goin' out. We move."

"Where to?"

"Out on the Basin floor." Ed was reaching for his Winchester. "I don't want no more hole-in-the-rocks hide and seek. We can camp in the brush along upper Cherry Crick till we get a chance to hit for the cabin and get hosses."

"Suits me," agreed John hastily. "The hell with this damn mountainside stuff. Gimme the brush anytime."

"All right, let's go then," said Jim.

"After you," growled Frank, cursing under his breath as he followed the three half-breeds down the narrow trail.

He had had about enough of this infernal Apache sneaking around. Damn these crazy Indians anyway! The time was fast coming, if it had not already arrived, when they would, all of them, have to stand and make a showdown of it.

To the dangerously trained hands and deeply hurt heart of Frank Rachel, that time could not come any too soon. In the big rider's belly, as he trailed the Fewkes across the valley floor, the old pinch was growing.

Why did they want to kill me?

Billy Graden was shot on the 17th. He died the following night the Graden Ranch. His last words to his grief-stricken older brother were, "Tom, I still don't know why the Fewkes would want to kill me."

Those thirteen pathetic words forecast the final die of the Peaceful Basin vendetta.

The boy had died in Tom Graden's arms. From that tortured moment, the owner of the JT turned on the Fewkes like a wounded grizzly. Up until then it had been his strong will and iron refusal to be pulled into the feud on a personal basis which had kept its casualties to their present, grim minimum.

Now, and suddenly, he seized belated control of both his own hired gun fighters and of the so-called "honest cattlemen" who made up the Graden side. Terror swept the Basin anew. The outburst of feeling which had flared following the killing of Harp Bivins paled by contrast.

The Fewkes and Frank Rachel were men doomed as surely as though by a constituted court of law. Their sentence was death, Tom Graden their judge, prosecutor and self-appointed executioner. The fact that Hook, not Jim Fewkes, killed Billy Graden was not known until the former returned to St. Johns nearly a month later.

Of the many unsolved puzzles of the Peaceful Basin War, Deputy Jim Hook's part in it remains one of the most frustrating. Old-timers are still arguing his role in the feud. Was he really allied with the Fewkes? Was he, in the beginning, actually one of the Skaggs Brothers' hirelings? Did he honestly mistake young Billy for Judd Graden? Did he ever really have a warrant for the latter? Or did he have some never-revealed personal reason for wanting the war enlarged and brought into the open? The questions are as unanswered today as they were in their own time. The known fact of the long delay in Hook's return to his Apache County office in St. Johns has had only one explanation—one put forward years later by a surviving Fewkes partisan—that the Apache County deputy had remained in hiding in the Basin itself for almost four weeks, fearful to move out of it until the wave of terror put in motion by his brutal killing of young Billy Graden had subsided.

Two things alone are clear. Except for one minor reappearance in the closing hours of the war, Jim Hook bowed out of its grim history with the killing of Billy Graden.

And it was, indeed, almost a month to the day, before he reappeared in St. Johns officially to report that killing.

By that time the *Fourth Horseman* had already thundered across Peaceful Basin's "dark and bloody ground."

A week passed and grew into ten days. Still the Fewkes remained apparently absent from the Basin, and still the restless riders of the Graden cattlemen combed the valley in vain for a trace of their disappearance.

It was the morning of August 23rd when a scout rode into the headquarters ranch beyond Parker's Store to report seeing the Fewkes brothers and Frank Rachel leaving old John Fewkes' place before daylight.

In eager response to Tom Graden's barking orders, Anse Canaday rounded up every hand on the Graden place. This group was joined by a dozen ranchers from Parker's Store. By nine o'clock the avengers of Harp Bivins, John Payton, the nameless Rock House cowboy and young Billy Graden were riding swiftly for old John Fewkes' cabin.

They had not gone a mile down the Cherry Creek trail when they met, head-on, with another even bigger, more determined group.

Anse pulled his pony in, his followers holding up behind him. The composition of the approaching group warranted the discretion.

Anse, along with more than a few of the horsemen behind him, was well enough acquainted with the official personnel of the duly elected law enforcement bodies of the immediate southwest, to recognize such "P for promi-

nent" peace officers as Billy Mulvehey of Prescott and
Jules French of Flagstaff. When the sheriff and deputy
sheriff of Yavapai County rode into you backed by con-
stables of the cut of Emmett O. Dell, Johnny Wexford
and Fletcher Fairhurst, you pulled in your ponies and
waited. And while you waited you wondered. Wondered
if that damn Jack Maddows had wired Mulvehey at Prescott about the Mittelson Ranch killings like he'd promised
Charley Parker he would, and if Mulvehey was now riding into you as a result of Maddows' report. And if so,
what he meant to do about it.

Anse was given only time to get his wondering started,
when it was cut pleasantly and soft-drawlingly off.

"Mornin', Canaday." Mulvehey did the talking. "Where
you bound?"

Anse thought a minute, then let him have it straight
out. "After the Fewkes. What brings you?"

"More of the same," said Mulvehey easily, and watching him with his eyes as hard as his voice was soft. "I got
ten bench warrants over my own signature. For the lot of
them: Ed, Jim, John, Frank Rachel, Joe Boyce, Jacoby,
Roady, Billy Beshar, all of them."

"For what?" sneered Anse. "Runnin' sheep?"

"For the murder of Harper Bivins and John W. Payton," answered Mulvehey evenly. "Any objections, Mr.
Canaday?" Anse didn't miss the little inflection.

"None, sheriff!" The crazy laugh broke quickly. "It's
about time. Good luck!" He was turning his mount with
the words, when Mulvehey cut in.

"Hold up, Canaday. Where you think you're goin'?"

"After the Fewkes, like I said. You do it your way, I'll
do it mine. Warrants has been brung in here before."

"So?"

"Sure. Bringin' them's easy. Servin' them's somethin'
else again."

"I'll serve mine. You want to ride after the Fewkes,
you'll ride after them back of me, legal and proper, or not
at all. I've had my bellyful of this mess in here."

Mulvehey paused, his quiet eyes sweeping the crowded
ranks of the nervous cattlemen behind Anse.

"I want somethin' got straight by all of you, right now.

See you remember it and don't say you wasn't warned. I back nobody in this goddam feud you got goin'. I'm sheriff of this county and the only thing I back are its laws. One of them laws deals with murder. Where I can prove a murderer in here, somebody's goin' to hang for it. It happens I got warrants for the Fewkes this time. Next time they might be for you!" It was a general statement, but his eyes drove it squarely at Anse Canaday.

"Now don't let me rush you, boys," he drawled softly. "You want to take the Fewkes, you're welcome to ride along and see them took, legal. Otherwise, turn around and drag your tails."

Anse eyed him, let his nervous glance slide to the sobering faces of the big group of horsemen backing him, saw no reassurance there. "Suits me!" The laugh again, high and quick. "How about you, boys?"

The Basin cattlemen nodded, most of them glad enough to have official backing. "All right, sheriff," the crooked grin spread, "let's go."

"There'll be shootin'," grunted Mulvehey, "when I say so and not before." There were no arguments. The thirty horses splashed across Cherry Creek, turned south, picked up to a high lope.

They got onto the trail at the Fewkes ranch and followed it northward until late afternoon. By that time and from the way the tracks lay, Mulvehey was convinced the Fewkes were heading for the old Navajo trail and Holbrook, probably to stock up on ammunition.

Knowing the old trail was the only break in the north rim, he announced his intention to camp astride it and await the return of the fugitives. Anse objected at once and angrily. And in vain. The posse, and most of his own men, sided with Mulvehey. Camp was made.

At eight o'clock that night, with the supper fire banked and the last cigarettes being built, the sound of a shod horse was heard along the upper trail. Seconds later, the horseman rode into the reach of the firelight.

Anse started for his gun but Mulvehey moved in, striking his arm up.

"Thanks, Sheriff." The big horseman eased in the saddle. "I aim to let the little man make his play one day, but this ain't the day."

Mulvehey kept it quiet, making no move with his Winchester. "I've got a warrant for you, Frank. You're under arrest."

"Suits me," nodded the other, "only don't pull it on me just now. I got a friend wants to see you first."

"Name of Jim Fewkes?" asked the officer.

"Didn't catch the name, Sheriff." The brief grin flicked his mouth corners. "Some feller I bumped into in the dark. You comin'?"

"I'm comin'," said Mulvehey, and moved for his saddled pony.

There was an immediate argument among the posse. Any man who would follow Frank Rachel off into the dark alone was an idiot. The classification held for Billy Mulvehey or anybody else.

The quiet officer waited. When his followers had stopped talking, he turned to Frank.

"You've got a friend, Frank. Any objections to me bringin' one?"

"Pick your man," nodded the big rider. "My pal don't like to be left alone. He's scared of the dark."

"I imagine," murmured Mulvehey, making no effort to hide the grin. "Come on, Jules. Leg up."

"Bring the warrants," said Frank. "My friend's purely human. He'll want to see his name in print."

"I'll show it to him." The grin was gone. "Lead off."

Frank went first, Mulvehey and his deputy crowding their mounts behind his in the darkness. As he guided them north along the Holbrook trail, Frank's mind turned restlessly on two questions: where did Sheriff Bill Mulvehey stand in the feud, how did Deputy Jim Hook fit into it?

Actually, he thought he knew where to put Hook. Jim had said he was a killer. Coming from Jim Fewkes that was a professional opinion not to be ignored. Real man-killers didn't need any reason to make a war or keep one going. The West was full of men who wore badges for one purpose only, as a permit to kill and a legal shield against getting strung up for it. A man could no doubt run

Hook right along with that dirty herd and forget about him.

But Billy Mulvehey was something else. He was not a professional killer and as far as a man could figure or find out, he was, like Jack Maddows, backing nothing in the Peaceful Basin feud but the cold law. Judging him for yourself, just as a man, you had to figure he actually meant to pick up you and the Fewkes on those murder warrants, legitimately, and to do his level best to see you got a fair shake in court, too.

But the whole tangle of sheriffs was one too many for Frank Rachel. You only knew one thing. Mulvehey, nor Hook, nor Maddows, nor nobody, was going to pick Frank Rachel up before he had served his own Winchester warrant on the Gradens. That was for certain as a .44 slug through the kidneys would kill you.

"That you, Rachel?"

The low call came out of the dark, checking the shadows of the three horsemen.

"It's me. We're comin' in."

"Who's with you?"

"Billy Mulvehey, like you wanted. And Jules French."

"Come along in."

They guided the horses around the big boulder and in under the thick piñon clump backing it. Mulvehey swung down, asking softly, "That you, Jim?"

"Yeah. Hello, Billy. I got a deal, happen you want to hear it."

"What goes, happen I don't?"

"You do," gritted the half-breed. "Right on back to where you come from."

"Fair enough. What's your deal?"

"We heard you was comin', and with warrants for the lot of us."

"You heard right. That Jim Hook gets around." The reference was acid. The Apache County deputy was not only a sheepman and a known Fewkes partisan, but a trouble-maker of long standing in his own hard right.

"Hook's my friend, same as you," said Jim slowly.

"Leave me out of it," replied the officer. "What's this

Anse tells me about you pluggin' young Billy Graden?"

"Hook done it." The half-breed did not flinch to the sharp barb of the unexpected question. "He'll back me on that soon as he reports back to Odens at St. Johns. Right now he's scared to move. He's hidin' out in the Basin till things cool off, same as us."

"He with you?"

"No sir, he ain't."

"All right, we can check your story. I'll wire Odens when I get back to Prescott. Meanwhile, what's your deal?"

"You got them warrants with you?"

"I got them. Maddows wired me what he'd found at Mittelson's. He named Frank and you, along with Ed and John. I didn't have no choice but to charge you boys with the killin's."

"All right, show me the warrants. If they got our names on them, we'll come in on one condition."

"Name your condition and maybe you can have it," said Mulvehey. He made no move to produce the warrants.

"You arrest the Gradens first. All of them. Judd, Tom, and that goddam Garth when he shows up."

"Where's Garth figure in it?" asked Mulvehey, puzzled. "He ain't been in the Basin since '84, and he ain't in it now as far as I've heard."

"He ain't yet, you're right," nodded Jim. "But you just ain't heard far enough."

Frank felt his belly pull, hard up. Felt the muscle in his jaw twitch and run. That damn Indian-mouthed Jim! He hadn't said a word to *him* about Garth. He waited, pale eyes narrowing, for Mulvehey's reply.

"Such as how far ain't I heard?" said the Yavapai sheriff quietly.

The half-breed spoke quickly. "Hook told me their office over to St. Johns got a wanted flyer on Garth from down Tularosa way two weeks ago. He was last seen in Alamogordo, headin' this direction."

"Damn funny Perry ain't wired me . . ."

Mulvehey meant Perry Odens, famed, fancy-dressing, long-haired sheriff of Apache County and, Frank knew, Deputy Jim Hook's immediate superior.

"It ain't funny," said Jim. "How about my deal?"

Mulvehey eyed him through the dark, pausing.

"Lemme see if I got you right. You're sayin' if I get out warrants and pull in the Graden bunch, too, you'll come in peaceful. That it?"

"That's it."

"How about otherwise?"

"Otherwise, unpeaceful," grunted the half-breed.

Again the officer paused.

Billy Mulvehey was afraid of no man, Jim Fewkes included. But he was squarely up against the biggest fight of his official life, and he knew it.

He also knew he was up for re-election and that his Yavapai County constituency had had about all it could hold of the Peaceful Basin killings. The murder of Billy Graden, hardly more than a blood-related bystander, would raise hell back in Prescott.

Billy Mulvehey was that rarity among peace officers, the duly elected minion who understood his job to mean the maintenance of law and order at any cost. In the present case that maintenance had meant finding and arresting a personal friend, Jim Fewkes, on a sworn charge of murder, and to bring him in, innocent or otherwise, to stand trial on the charge.

Thinking rapidly now, Mulvehey also knew that the trouble in Peaceful Basin would not be over so long as one Graden and one Fewkes were left free in it, that neither side was all black or all white, and that in arresting the Fewkes the inevitable, final clash between the two factions was only being put off.

Now, suddenly, in Jim's simple suggestion that were he to arrest the Gradens as well, the Fewkes would surrender on demand, the Yavapai sheriff saw a way out that would clearly serve the ends of impartial justice and his own stern sense of law enforcement at the same time.

With the decision, he spoke at last, and quickly.

"What do you think, Jules?" The question on legal ethics went to the silently waiting deputy.

"Same as you, I reckon. It might work, at that. I don't see no better way offhand. The boys in the posse will holler, but I allow you can handle them."

Mulvehey knew French was right, that the posse would

make trouble if he didn't return with the men named in
the warrants; decided, as quickly, it was worth that gamble;
spoke short and hard.

"I allow I can. All right, Jim," he turned to the watchful
half-breed, "it's a deal. Twenty-four hours after I take the
Gradens, you be at your old man's ranch. All of you."

"Ed and John and me," corrected the half-breed. "I
can't speak for Frank or Joe Boyce or any of the others
of them."

"The others'll come in. I ain't worried about them.
Frank," Mulvehey wheeled on him, "what about you?"

"I'll be there," he nodded. "Providin' . . ."

"Providin' what?" The officer's voice tightened.

"Providin' I get Garth Graden meantime."

Mulvehey looked at him, nodding thoughtfully.

"I'll buy that. The odds favor me."

"They do," grated Frank, his own voice suddenly harsh
and deep. "You can find your way back all right, I reckon?"

Mulvehey swung up. "I reckon. I got Jules to hold my
hand, happen I get worried. So long, Jim."

"So long, Billy."

"See you, Fewkes." Jules French heeled his pony to follow Mulvehey's. "So long, Rachel."

There was no answer from Frank or Jim, both having
faded back into the brush. The two officers looked at one
another and shrugged. Guiding their ponies around the
boulder, their shadows were quickly lost in the darkness
down the trail.

Frank waited until the ironshod clip-clopping of their
mounts' hooves had died away, then turned to the shadow
siding him in the piñons.

"Jim, how come you not to tell me that bastard Garth
was headin' back into the Basin?"

"Maybe he won't show. I didn't want to spook you for
nothin'."

"He'll show. They always come back."

Jim shook his head. "Tom told me he wouldn't let him
in the Basin, if he did, Rachel. Garth's a killer. Tom never
had no use for his breed. I got to give him that, no matter
I hate his slick guts. He's held right along against killin'.
You know that."

"A man don't do no work he can hire done," snapped Frank. "My God, Jim, you know this Billy Graden killin' has changed everything for Tom! He's already blowed sky-high. What in the name of hell do you think's been keepin' us in the brush the last ten days? Mosquitoes?"

"On horseback, with guns," grunted the half-breed, unsmilingly.

"Why, hell," Frank continued angrily, "Tom will already have sent for his 'killin' brother' the minute Billy died. He will, providin' he knew where to send."

"He'll likely know. It's a close clan."

Frank nodded. "He'll be back," he said thickly. "I always knew he would. His kind always circles the bait, comin' back to it sooner or later. By God, Garth Graden could no more keep away from this trouble than a buzzard from a bear-killed colt! I knew it all along, Jim. I feel it strong now."

"Well, it's what you want, ain't it?" The half-breed's voice was suddenly bitter. "To have him back here in the Basin?"

"It's all I want," said Frank, low-voiced.

Jim Fewkes bobbed his head. "Let's go," he muttered. "You worry about Garth Graden. Me, I'll stew about Mulvehey and that posse. I ain't bought that easy deal with them warrants just yet."

"Meanin'?"

"Meanin' I aim to lay out and trail him and his bunch tomorrow. You with me?"

"Right behind you," grunted Frank, then added softly, "Or maybe so way ahead of you!"

Sun-swollen and fly-blown

The following morning the Prescott posse broke camp, Anse and his followers having left in anger the previous night when Mulvehey returned without Frank Rachel or Jim Fewkes.

Frank had wanted to tail Anse when he had left, but Jim had insisted they stay with the posse until it left the Basin. Now they were shadowing the posse, seeing from its direction that Mulvehey apparently meant to ride by and check the scene of the Bivins and Payton killings at Mittelson's Ranch, for himself.

The posse arrived at the ranch shortly before noon of the 24th.

Desolation and the smell of death were on every hand. About the whole, drear landscape hung an invisible pall of hidden menace difficult to account for, and the uneasy members of the posse eased their guns in their holsters, casting continual, nervous glances into the silence of the surrounding hills.

The cabin had been burned to its sills, only a sifting pile of wind-blown ashes marking its site. A solitary pig and half a dozen forlorn chickens wandered in the emptiness of the yard. Two dead horses lay sun-swollen and fly-blown beyond the cabin sills. And beyond the horses the raw scars of the two new graves showed, loosely piled with the rocks heaped over them by Charley Parker and Jack Maddows, the Payson justice of the peace. Even as the posse approached, a big dog-coyote and his whining mate, already drawn by the decomposition invading the shallow sepulchres, left off their impatient pawing of the frustrating stones and slunk away through the greasewood bushes.

Mulvehey and his men did not open the graves, nor

did they linger in the vicinity of their brooding silence. Minutes after they had ridden up, the Yavapai sheriff led them away, his direction west by north, for Parker's Store, Payson and Prescott.

On the wooded ridge south of the ranch, Jim Fewkes cursed viciously.

"It's that goddam Anse did it! That's what the son of a bitch was doin', sneakin' away from the posse last night. You was right, Rachel. We should have tailed him."

"Oh, what the hell good would it have done, Jim? He had a dozen men with him."

"Not when he burned that cabin, by Christ. He come back and done that by hisself. To make it look like some of us done it."

"The hell with it," said Frank. "Whoever done it is goin' to say we did." He paused, waiting to catch the half-breed's eye. "Jim, I been thinkin'. I been thinkin' hard, all night. I reckon you and Ed and John better get outa here. Nobody will bother your womenfolks with you not around, and them and the kids can follow you out of the Basin later on."

"How about you, my friend? They're after you just as hard." Jim's voice showed no sympathy as yet.

"With me it's different." Frank, like all men used to doing their talking with firearms, was having difficulty with the words. "I ain't got nobody cares about me. Nobody to look out for. Nobody that's goin' to miss me. Ed and John have got their kids. You've got your pap."

His listener still was not impressed. "Ed and John will never leave so long as there's a Graden left in the Basin. And neither will Jim!"

Frank shrugged then. "Well that makes it unanimous. Let's get outa here. That place down there gives me the willies. I don't like the smell of a dead man."

The half-breed looked at him, dark-faced, then slid back from the ridgetop and stood up. "You should have thought of that before you chose your life's work," he said frostily.

"I didn't have no choice." Frank was following him down the ridge, grinning a little now. "I was born with a Colt in each hand and a silver slug in my mouth."

"Uh huh," Jim's head bobbed understandingly, "and you'll die with a lead one in your belly."

They had reached the foot of the ridge. Frank put his hand out, laying it lightly on the other man's shoulder, his voice suddenly serious.

"Jim. That talk of dyin' is what's been on my mind. It's why I wanted you boys to clear out of the Basin."

"What the hell are you gettin' at, hombre? We been handclose to dyin' for the past thirty days, every one of us. You gettin' spooked or somethin'?"

"It ain't about me dyin'," said the big rider slowly, "that's got me spooked. It's about you."

"Me, for Christ's sake!"

"You or Ed or John, one of you."

"Now hold on, Rachel. Don't tell me you've been a preacher all your life and only belted on your guns to save us ordinary sinners? I done read that one in Ned *Buntline* when I was knee high to a short hoss."

"I'm not funnin' with you, Jim."

The half-breed sensed he was not, let his answer sober. "I'm listenin'. Go ahead."

"You've seen your share of men die, ain't you? And there's been times when you've knowed beforehand that you was goin' to help some of that share along yourself. Ain't that so?"

"I reckon."

"Well, didn't you get a 'feelin' about it, I mean before it happened? That somebody was goin' to die and that it wasn't you that was goin' to be that somebody?"

"Can't say as I have. You sayin' you do?"

"My whole life," nodded the other softly. "From the first man I seen go down to the last. I read somewheres once about how animals can smell it comin', like dogs do. You know how a dog will sometimes take to howlin' before his master, or even just somebody in the house or a neighbor or anybody he knows, is goin' to die?"

"Sure," said the half-breed quickly. "I seen them do that myself. What's that to do with you? Or John, or Ed, or me?"

"I got that 'feelin'," said the big rancher. "One of you is goin' to die."

"Hell, it don't take a genius to figure that. Nor a nose like a death-smellin' dog." Jim's voice was back in its Indian-deep guttural, his momentary uneasiness gone. "I got you beat. It ain't one that's goin' to die. Nor two, nor six. There'll be a dozen dead before another month. Let's go."

Frank chucked his head, saying no more.

As he followed the half-breed back toward their Cherry Creek camp his pale eyes were set and expressionless, showing no feeling.

But inside of him the dog was howling and it would not stop.

Billy Mulvehey and his posse left the Basin the following day. The Yavapai sheriff had stopped at the Graden Ranch and warned Tom Graden that the next killings in Peaceful Basin would bring him, Mulvehey, back with the biggest posse in Arizona. And that that posse would be coming to arrest and take every man on both sides. He promised, meantime, to keep after the Fewkes and to come back any time he heard they had returned. In return, he charged Tom and Judd with the responsibility of keeping the cattlemen quiet and leaving the Fewkes boys to him and the legal law.

Tom Graden had looked him in the eye and told him, flat-out, that he and the "honest cattlemen" of the Basin meant to "wipe out every living male member of the Fewkes clan, law or no low." Hearing the wild threat, and mistakenly cataloguing it as such, Mulvehey had repeated his original warning, and pulled out for Prescott.

When not riding back of a temporary tin star, most posse men of the day had lives and livings of their own to worry about and could not, accordingly, sit around all summer in Peaceful Basin waiting for a war that had been threatening for five long years. Forty-eight hours after its forceful appearance "the law" rode back out of the Basin. The brooding field was left to the vengeful cattlemen.

For the following three days, Frank and his three half-breed companions continued to keep to the brush. And around the clock, the eager scout parties of the cattlemen kept after them, goaded on by the raging Tom Graden.

Then, suddenly, on the sixth day, the search was called off.

Ed, sent out as darkness fell that night to scout the store and the Graden Ranch, reported an unusual number of horsemen gathering at the enemy's headquarters. He was unable to give or even guess a reason for this flurry of activity in the face of the mysterious calling off of the search parties.

Two more days crept by and then, on the evening of September 1st, a quail whistled a little too loudly downstream of their hiding place. Jim answered it and minutes later they were getting their explanation.

Frank did not know Jacoby or Joe Boyce, except by sight. There were no introductions now. The two men drifted up through the creek brush on foot, spared one general nod to the four of them and began talking.

The close-cropped nature of their discourse was at once enlightening and entertaining, if a man were hungry enough for entertainment.

The ruckus at the Graden place had been occasioned by the arrival there, the previous night, of Garth Graden. The long missing Garth had evidently taken over command from Tom, as it was his order which had called in the search parties. His orders, too, were those now causing the comings and goings at the ranch, though what those orders might be a man on the Fewkes side could only guess. Unless, of course, he wanted to listen to the threat now being openly made down at the store.

Boyce had been doing most of the talking and as he made the ominous terminal reference, Jim braced him.

"And what are they sayin' at the store, Joe?"

"They're sayin' Garth is goin' to give your place what Mittelson's got, and that Tom's backin' him all the way."

"They wouldn't dare, by God." Ed said it slowly.

"Maybe, maybe not. But that's what they're sayin'."

"What else they sayin'?" It was still Ed.

"That they're goin' to take your old man and all your women and kids out of the Basin. Goin' to set them afoot in Globe or Holbrook. They're sayin' they ain't goin' to have a Fewkes, not even a two-year-old one nor a growed female by marriage, left in Peaceful Basin when they're done."

"They're sayin' quite a bit!" cursed John Fewkes. "It might take a little *doin'* as well. How many men they got, you figure?"

"Maybe forty. Plenty enough anyways."

"We got no choice." Jim, as usual, made the decision. "We'll have to go down to the cabin."

"It's a trap."

Frank's flat statement broke in, stilling the others.

"It's a trap and a damn bad one. You're walkin' right into it if you go down to the cabin. They'll not burn your place nor harm your women and young ones. That's just talk, to pull you out of the brush. It's crick-clear, Jim. You can see that, for God's sake!"

"Seein's one thing, believin's another. Garth ain't like Tom and Judd. He'll do it."

"Maybe." Frank was moving with the word, levering and checking his Winchester, easing the big Colts in their leathers. "Where'd you boys leave your hosses?"

"Half a mile downcrick. Why?"

"I'm aimin' to borrow one of them, the best one."

"You're aimin' wrong." Jim moved too, now, stepping in front of him. "You can't get to Garth with all them others around him."

"You might," qualified Joe Boyce. "Providin' you had the time."

"Which you ain't," added Jacoby tersely. "We hear they're ridin' late tonight, figurin' to be around old John's place before first light. I've heard you're somewhat with a gun, Rachel. You'll need to be, to drill one of forty in the pitch black!"

"We ain't got no choice," repeated Jim harshly. "We'll go on down to the cabin."

"I'm still goin' after Garth," said Frank. "If they catch you in them cabins, you're dead and done. You ain't only got no choice, you got no chance."

"We got one," contradicted Boyce. "Just one."

"Such as?" rasped Frank impatiently.

"Soon as I heard Garth was back, I sent John Roady to fetch Jack Maddows. That was day before yesterday. If Roady made it to Payson and Maddows listened to him, Jack and a posse could be here sometime late tomorrow."

"They'll be sometime late," grunted Frank. "Tomorrow or otherwise. I'm goin'. If I can't get to Garth, I'll see you at the lower cabin. Which hoss do I take, boys?"

"Take the bay," said Jacoby. "I pulled his shoes yesterday. He goes real quiet in the dust."

"He'll need to," growled Ed Fewkes.

Frank did not hear him. He was already gone, sifting off through the dark, downstream, toward the tethered horses.

He lay half the night, belly-flat, on the ridge above the Gradens' ranch, the borrowed bay nose-wrapped and reinstied in the brush below. The light in the main cabin burned late and mounted men continued to come in until long past midnight. In the whole time he caught only occasional glimpses of Judd and Tom moving inside the cabin, and none at all of Garth or of any stranger who would match the description given him of the mysterious fourth Graden by Old Jim Stanton.

With the four o'clock dawn beginning to streak the east and the ground-sleeping men around the cabin beginning to stir and saddle up, he knew he was not going to get his shot.

He knew too, that it was long past reasonable time for him to clear out.

Still, he stayed, thinking not of Jim or Ed or John, or even of any of their women or young ones. But thinking only of a twisted juniper and a silent pile of granite boulders waiting high and lonely above the deserted sweep of Apache Bench.

At 4:15 the Gradens came out of the cabin, Judd first, followed by Tom.

And then he came.

He was tall, taller than Tom by half a head. And big, hard-big, just like Old Man Stanton had said. He moved quick and easy, coming to his saddled horse and easing up on him in a way that let a man know he did not have to look to the low set of the cross-belted Colts to know he had his hands full with this one.

Frank found the broad back in the rear sight, checking the Winchester hard and close. He brought his finger into the light touch of the trigger, felt the short travel of the 'reep ease away and come up, crisp and clean, against the last hairline of the let-off.

He held a long three seconds, then cursed viciously.

The stock slid away from his cheek. He waited another moment, then pushed himself back and down from the skyline. He left the nosewrap on the bay, guiding him quickly along the base of the ridge and off through the backing timber of the flats below it. Again the curse came, hard and bitterly head-shaken.

In the end a man always came squarely up against himself. Against the warped way he had lived and would no doubt die. And against the gall-bitter, senseless pride which had time without memory made him ride with the pot when he could have cleaned the table with one sandbag bet.

In the end, he could no more shoot Garth Graden in the back than he could have done so to any man on the long list before him.

The double-bitted ax

The clear dawn, just before the sun comes, is always beautiful in central Arizona, particularly so in the high, warm days of early fall. Five o'clock in the morning of September 2nd, 1887, was no less serene in the jeweled clearness of its pre-sunrise stillness than any day before or after it.

As Frank drove the unshod bay across Cherry Creek and southward along its sandy bottom lands, the coming sun was just tipping the ancient, barren shoulders of the Mazatzals. To the east, still shadow-black against the growing daylight, the Mogollon Rim reared its thousand sheer feet skyward.

The only sounds carrying beneath the muffled hammer of the bay's hoofs were those of the accompanying, foaming splash of the creek and the distant, time-delayed chonk of an early rising settler's ax far over among the pines of the flat. Passing Jacoby's and Boyce's cabins, he noted the tenuous hang of the smoke wisps issuing straight up from the blackened chimney pipes, and knew from them that the fires were long banked and many hours old.

He nodded, grimly pleased. Good. Bill and Joe were with the boys down at old John's cabin.

He swung the bay away from the creek, quartering him up and over a pine-clad ridge, bypassing young John's place and shortcutting straight for the old man's. Five minutes later he pulled him up, stepped off of him. Hazing him into the split log square of the empty hogpen where the saddled horses of the others were already standing, he raced for the cook shack. He had time to wonder, even as he did, why there were but three of these prepared mounts where a man would have expected at least six. He was inside the cook shack then, and Jim was meeting him with a piece of information to match and shadow his own, and to explain the chilling whereabouts of the missing horses.

"They're comin', Jim," he said. "Tom, Judd, Garth—the lot of them. You ready here?"

"Will be," replied the other, "soon as John gets back." There was no excitement in the statement.

"Where'd he go?" Frank's question fell harshly.

Jim Fewkes shrugged. "Him and Jacoby went up to John's place with Billy Beshar. The kid wanted his hosses brung down. Didn't want them run off by the Gradens. They'll be back right off."

"The dumb bastards! Why did you leave them do it!"

"You ever try to stop John?" queried the half-breed coolly.

"Not up till now." With the bobtailed comment Frank was moving for the cowskin doorway. "But I reckon there's a first time for everything . . ."

"Where the hell you think you're goin', Rachel? They'll be back in ten minutes. They only got to run them out of the front pasture."

"Ten minutes won't cut it by half, amigo. Garth and his bunch wasn't more than five minutes behind me. I'll be back. Cover us in case we have to cut it a mite fine on the return trip."

"Rachel! You can't go up there, with them bastards followin' you so close. You'll run square into them."

"Ever try to stop Frank?"

The big rider mimicked him acidly, then grinned and slid out past the hanging cowskin. Heeling the bay back past the cabin, he saw Jim break from the cook shack and scuttle toward the main building. Again his head bobbed in the grim nod. Boyce must be in the cabin with Ed and old John. With Jim joining them, that made four top guns. Now if he could get to young John in time . . .

Breaking around the brush clump which hid the upper cabin from the lower, he threw the bay on its haunches, seeing in the brief second of the action that his time had run out.

Jacoby, Beshar and John Fewkes were just coming clear of the cabin's corner, hazing John's horses ahead of them. They saw Frank at the same time he saw them. But half a breath sooner, they had seen the others: Anse Canaday, Clint Bivins and a dozen of the Basin cattlemen from Parker's Store, already well into the clearing from the opposite, north side.

Frank, seeing Anse's group in the same instant, and seeing its members had seen him and meant to ride between him and John's little bunch, levered his Winchester into the galloping cattlemen. At the same time John and his two companions spurred toward him, adding their fire to his.

There have possibly been better men with the saddle-gun than John Fewkes. If so, with the notable exception of his own brothers, Ed and Jim, history has failed to record them. Three of the stockmen's ponies were down in the first seconds. Two other riders had twisted and spun in their saddles, staying on their pitching mounts but squarely hit and looking for nothing but leather to keep them on them.

Broken up by the sudden appearance of Frank Rachel and the wild burst of rifle fire which had followed, the cattlemen split forces and pulled away, a third of them wheeling back up the creek trail north, the remainder, under Anse, swinging off in mid-gallop to race southward toward the lower cabin.

Frank kicked the bay around, getting him in stride as his companions thundered up. "It's straight on in from here, far as I can see!" he shouted to them.

"I can't see no farther than you!" John's eyes were slits, but the family wolf-grin was working. Frank threw the grin back, slashing at the bay with his rifle barrel, turning to shout at William Jacoby.

"How's it with you, pardner?"

He knew the taciturn rider had been hit twice through the body. He had seen him jolt and twist as the slugs tore into him.

"Two in the back," grated Jacoby, "both on the same side. Can't move my left arm." He tried to gesture with the paralyzed member. "I can still shoulder and aim, if somebody'll load and lever . . ."

Then their mounts were breaking into the open of the main cabin clearing, and just into it.

They had only time to see that Anse was there before them, when the crossfire of his small group and that of Garth Graden's main bunch on the ridge south of the cabin, hit into them.

Anse had executed his ambush with calculated viciousness. He had held up in the border pines, letting them get past him and forty yards into the clearing; just far enough for the cross-clearing fire of Garth's men to hit into their horses. As their mounts reared wildly to the frontal fire, Anse had given it to them where he liked to put it—in the back.

Billy Beshar spun off his horse, knocked free of the falling animal by a bullet through the shoulder. He lit on his feet, apparently not badly hurt, and ran crouching for the pines.

Frank, riding last, saw the heavy dust-puff smack into Jacoby's spine, knew from the oat-sack slump of his body that he was dead.

John was twice missed by shots which ripped through his shirt before the final slug tore off the back of his head. He slid into the clearing dirt not ten feet from the stumble and fall of Jacoby's horse.

Frank leaped his bay over the struggling animal and drove, still unhit, for the cabin. He hit the ground, running doubled over, dove through the opening door, rolled to his feet and ran for the north window. He was in time to see the grisly climax of one of the most brutal killings on Western record.

Billy Beshar had made the cover of a corded stack of logs where Old Man Fewkes had been cutting stovewood among the fringe pines of the clearing. The splitting block, crossbuck saw and double-bitted ax lay where the old man had dropped them the night before. The wounded man's attackers now worked swiftly toward this refuge, spreading through the sheltering timber in a closing, three-sided net.

As Frank watched, the cornered fighter's ammunition ran out. He saw him snap the empty guns, jam them back into the holsters, drop behind the woodpile, cursing.

Jim Fewkes, joining him at the window, saw it at the same time. Both watching men knew what was coming.

The trapped man knew better than to try to surrender. He knew, also, that the moment his fire fell off the enemy would rush him. The next instant he had slipped around the woodpile and was racing in a zig-zag run for the cabin. They could only watch helplessly. The hidden rifles in the pines offered no mark for covering fire and the range was overgreat in any event.

Beshar wasn't ten feet from the chopping block before he had been hit half a dozen times. He spun crazily, somehow managed to stay on his feet, lurched drunkenly back toward the woodpile, collapsed against it. The weight of his body broke the pile and he fell over and behind it.

Three men slipped from the pines and dove after him behind the pile, the first man scooping up the ax as he ran past the chopping block. For a minute Frank thought it was Anse. Then he was not sure. He and Jim fired swiftly, snapping the hopeless shot, snarling their helpless rage. The range was too much. Skill and anger were not enough. The arching, two-hundred-yard trajectory of the blackpowder rifles spewed the falling lead harmlessly into the ground around the woodpile.

Beshar stumbled out from behind the pile, still alive. The first of his tormentors was behind him like a cat, the sickening swing of the ax catching the wounded man between the shoulders and driving him to the ground. The axman hit him twice more, crunching, bludgeon blows, aimed at the slack head. Then he was leaping back for the shelter of the woodpile, Frank's and Jim's futile lead mushrooming the ground behind him.

But even across the eighth-mile meadow the crazy, high laugh carried jarringly. In early light like this, with the blackpowder smoke drifting heavily and his own nerves standing on edge, a man's eyes might fool him. His ears never would.

That had been Anse Canaday with that ax.

The sudden, cabin-close explosions of Ed's and old John's rifles from the opposite window, brought Jim and himself leaping to their sides. The next moment their Winchesters were levering over the heads of the former. The whole meadow, from the southern ridge halfway to the cabin was swarming with the mass rush of Garth Graden's men.

There was no time to pick a target. The four defenders, joined a second later by Joe Boyce, poured their fire blindly into the front of the racing cattlemen, shooting into the horses to break up the attack.

Three mounts were down in the first volley, their riders rolling free to race back for the safety of the ridge. The other riders, four of them slumping in their saddles, pulled their horses wide and galloped out of range toward the back pasture.

Jim and Frank leapt back across the cabin to the north window but Anse's men had been slowed by the necessity of getting back to their horses after finishing off Billy Beshar. They had just broken free of the pines when Jim's and Frank's fire began to get into them. Like the main force, they swung wide, sent their horses eastward for the cover of the pasture fence.

Frank's glance swept instinctively toward the woodpile, seeking Beshar's body. His eyes widened and he cursed. "Where's Beshar? They must have drug him back into the timber. I don't see him nowhere, do you?"

"No," Jim muttered. "They've moved him all right. I had him marked by that big pine back of the bucksaw."

"By God, you don't suppose he made it by hisself? Still alive?"

"Do you?" The half-breed threw him a hard scowl.

"No. Not after what we seen Anse do with that ax. It's funny they'd bother to move him though."

"It ain't," said the half-breed darkly. "They've hid him somewheres for right now and they'll pack him out when they go. There ain't nobody but me and you that's ever goin' to know what happened to Billy Beshar. You'll see . . ."

"Well, Billy's past worryin'," said Frank grimly.

"So are John and Bill Jacoby," added Jim softly.

"Yeah," the big rider's eyes shifted to the other men across the cabin, "but we sure as hell ain't." He shrugged. "Five-to-forty, and us with your women and kids. It's like drawin' three cards to an inside straight."

Jim Fewkes said nothing. Their situation was beyond the need of reply.

The cattlemen had spread their forces completely around the meadow. The south ridge, the elevation of which commanded all four sides of the cabin, bristled with rifles. Eastward, the heavy poles of the pasture fence protected another group of guns. To the north and west the dense pine timber hid other keen-eyed, deadly marksmen. Fewkes' meadow, as Frank had foretold it would weeks before, had become a death trap.

For the next five hours and until the sun stood noon-high overhead, the besiegers kept the little cabin under ordered, constant fire.

They had plenty of time, plenty of ammunition. They were in a position, if need be, to spend a week of one and a wagonload of the other. That the need would never arise was as clear to the men trapped in the cabin as it was to those waiting on the hillside.

With nightfall and using the cook shack and hogpen as approaching cover, resolute men could get to the main cabin and fire it. There was no paucity of resolute men in the field in that day's battle: Anse, Clint, Simm and Jake Bivins; Tom, Judd and the mysterious Garth Graden; Ollie Weston, Clayte Samuels and a baker's dozen of their hired Hash Knife gunmen: it was a killer crew and more than enough of a killer's crew to raise the hackles of apprehension on any fighting man west of Fort Worth.

Nobody had to tell Jim Fewkes and Frank Rachel they were fighting men. Nobody had to tell them, either, how far west of Fort Worth they were.

Providing Jack Maddows did not get there before sundown, Tom Graden's threat made openly to Sheriff Billy Mulvehey before the latter left the Basin following the Mittelson Ranch killings—to wipe out every living male member of the Fewkes family—was going to go into the books.

One o'clock dragged slowly toward two, and the sun blaze of the meadow's heat mounted insufferably.

Inside the cabin, the defenders cursed and shifted from window to window, the calm voices of the Fewkes women and the white-faced queries of Ed's and John's small children, compounding the helpless fury within them. Outside, Graden's men lay among the rocks of the ridge, waiting and watching, their rifles never quiet, their positions and the intensity of their fire constantly shifting and probing, daring and drawing the return fire from the cabin, steadily wasting away the defenders' precious ammunition.

Frank knew from this that Garth and Tom meant, if they could, to force a surrender *before* sundown.

He cursed, giving the stolid JT owner a grudging credit. Determined as he might be to see Ed and Jim Fewkes dead, Tom was fighting it fair right down to the wire. If he could avoid firing the cabin, with that act's resultant and certain disaster to at least some of the innocent women and children inside, he would do so. If he couldn't . . .

With two o'clock sweated under and the heat and the fly drone and the choking stifle of the gunsmoke in the cabin thickening by the minute, it happened.

No more inhuman an action is remembered in Arizona's history, not excepting the more flagrant atrocities of the old territorial Apache raids. It represented a boundary of barbarity any red savage would have hesitated to step beyond. Yet, with a callous morbidity scarcely credible even from the distance of sixty years, forty white men that day stepped across it.

The justice of the peace

      The bodies of John Fewkes and Bill Jacoby lay in full view of the cabin's occupants, midway between their shelter and the meadow's edge, and directly under the fire of the attackers' guns. At twenty minutes past two—they remembered the time because Old Man Fewkes had just pulled out his pewter watch to check the hours until sunset —Mary Fewkes spoke in sudden horror from the north window.

"My God, Jim, here comes the hogs!"

They rushed to the window, joining John's white-faced wife. Driven out of the timber's shade by the rifle fire of Graden's men stationed there, the Fewkes' pig herd was moving across the clearing toward the sanctuary of its pen. Halfway, its leader, an enormous-teated old sow, stopped, her glistening snout swinging across the dead air, her near-sighted eyes squinting uncertainly. Presently she grunted, altered her course to bear westward, her ugly snout sampling the air excitedly.

"The sow has spotted them." The slow words were Jim's, their simple announcement stating the dread fear growing in the minds of all of them. Seconds later that fear became a grisly fact.

The sow shoved her nose under John's slack body, turning it and rooting at it eagerly. Behind her, the other sows and the herd boar moved in quickly, the sucking pigs and weanlings milling curiously at their rears, the deep, slobbering feeding noises of their elders exciting their nervous, high-pitched squeals.

"Get away from the window." Jim turned as his order went to the blank-faced Mary. She did not move and he took her arm, forcing her roughly. "I said get away from that window, woman!" He hissed the words. "And keep the kids away from it too! Frank . . ." he wheeled on the big rancher. "Cover me. I'm goin' out."

"By Christ, you're not!" It was Ed's voice which answered him. "You'd never even make it to the cook shack. Listen to that fire out there! The bastards are heapin' it up, deliberate, to keep us pinned in here while them hogs eats."

"Jesus, it ain't possible they'd stand by and see them hogs eat John and Bill . . ." Joe Boyce trailed it off, white-faced.

"Maybe it ain't," Frank was at the window, "but they're standin' and them hogs is eatin'."

"It ain't like Tom, it ain't like him. It just ain't, it just ain't . . ." Old Man Fewkes stood at the window shaking his head dully, the words coming over and over. The whang and scream of the rifle slug ripping the casement inches from his dazed father's head brought Jim's shoulder into him, knocking him away from the opening.

"That ain't like Tom neither, I suppose," he snarled. "By God, I'm goin' out there!"

"Mary, oh my God . . ." It was Lydia Fewkes' voice, high and sudden and sharp."

"You won't need to, Jim." Frank's quiet words fell into the harsh silence following Lydia's startled cry. "Mary's beat you to it." No one answered the big rancher, the abrupt cessation of all firing from the ridge intensifying the stillness within the cabin.

Already halfway to the cook shack, Mary Fewkes continued her slow, straight-staring walk. Still no one spoke, no one moved. The cabin door, left wide in her shock-stricken exit, hung motionless on its rawhide hinges. In its unprotected frame, in full view of the silent riflemen on the ridge, stood Lydia Fewkes. Behind her the Fewkes men waited wordless and narrow-eyed, the black anger of the moment welling bitterly within them.

The dead man's wife was coming out of the cook shack now, moving head up across the meadow, the rusted shovel rigid in her right hand. On the ridge and in the pines other men watched and waited, their guns forgotten, their eyes tight, their thoughts their own. Even the brute hogs seemed to sense the coldness and calm of the woman's approach, the herd pulling back and away from its ghastly feast as she came up.

Only the old sow lingered in defiance, squealing and chopping her tushes savagely.

The echoing roar of the Winchester rolled out from the cabin. The sow lurched forward, drooping soundlessly, and Jim Fewkes levered the empty case from his rifle's action, his eyes never leaving the window. The shell spun against the cabin wall, hit the stove, bounced to the floor and lay still. It was the only shot fired by either side in the shame-still quiet of the gruesome truce.

Mary Fewkes buried the two men in a common, shallow grave, heaping the spongey clods of the meadow turf over them. When she had finished she dropped the shovel across the mute pile and walked slowly toward the cabin. The moment she disappeared within, the cattlemen resumed their fire.

The volume of the renewed fusillade seemed to increase in fury rather than diminish, following the truce. But such were the thickness of the cabin's pine-log walls, and such the deadly accuracy of the fire returned from within those walls, the besiegers could force no further move from the embattled Fewkes. By the return token of the hail of lead being rained down by the cattlemen, no move, forced or otherwise, was available to the defenders.

With the sun dropping swiftly, Tom Graden readied his final action.

"Garth!" The tall gunman lounged forward in response to the summons. "You take the bunch that will move up from the pasture to fire the place when dark sets in. Take your time and wait for full dark now. When you're ready to go, send a man up here and we'll pour it to them while you sneak in."

The tall man nodded, moving for his horse. He said nothing, being of the kind to whom words were largely a waste and simple action was the mother tongue.

Anse Canaday was of a different breed. He moved forward, confronting him instantly and noisily.

"Hold up, Graden. I reckon Tom's got his names a little mixed. I'm takin' that pasture bunch."

Garth held his silence, glancing over his challenger's shoulder to look at Tom. The latter's big head shifted to

the barest perception of a nod. Garth returned his gaze
to Anse.

"Somebody's a little mixed up." He had a flat, dry voice,
strangely foreign to his towering size. "Likely it's not
Tom."

"Don't call me, Graden! Get out of my way!"

"I never call your kind," said the big man softly.

He hit him low, the balled left fist driving into the thin
gunman's groin, the right smashing with twisting power
into the side of his head. Anse spun and fell, his side and
shoulder crushing into a boulder behind him. He bounced
off the rock, slid to the ground, came halfway to his knees,
clawing for his guns.

Garth stepped into him, driving his knee upward.

Anse's head flew back and this time when he struck the
ground he stayed there. Garth put his boot into him,
shoved him over contemptuously. He did not hurry as he
bent to pull the Colts from their holsters, and passed them
to Tom. "Like I said," he nodded to the unconscious Anse,
"your kind don't take callin'."

"Jake!" Tom stepped toward the fallen man's brother,
handing him Anse's weapons. "Take these and give them
back to him. Haul him back to the picket line and when
he comes around put him on his hoss and head him out of
the Basin. I told him if he ever put off on me again, he was
through. See he understands it."

"Hold up, Mr. Graden." The sullen Jake took the guns.
"Anse's got a right to get at them Fewkes. We all have.
You're forgettin' Harp."

"I'm not forgettin' Harp, nor my own brother, Billy.
I'm rememberin' somethin' else."

"Such as what?" It was the hulking Simm, moving forward to side his brothers.

"Such as Bill Beshar."

"Beshar, for Christ's sake!" Jake's heavy voice showed
honest surprise.

"Beshar," repeated Tom Graden flatly. "Get Anse out
of here, Jake."

"Get him out yourself." Jake backed off, Simm stepping
away to give him room. "I ain't touchin' him."

"Pull your pin, Bivins."

Jake and Simm were watching him when Garth eased forward with the quiet order. Still they could not follow the slight motion of the wrists which brought the Colts out and up. "Pull it," the tall man repeated evenly. "I got a cabin to burn."

The bull-like Simm nodded sullenly and swung Anse's limp form over his shoulder. Jake, turning to follow him toward the picket line, paused long enough to snarl at Garth. "We'll be back. Anse and Simm will side me. We'll be back."

Garth nodded, easing his guns into their leathers. "You and Simm might," he drawled. "But Anse won't." Pausing, he eyed the glowering Jake thoughtfully. "But if he should feel 'called to,' be sure and tell him to bring his ax!" Again the little pause, then the quiet conclusion.

"The dirty, murderin' bastard."

With the western shadows running long and black across the meadow, the firing from Graden's men suddenly slacked off. Within seconds, their lines had fallen completely silent.

"Somethin's up," growled Jim, sliding across the darkening cabin to join Frank at the south window. "You figure they'll try another big rush?"

"No. That don't make sense. There's still good shootin' light and they only got another forty-five minutes to wait for dark. I don't get it."

Ed came across the room to crouch with them, peering across the sill toward the silent hills. "Nothin' movin' on my side," he grunted. "Whatever's doin' is goin' on with the main bunch on your ridge yonder."

"Yeah, I reckon," muttered Jim. "We'll know soon enough."

"Soon enough's right now!" snapped Frank, suddenly tense. "Who's that cuttin' across the meadow?" His quick gesture swung their eyes to the right. A lone horseman, riding out from the pines to the east, was jogging his mount slowly down the middle of the clearing.

"I can't see him to call him," said Ed, cheeking his Winchester. "But I can to drill him."

"Let him come in," rasped Frank. "He's alone."

"It's a trick," growled Ed, lining his barrel and laying his sights. The rifle steadied and held. In the last moment, Jim's eyes widened.

"Hold off, Ed! It's Jack Maddows!"

Ed's eyes narrowed. "It's Jack all right. We'll see what he wants."

"I hope to God he's got a posse along!" It was Joe Boyce, coming quietly up behind them.

"It's a beautiful thought," agreed Frank caustically. "Let us dwell upon it."

The Payson justice of the peace pulled his horse up in front of the cabin. He kept him well clear of it and where he could be seen from both sides of the meadow. "Hello, the house!" His deep voice carried echoingly in the clearing silence. "Who's inside and what's the trouble?"

Jim nodded to Frank and the latter slid the door open just far enough to let his answer out. Tersely he named the cabin's living occupants and called the brief roll of the meadow dead. In all, he used less than twenty words. The quiet-faced officer returned the favor with less than ten.

"All right, you folks, set tight. I'll be back."

They watched him as he loped his horse toward the ridge from which the main fire had been coming when his arrival and subsequent recognition by the Graden forces had stopped it. He brought the pony up at the base of the rise, his slow voice carrying to the topmost of the silent rocks.

"You boys know me, so don't waste my time. I've got a posse of twenty men comin' down Cherry Creek. They'll be here in fifteen minutes. Any man left within rifle range of this meadow in five will be indicted for the murders of John Fewkes, William Jacoby and Billy Beshar."

There were no answers from the rocks, and no sounds of any kind to break the listening stillness save the hoof stampings and harness jinglings of the picketed horses beyond the ridge. Maddows nodded.

"All right, boys. You play it any way you want. I'll be holdin' a coroner's inquest out past that hogpen in exactly one hour. Any one of you wants to attend and speak his piece is cordially invited. If you got nothin' to say past what I've been told by the Fewkes yonder, I'd advise you to find other entertainments this evenin'." He paused, letting the silence soak it into them. He turned his horse with the final nod.

"You got fifteen minutes. Use them any way you want."

When Jim Fewkes had said Maddows was "tough" and "fair," he had made one of his typically Indian understatements. No braver, more honorable law officer ever rode the old Arizona Territory than Justice of the Peace Jack D. Maddows of Payson. And the skulking cattlemen knew as well as Jim Fewkes just how "tough and fair" he was.

It was one thing to trap and kill enemies who were as far beyond the law as themselves, and who would in quick-triggered turn kill them as quickly as they would expect to be killed by them. It was quite another to consider the uneasy proposition of taking on the constituted law and order of the land as personified by an officer of Jack Maddow's cold courage, most particularly when that officer came backed by a heavily armed posse of first class fighting men.

The withdrawal was sullen but notably swift.

Ten minutes after the last word of the called-out ultimatum had fallen, the ridge and the surrounding meadow edges stood in full and final silence.

Somewhere back along the pasture fence a hunting coyote, out for mice in the sunset grass, lifted his head and sampled the freshening breeze moving eastward across the meadow. He yapped once, noisily, and was answered only by his own echoes. He whined nervously, not liking the too-quiet feel of Fewkes' Meadow this particular evening. Well, there were other mice and other meadows. He turned, slinking quickly westward through the tall grass bordering the split rails.

It was best to work far windward of that rising meadow breeze tonight. It was stale and disturbed, hanging badly in the nostrils.

And the smell of death lay heavily in it.

The moon had not yet risen. The guttering flare of the coal oil lanterns was the sole candle of the dead Mass that night spoken over the shallow graves of John Fewkes and William Jacoby.

The officiating priest was Justice J. D. Maddows of Payson, his altar assistants, his hard-eyed coroner's jury of twenty rifle-bearing deputies, his congregation, the five still-faced Fewkes men and their three, gaunt, head-bowed women.

Acting under his authority of justice of the peace for Yavapai County, Maddows exhumed the bodies.

The inquest was mercifully short. Jacoby had been shot three times in the small of the back, two bullets nicking the spine, the third shattering it. John Fewkes had been hit only once, the slug entering the base of the neck, ranging upward and disintegrating the back of the skull. The forepart of the head appeared to have been smashed in with a rock, but whether this wound was the result of his fall from his horse or of a brutality unseen in the excitement of Frank's arrival at the cabin, was not established.

The body of Billy Beshar could not be located and Maddows refused to include his killing in the jury's findings.

With the lantern-lit inquest concluded, the men quickly deepened the graves, digging them narrowly side by side. The bodies were rolled in, unwrapped. Minutes later, the wordless group filed away, leaving the dead alone in the meadow, separated from their God and His eternity by two feet of loose-shoveled, boot-stomped dirt.

Maddows and his posse left the Basin that same night. It is not known whether any warrants were ever drawn or served against the murderers of John Fewkes and William Jacoby. The records of Justice of the Peace John D. "Jack" Maddows, were destroyed some years later in a courthouse fire in Payson. The nature of the inquest exists, however, in the numerous first-hand accounts of old-timers present with the Payson posse that long-gone day. The date was September 2, 1887.

The finding of the enemy

Once again the three men slipped into the brush. But this time they went well mounted and heavily stocked with ammunition and supplies.

Their return to the Cherry Creek hideout was made during the early morning hours of September 3rd. Joe Boyce accompanied them as far as Stanton's abandoned ranch, then left them to scout the valley store to pick up what news he could of Anse; Jim having announced his intention of killing the Texas renegade if he had to "walk into Parker's Store in broad daylight" to do it.

Boyce returned to the hideout before dawn of the 3rd, his news bringing a dark smile to the half-breed's face. Tom Graden had called Anse over the ax-murder of Billy Beshar and given him his permanent riding orders. And more. Those orders had been issued across the slick guns of Garth Graden, and they had stuck. Anse had left the Basin the night of the cabin siege, accompanied by Jake and Simm. Clint, not having been involved in the argument and being a particular crony of Judd's, was still at the Graden Ranch. The word was that Anse had headed for Holbrook, where his foster mother, Old Mark Bivins' widow, Mary Bivins, kept a town cottage.

It was more than enough for Jim Fewkes. At the last minute Ed decided to go with him and the two brothers left by the North Rim trail before daylight. Boyce drifted back into the Basin to contact the Fewkes partisans still in residence near Parker's Store, and Frank was left alone.

Just before he left, and after Jim and Ed had gone, Boyce had dropped one last bit of information. One of the JT hands, on a high lonesome down at the store, had boasted drunkenly that, "By God, Garth had got the hoss, he'd likely get the man too!" This had been in reply to

another Graden hand's statement that he had heard Frank
Rachel was looking for the taciturn Garth.

Boyce had got the report from a reliable eye-witness,
but the witness could not supply any more detail. Just that
one cryptic comment from the drunken cowboy. For a
moment Frank's heart had leaped, then as quickly subsided. Even if Garth had been in on the lifting of Red Boy,
it was a certainty he had not brought the horse back into
the Basin. Not unless he had him stalled-up in secret on
the Graden place, and even that did not figure. And, if by
some long chance it might, it could have no bearing on
what Frank had to do now. He had possibly two days before Ed and Jim would return. It was borrowed time. All
a man could do was make the best of it.

Frank Rachel did.

All that day and the next, for forty-eight catnapping
hours, he lay on the ridge above the Graden Ranch, waiting for Garth to return, his mind far from Red Boy and
the big stallion's possible fate.

But the cabin remained dark, its chimney cold. The
stock in the corrals bawled ceaselessly, complaining against
their hunger. No one appeared to feed them. Not a solitary
rider passed up the Payson trail north of the ranch.

The night of September 4th was moon-dark until ten
o'clock. About nine, he thought he heard some undue stir
down in the corrals but he heard no horse or harness
sounds to indicate the approach of riders. He shrugged it
off. At ten-thirty, with the moonlight clearing the ridge
and hitting into the corrals, he saw that the gate bars were
down, the stock spreading out to graze the main pasture
south of the cabin.

He knew then that the Gradens had somehow sensed
his surveillance and were planning to stay clear of the place,
for if they had not, and were not, they would not have
troubled to send somebody in on foot to turn the stock out.

The birds were gone and he was watching an empty nest.

Back at the hideout there was no sign that Ed and Jim
had been there, but an hour after his return they slipped
in through the downstream brush. In twenty seconds of
Indian-short grunts, they had made their blank-faced report

of the fight which to this day remains the granddaddy gun battle of them all.

"Lemme trail you back through that once more," said Frank unbelievingly. "You say Simm is dead, and Anse and Jake gutshot and good as the same!"

"Simm, plus the boy, like we said," nodded Jim. "The kid was a nephew of theirs. Big kid and wearin' a gun, but only maybe fifteen, sixteen. Name of Sam Hairston, somebody told us."

"And this crazy sheriff braced the houseful of them all by hisself?"

"By hisself and carryin' only his saddlegun."

"It's pretty damn hard to believe."

"Easy enough if you'd seen them sprawled around on that front porch like we done."

"I never seen so much blood in my life," shrugged Ed. "Place looked like our cook shack after Pap's butchered a hawg. Simm and Anse was both shot in the belly and bleedin' somethin' fierce. Like Jim says, they'll never make it till mornin'."

"How come the fracas to start?" asked Frank, still dubious.

"Odens had a warrant for Anse," Jim replied. "Not one of them phony old Yavapai County ones, but brandnew one, drawed on Apache County. He seen Jake and told him to go fetch Anse in. Jake dusted for the cottage and Odens trailed him. He called them out before they could get to their hosses."

"It went quick then, eh?"

"Somewhat! They was all down inside of fifteen seconds. He nailed two of them comin' out the front door, one jumpin' out a side window, the other one comin' around the side of the house from the back. All with the Winchester."

Frank shook his head. "Odens is the bird you was tellin' me wears the Buffalo Bill suit and the long hair and belts just one gun high on the left side, butt forward, ain't he?"

"He is. But he's the fastest goddam deadshot you ever saw. And guts won't touch what his belly's stuffed with."

"Well," said Frank slowly, "hats off to Sheriff Perry

Odens of Apache County. And amen. Now, how about us?"

Jim looked across the rush and bubble of Cherry Creek a long time before he answered. "We stay in the brush and in the Basin until the last Graden is dead or the last Fewkes buried."

"Amen again," said Frank. "Let's get to it."

The getting-to was not as easy as the amen-ing.

The Gradens had returned to their home ranch east of Parker's Store, but with the withdrawal of Maddows' posse from the valley the Basin War passed into its final stage.

The ranch was operated on a siege basis and its hired gunmen were back in the field on a round-the-clock schedule. The price lay heavy upon the head of any Fewkes and the bounty-hunters never slept. Frank and his slant-eyed fellow outlaws were pinned to the Cherry Creek brush, not daring to move by day, helpless to do anything but contact their few remaining sources of information during the night. Twice in the first three days mounted search parties passed so close to their camp the hidden men could hear the blowing of the horses and the squeak and jingle of their cinch straps and bit chains.

The only news from the outside was that Garth Graden was still passing the terms of Tom's last sentence from one end of the Basin to the other, death for the Fewkes and their pale-eyed henchman, Frank Rachel.

The fourth day of their hiding, and the sixth one of that fateful September, came and was ridden under by the tireless mounts of Garth's prowling gunhounds. Frank and the brothers lay close in their perilous cover, thinking little, saying less, their tired, trapped minds unable to progress beyond the blind terminal of tomorrow. And from where they lay and from what they could see and hear that sixth of September, tomorrow was going to be like yesterday and the day before: nervestrung and endless and without hope.

Their trouble was one of human limitations. They simply could not hear or see far enough.

In 1887 Peaceful Basin and all of what is today Coco-

nino County lay in old Yavapai County. And the sheriff of
Yavapai County in that far-off day and year was slow-
spoken Billy Mulvehey. The fact of that matter may appear
to have little to do with the limits of human sight and
hearing. Appearances have killed many a curious cat.

On the fourth of September, Justice of the Peace Jack
Maddows reached Payson. On the fifth, he wired Mulvehey
at Prescott. And on the sixth the latter was exchanging
wires with District Attorney John G. Harnden. On the
seventh, both Mulvehey and Harnden were meeting with
Governor C. M. Zellick in Maricopa County.

The upshot of this conference was the chief executive's
historical decision ordering Mulvehey to raise a posse large
enough to go through the Basin from end to end, arresting
every man of either side encountered; the invading force
to be of such number and selection as would enable it to
overwhelm both the Graden and the Fewkes groups should
those forces be inclined to "want it" that way.

Billy Mulvehey's gunblood was boiling over. He had
been duly elected to keep the peace in Yavapai County
and he was now officially ordained to do so by the highest
authority in the territory; and to the necessary extremity of
killing as many "honest citizens" as might choose to get in
his angry way.

On the ninth, he wired Deputy Sheriff Jules French at
Flagstaff to meet him at Payson with all the men he could
deputize from his area. On the tenth, he left Prescott with
his own famed deputies, George Brisling, E. M. Tucker
and Ed "Shanghai" Sullivant.

The following day he was in Payson meeting with Jack
Maddows. The two officers went at once about the grim
business of raising, equipping and co-ordinating the biggest
peacetime fighting force of law officers in the territory's
history. It was a task which took precious time, and time
for the Gradens and the Fewkes was not something to kill,
but something with which to kill.

Mulvehey waited and cursed and struggled with his
marching order, and the Fourth Horseman struck again in
Peaceful Basin.

The second week drew to its close. The three men

trapped in their tiny camp on Cherry Creek were near the breaking point. That raw nerve-edge which is never far from the surface in cornered fighting men was already frayed to the last shred when Joe Boyce rode up the creek in the early evening of the 17th.

His news snapped the end-thread for Frank Rachel.

Garth Graden had just been spotted leaving the ranch for Parker's Store, riding alone. There was no one at the store except its proprietor, Charley Parker, and two non-feuding cattlemen from the upper valley.

Against Jim's vehement objections that he might be spotted in turn, and trailed back to their hideout, Frank mounted up. Minutes later he was loping past the old Stanton place and moving down on the store.

But a quarter of a mile uptrail of the store he was throwing his horse into the brush and sliding off of him quick and quiet.

Maybe Boyce had had it right to begin with. Garth may indeed have left the ranch alone and the store might indeed have been nearly empty when he did. Times change. Circumstances alter. And men curse bitterly and in vain over them. That damn store was a blaze of lamplight and no less than eight saddled horses, in addition to Garth's familiar buckskin, stood hipshot at its hitching rail.

Frank tailed off his curses, turned to his pony. A man does not survive riding the highline for ten of his twenty-eight years by fancying the long chance. Nine-to-one was a shorter end than he cared to be holding up. When he went for Garth he had to know it was fifty-fifty, with the fastest fifty cashing in the chips. And more. Garth had to know who he was bucking and what was in the pot. He had to have time to look around the table and remember the third, forgotten player in the game. The one whose last raise had been high enough to lead a lonely man to bet his life on it.

He had to remembered Libby Fewkes.

Frank eased his mount out of the brush, turned him north again, away from the store. The fading clip-clop of the pony's swift singlefoot was still audible when the two other horsemen pulled out of the pines a hundred yards downtrail of his hiding place.

The men stared through the early darkness, listening until the pony's hoofbeats died completely away. The taller of the two nodded to his companion.

"Harry, you get on back to the store. Tell Garth his gamble to pull them out of the brush paid off."

"Yeah, by God, it did. I'd have bet my next month's pay it wouldn't, too. I'm glad that Garth's on our side. He's slicker than green axle grease."

"He's a heap different than Tom or Judd all right."

"Yeah," the other turned his pony. "Which one of the Fewkes you suppose that was? Ed or Jim?"

"Neither," his companion said. "Too big in the saddle. Get goin'. That was Frank Rachel!"

"Garth will be glad to hear that," the second rider grinned.

"He ain't goin' to hear it, the rate you're not movin'. Get goin' now, Harry. I'll tail Rachel to their camp and drift right back. If it ain't too far we can still hit them tonight!"

The other nodded, wheeled his pony for the store. His companion watched him go, then turned his own pony uptrail. He passed quickly out of the pine shadows, into the open starlight.

It was Joe Ellensburg, the cowboy who had been with Billy Graden.

The Cherry Creek camp lay still under the morning stars. The tiny fire, long banked but slow dying, wisped a thin streamer of blue woodsmoke. Close by, the whirl and splash of the creek comforted the bone-weary sleepers. Up and downsteam there was no other noise. The men slept on, but history was awake.

It is the little things which count in life. And in death.

Jim Fewkes came up on one elbow, the disturbed chatter of the sleepy mountain jay dying away as he did. The next instant his guarded whisper was going to his companions. "Ed. Frank. You awake?"

"I ain't slept for six weeks," growled Ed, his own half-breed instincts treading the heels of his brother's. "That was a jay, wasn't it?"

"It was. Frank!"

"Yeah? What's the matter with you goddam Injuns now? Can't you let a white man sleep?"

"We heard a jay chatterin' downstream. Roll out, somethin's movin' down there."

Frank was still in his blankets, reaching for his rifle, when the first of the looming horsemen crashed into the camp.

He fired from the ground, into the horses, Ed and Jim diving free of the tiny clearing and into the brush. Their Winchesters roared. The yells and curses of the attackers rode in over the smashing hooves of their mounts and the blinding explosions of their guns. The whole, wild melee was cleared in a matter of seconds, the uncontrollable horses of the cattlemen careening on through the camp and into the upstream timber.

Frank lay, breath held, in the darkness, not twenty feet from the scattered firebed. Behind their chosen trees, within the same scant perimeter, Ed and Jim crouched motionless, rifles levered and waiting. The seconds ticked away, but the only sounds from the cattlemen were the continuing curses and counter-curses being called across the night from the darkness two hundred yards above.

After an endless minute, Jim moved, gliding through the trees toward Frank. Ed's shadow joined his and together the half-breed brothers slid around the boulder behind which the big rancher lay.

"Follow me," was all Jim said.

It was more than enough. The time and place admitted of no lengthy debate. The three shadows melted away from the clearing. Quickly they moved up the granite outcrop which their hideout footed, bellying down in the rocks atop it, their guns and glances trained upstream.

With only the starlight for illumination, they could make out little more than the blurred movements of the horse and man-shadows gathered in a nebulous shifting group along the near side of the creek. There was little chance and less reason to shoot. They could make out at least twenty riders in the attacking force. If these riders chose to spread out around the granite rise and wait out the night, the feud was going to be over, come sunrise. The three men in the boulders above had no option. They could stay where they were, saving their few shots until daylight could let them find their sights and make those few shots count.

In the minds of the three there was no community of doubt.

The first attack had failed but clearly nobody had been hit or hurt, and the cattlemen would either chance it again right now, or merely wait for daybreak to take the chance out of it, making it dead certain.

Once again the certainty of human supposition fell a little short of simple fact.

Ten minutes after the opening assault, the cattlemen forded Cherry Creek above the camp, struck the open trail of the Parker's Store road and turned quickly south. In the brief moment of their crossing, the watching eyes above had seen its reason: two led horses, their riders sack-limp and motionless across the swaying saddles.

They were Joe Ellensburg and Harry Mattson. The former was to survive his wounds and leave the Basin, Harry Mattson to die two days later and be buried alongside Billy Graden; the eleventh known man to die in the Peaceful Basin War.

The cattlemen had found the enemy, and found him deadly. Even in the dark!

Of sheriffs and shotguns

Three days later, the evening of the 20th, Frank, with Ed and Jim Fewkes, appeared at Joe Boyce's cabin in answer to a message sent by the latter. Big Jake Lohburg, the bearer of the message, could give them no reason for the mysterious summons, or in any event would give them none. All he said was that there was "a man at Joe's wanted to see them."

The "man" was Jim Hook, Sheriff Perry Odens' omni-present deputy.

They faced him now across the cabin's one room, Win-chesters in hand, alert for anything. Hook spoke quickly and guardedly.

"The war's over, boys. Billy Mulvehey is hid out up at Haggler's ranch with Jules French, Emmett Dell and forty men.‛Billy sent me to call you in on that deal he made with Jim."

The half-breed did not answer him, speaking instead, and quickly, to Ed. "Ed, get outside and keep a watch. I don't like the smell of this." His brother nodded in reply, slid out the door. Confronting the deputy again, Jim growled the two words, blank-faced.

"What deal?"

"You ain't made more than one, likely." Hook eyed him steadily.

"Go on," Jim said.

"Billy's goin' to pull the Gradens in first thing tomorrow. He wants you and your bunch to get out of the way and stay out of the way. We've got warrants for every man on both sides, remember that. You're to have your whole bunch at your old man's place by sundown tomorrow like you agreed."

"Where'll the Gradens be?" Frank asked it automati-cally, slow to realize the full import of what Hook had said.

"They'll be there," said the deputy grimly. "One way or the other."

"You sayin' that Billy's guaranteein' that?" Jim, like Frank, was having difficulty grasping the swift finality of the moment.

"Governor's orders," rasped Hook. "Billy's to bring them in on their horses, or across them. Either way they want it. You and your boys are gettin' a special discount on them orders, courtesy of William Mulvehey by way of James Hook. It's the deal he made with you, Billy says."

Frank watched him closely. "That all Billy said?" he asked quietly.

Hook took the hostile stare in stride. "Not quite," he said. His eyes stayed with Frank's.

"It's your speech." The big rider grunted it, moving away from the door a little. "Tail it off!"

"He said 'take it or leave it,'" Hook answered. "I'm to be back at Haggler's in an hour, either way. If it's 'take it,' you be at Old John Fewkes' place like I said."

"Otherwise?"

It was Jim Fewkes who asked it, narrow-eyed and suspicious, his glance darting to Frank.

"Otherwise, we serve them warrants on you the same as on the Gradens—with a Winchester."

"It's big talk," said Frank, returning Jim's uneasy glance.

"It's a big posse," shrugged Hook. "What'll it be, Jim? Take it or leave it?"

Jim Hook was a hard man, by his own or any other standards. A professional killer, he chose to operate his trade within the law. He had at the time, and was destined to have in the future, the most sinister reputation of any partisan on either side of the Graden-Fewkes Feud. But his dealings with Jim had been, for some reason of his own, consistently friendly. Hunted, desperate, his sister and one of his brothers dead, his few cattle gone and his ranch ridden in on all sides by relentless enemies, the half-breed hesitated. As he did, the big man at his side spoke quickly.

"You do it, Jim." Frank Rachel had been thinking too. He moved closer now, putting his hand on his friend's shoulder. "It's the only chance you and Ed have got to get out of the Basin alive. You take it now, you hear me?"

The half-breed's shoulders sagged. He stood a moment more, then turned to the waiting Hook, head down, voice dropped. "We'll take it," he said.

Hook nodded, his eyes holding on Frank. "The deal includes you, Rachel."

Frank moved into him. "I make my own deals, friend. And not with *deputies!*" He stepped back. "Hop your hoss, little man."

"Hold up, Rachel!"

"Hop it!" grated Frank, dropping his hands. "Your hour's runnin' out!"

Mulvehey moved on Parker's Store at midnight.
The horses were left in the timber south of the creek

road and out of sight of the Graden ranchhouse which, from its mid-meadow knoll commanded a full view of the crossroads and the store buildings.

His plans had been made with utmost secrecy and he was satisfied no word of his coming had reached the Basin ahead of him. Every chance rider encountered since the posse had left Payson on the 19th had been taken into custody. His own huge group had been further swollen by its chance meeting with another, smaller group under Deputy Sheriff Joe McKimson of Apache County, at Haggler's. The Apache County deputy had been trailing fugitives from a Santa Fe train robbery at Navajo Springs and his presence in the final hour of the Peaceful Basin War was simply a happy accident. But of such "happy accidents" is unhappy history fashioned.

McKimson's posse had been sighted coming into the valley. The Graden forces were alerted.

It remains uncertain if they knew, also, of Mulvehey's huge force. In the light of the stark tragedy which followed, it seems scarcely probable that they did.

In any event, Mulvehey secreted his own men in and around Parker's Store, one group under Jules French in the store itself, the other under his own leadership across the road from the store and behind a stone foundation Charley Parker had under construction for a residence cabin.

The choice of the deathtrap was a murderous one. The Peaceful Basin store had been built in the late 1870's for use as a fort against the then still active Apaches. Its walls were a foot thick, its windows narrow-cased and so set as to insure a field of fire in any direction. The crossroad foundations were breast-high and heavy enough to flatten a six-pound shot.

By 4:00 A.M. the mainsprings of Mulvehey's trap were cocked. The Yavapai sheriff was ready to plant his poisoned bait.

He called Joe McKimson to him and the two officers talked quickly. Shortly, the Flagstaff deputy and his five men mounted up and rode off toward the southern foothills. Minutes later the first daylight began prying with its gray fingers at the stones of the store and of the half-built

foundation across from it. But the last shadows had ceased
to move among those stones and the unnatural stillness
only mounted with the growing light.

Crouched in the four o'clock blackness atop the ridge
overlooking Graden's Meadow, Frank blew the chill from
his fingers, flexed them carefully, regripped the Winchester.

As yet he could see nothing, but Boyce and Big Jake
Lohburg had assured him the Gradens, at least Judd and
Garth, were at the ranch. Tom had not been seen for two
days but he too had last been reported at the ranch and
there was no reason to believe he had left it. There were
also, at last report, no less than three other men holing up
there, Clint Bivins among them.

Frank cursed the darkness and the cold. He cursed Jim
Hook and Billy Mulvehey and the whole, bad way the
thing was winding up.

With the Yavapai sheriff's posse due to jump the Graden
place as soon as there was light enough to make the leap,
he might never get his chance at Garth Graden. Once
Mulvehey took Garth into custody it was all over. He was
not the kind of officer who got careless with his prisoners.

For the hundredth time since Libby's flight from the
Basin, he thought about Garth.

The big man did not figure, any way you wanted to look
at him. Especially, when the only look you had ever had
at him had been over the sights of a Winchester at two
hundred yards.

Frank knew he had been named with the other Gradens
in those St. John's rustling indictments in '83 and '84. But
he had not appeared with the others in answer to those
indictments at the time, and he had been seen in the Basin
only once since then. Most of the people in the valley
had never seen him at all, and half of them still did not
believe there was another Graden. If he had not seen him
himself, and been warned about him long ago by Old Jim
Stanton, he would have to have agreed with them. He
was like a damn shadow at high noon. You knew he was
there, yet you could not see him. None of the ideas Jim
or the others had about him, such as his being the secret
money behind the whole Graden operation, seemed to fit

or make sense, and in the end you just had to cuss again, letting him remain a full-out mystery.

All a person could do beyond that, was what he was doing: staking out on that damn ridge and hoping and praying for just one clear sight of him before Mulvehey and the posse showed up. At that thought, Frank nodded wryly to himself.

With a growl, he blew on his hands again, shifting his position, eyed the eastern sky. It was tinging up with rose and gray, making the valley shadows blacker than ever. But it let a man know that four o'clock was past and five coming swiftly on.

Suddenly, he tensed. Was that a movement down there in those shadows in front of the cabin?

He could make out the smudge of the door and, watching it, he saw the other smudge moving away from it. He followed the blur with his Winchester, tracing it along the cabin wall and waiting for it to cross into the open toward the horse corral. When it did, he cursed again and lowered the rifle.

It was Tom Graden.

A man could not miss the wide bulk of him and the familiar, narrow-brimmed Stetson. Garth was taller, he knew, and wore a four gallon, high-crowned, Texas hat.

He watched the JT owner mount up and guide his horse out of the corral and across the meadow toward the store. Then he was watching something else, and so was Tom Graden.

From the rail in front of Parker's Store, six shadowy horsemen swung away, starting south down the Cherry Creek road. Passing the lower end of Graden's Meadow on the road, they cut away, riding southwest into the foothills. Below him, in the meadow, Tom let them pass, then sent his own mount after them, keeping well back and clearly trailing them. It was the last any man saw of Tom Graden that fateful day.

Frank stayed on the bridge, restlessly dividing his glances between the cabin and the store, sensing now that something was afoot at the latter place, yet not daring to leave the ridge or his surveillance of the cabin. Five o'clock came, and with it clear daylight. Still nothing happened. No sound or movement came from the store, no sign of break-fast smoke showed above the cabin chimney.

At five-thirty, he made ready to leave the ridge. He had missed. Tom had been alone in the cabin and Garth and the others were God alone knew where.

He had not moved a foot away from the boulders when he froze. Down at the crossroads things were picking up.

He watched the approaching horsemen coming north up the Cherry Creek road, knowing from their number and direction they were the same six who had ridden away forty-five minutes before. He recognized the leading rider as Joe McKimson, the deputy from Flagstaff, correctly figured his followers as possemen from the same town.

McKimson's men rode slowly and with apparent un-concern. Even from the distance he could hear their voices loud and careless in the morning stillness. At the store they tied their horses and went in.

Minutes passed and there was no movement from the Graden cabin in response to the appearance of the posse. Frank swung his glance across the store road to the cabin of Al Ross, one of Tom Graden's chief lieutenants, be-latedly thinking the rest of the Gradens might have holed up there rather than in their own place. The thought proved unproductive. Nothing moved at the Ross cabin.

His restiveness grew swiftly. Again the thought of leaving the ridge crossed his mind. And again it was as quickly frustrated. McKimson's posse was coming out.

The sun was tipping the Mogollon Rim now, splashing the whole crossroads with its daybright light. He could count the cartridge heads in the possemen's gunbelts, mark every detail of face and figure. They were the same five who had followed McKimson into the store. But the sixth man, swinging up on the Flagstaff deputy's horse, was not McKimson. He was Jules French, Mulvehey's righthand gun!

Frank's eyes narrowed.

A man could chew that up and spit it out any way he wanted. It came out in the same sized chunks. Billy Mul-vehey and his last chance posse were holed up in Parker's Store!

What followed came so fast he could only watch it, forgetting his own man and his own gun in the blazing suddenness of it.

The Flagstaff posse headed north, pushing its horses up the Creek Road with obvious urgency. Where their appearance had failed to draw the enemy out, their disappearance did not. They were still in sight when Frank saw the two smokepuffs break from Al Ross's cabin. A second later the flat reports of the rifle shots reached him. He had only time to wonder at their meaning when it was made clear to him by three answering shots from the Graden cabin below him.

Those shots had been signals, given and taken. There were Graden men in both those cabins!

He cheeked the Winchester, snapping its sights onto the Graden cabin door. He let Judd pass out, and then Clint Bivins, knowing the next man had to be *him!*

Full prescience is a sometime thing, and never foolproof. No third man came out. There was a quick shove of a booted foot from inside the cabin, fleetingly seen by Frank on the ridge above. Then the door banged shut behind Clint, and that was all.

Was it Garth who had kicked that door shut? By God, was it? The torture of the doubt had only time to twist once within him. Then his eyes and thoughts were forced to follow Clint and Judd.

The two men rode slowly to the store, circled it cautiously, pulled their horses up in the road south of the building, talking briefly. Frank saw Clint gesture toward the high stone foundation across the road from the store. Judd nodded and both kneed their mounts forward. Five seconds later they were looking over the rock wall and into the double-barreled face of death.

Frank saw them rise in their stirrups to look over the foundation, saw the quick haul-back of both horses, and the simultaneous stepping around of the corner of the breastworks by Billy Mulvehey.

"Throw them up!"

The heavy bark of the Prescott sheriff's command carried clearly to the ridge. The next sounds, and the last ones, were the blending of the roars of the blackpowder replies and counter-replies.

Clint drew first. His Colt had just cleared its holster when the 12-gauge buckslugs tore his belly out. He was dying the instant his horse reared, and dead before his ruptured body struck the ground.

Judd, a half second slower, never broke his pistols loose. The second barrel of Mulvehey's shotgun missed him, smashed into the head and neck of his mount. The animal reared and fell backward, Judd getting away from him and landing on his feet. He twisted toward the wall, still clawing for his guns. The belch of the posse's rifle fire rolled once across the foundation and after that there was nothing save the echoing stillness of sudden death occupying the Parker's Store crossroads.

Judd lived long enough to ask for a drink of water. And for Mulvehey to tell him he was sorry; that he had missed his second shot deliberately, shooting for the horse rather than the man, hoping till the last that Judd would surrender. Whether the second Graden brother heard or understood was never known. He died with the first taste of the water unswallowed in his slack mouth.

Frank, watching the huddle of peace officers around the dying man, broke his eyes suddenly back to the Graden cabin.

Two men ran out, raced to the corral, vaulted onto their saddled ponies, galloped off toward the southern foothills. They were Lew Parkins, a nephew of the Gradens, and Tom Bonney, one of the JT cowhands. Their appearance and flight brought a shout from the crossroads. Frank took his eyes off the cabin long enough to see a small group of the possemen mount up and start after them.

He could not have looked away more than ten seconds. But with a man like Garth Graden, ten seconds is nine and a half too many.

Frank saw the drive and hunch of the horse's rear bombard out of the boarded-up box stall behind the main corral, flash across the open of the meadow and disappear into the lodgepole pines flanking it. That was all. There was no time for a snarled oath, let alone a snapped-off shot.

One second he saw him, wondering how in God's name he had gotten out of the cabin and into that apparently abandoned box stall so fast, and the next second he had a hundred yards of post-thick pines between Frank and his half-swung Winchester.

But it was not the simple surprise of his speed which had dropped Frank's jaw and stopped the swing of his gun. It was not just seeing that eyetail flash of a man and knowing that it was Garth Graden. It was not anything about the man which stopped him.

It was his horse!

The mount Garth had ridden since his return to the Basin was a rangy, rawboned buckskin. The flash of that horse's rump just vanished into the pines was not buckskin, nor anything close to it. It was bay. Bright, satin-deep, blood-red bay!

Frank's face was white. The Winchester hung forgotten in his hands. It could not have been. By God though, *couldn't it?* That bright, blood color? The deerfast stretch and power of that matchless gallop? The remembered, wild black stream of that flinging mane? That hocklong tail?

Then he knew.

He still could not believe it, much less understand it. But the mare had not been foaled or serviced that could carry the twin of that crazy-running bay Garth was riding.

Horse ghost, hope mirage—name him any way you would —*that was Red Boy running yonder!*

For an uncertain moment he thought of mounting up and driving after them. Then the lonely years were paying off. The old belly pinch was pulling in, and the muscle tremor running his jaw. He waited, hard-eyed and deliberately, watching the upper end of the timber. He saw the stud break out of the pines half a mile up the meadow, skirt behind the low hills cupping the western side of the Graden homestead, come racing out on the Payson trail beyond.

He shook himself, the fierce joy of seeing the stallion once more putting its ache of sudden memory hard and tight in his throat. He forced his eyes back to the crossroads, knowing his next move had to be guided from there. He saw the main body of the posse gather, waited only long enough to see it start for the Graden cabin. He was sliding back off the ridge then, going for his horse.

Mulvehey and that posse were after Tom. And they thought they had him down there in that cabin. If not, they would never have let Lew Parkins and the other JT hand take off with only a handful of deputies following them. The quick grin hardened Frank's mouth as he reined the bay into the pines. They would have to close on that cabin mighty tight to squeeze Tom Graden out of it. For all his quiet ways and refusal to wear guns, the thick-shouldered JT owner was just what Jim Fewkes had named him, the slickest-gutted one of the bunch.

Breaking free of the foothills and coming out on the Payson trail, Frank threw a glance at the climbing sun, nodded his quick satisfaction and rode on quickly.

It was a day and hour patiently waited for. And long to be remembered.

Six A.M., September 21, 1887.

With his muddy boots on

It was perfect trailing weather. The ground was still damp from a mountain shower earlier in the evening of the 20th, the breeze strong and steady from the Mogollons. Where there was soil it held Red Boy's familiar, twisted prints in clean relief, letting Frank read them from the saddle with his own mount held on a high lope. Where there was sand or dusted silt, the wind blew it away and broke it up as quickly as a horse might raise it, keeping the man ahead from seeing that he was being closely trailed.

In this kind of country, tumbled and cut up and standing on end like it was, that was important. Once they had followed the Payson trail around Diamond Butte and the south end of Apache Bench, it would be different. The Basin opened up there. A mounted man riding it would stand out on its broad level as black as a restaurant fly on a custard pie. Either he caught up with Garth before they got out into that open, or he would lose him, for there was no question who had the top horse in this race. Red Boy was a runner, bred and trained; his own bay plug, a worn-out cutting horse which should have been pasture pensioned long ago.

Ahead now lay Antelope Saddle, a five-hundred-foot high granite crossdike, lying athwart the Payson trail. The trail went up and over Antelope Saddle and from its summit a man would get his last good view before the open lands began south of the bench. Once up that rise, he would have his one opportunity to know how far Garth had him headed. And he could weigh his chances of getting up to him short of Payson or Prescott, or maybe any place in Arizona!

He threw the bay off the trail just below the skyline, piled off of him and went sliding up into the rocks. He bellied over the summit, the curse coming as his squinted eyes adjusted to the dance of the sun on the bare granite below.

In this clear air the size of that mounted dot just breaking free of the last boulders, past Diamond Butte and into the open of the main Basin, meant your man was a solid five miles up on you. And it meant that another mile would take him free.

The simple beauty of the situation was that you could just sit there and watch him go. The old bay plug was still fresh enough. He could go the rest of the day if need be. But if he went the rest of his life, he would never head that red stallion.

Frank's mouth twisted. God and good luck had both put off on him. His only hope had been that Garth would hold Red Boy down, figuring he had gotten away from the ranch without being seen, and saving the stud for the long pull out of the territory. But Garth's breed had never flourished on figuring. His kind had to know a thing. He had pushed the big stallion all the way, had not only headed his slower-mounted pursuer but had opened up that heading by four full miles since leaving the meadow.

The realization of the fact tightened the twist of Frank's mouth. The big devil may have seen him early in the chase. But in his desperately moving mind he could place no spot along the backtrail where he could have done so. That early country was all too cut up, the trail through it too sharply turning and canyon-hidden. But the fact remained. Garth had pushed the stud. It left a man little to think but that he had been seen.

Even as Frank was thinking it, the hard-eyed gods of Western chance reversed themselves, smiled briefly upon him.

Brief and wry as the grimace was, it put the sudden hope of his hatred hammering within him. The distant horseman had not appeared beyond the far boulders which marked the edge of the Basin floor.

And he did not.

As Frank watched, unable in the first moment to absorb the full extent of his luck, Garth appeared west of the boulders. West of the boulders, and forcing Red Boy up and across the lower spur of Apache Bench! He disappeared beyond the spur, still climbing, and Frank knew what that meant.

Working to his hard formula of knowing what he had to do, Garth Graden had done the one thing, above all others, he should not have done. He had left the open safety of the Payson trail. And he had picked instead, the trail for the last place in Arizona Territory he should have chosen, Frank Rachel's Apache Bench Ranch.

Frank slid down off the summit, going for the bay. Swinging up, he heeled the animal hard right and into a full gallop. In less than five minutes he struck a dim cowpath angling north. He put the bay onto its level track, easing him down to a hand-gallop. The creases of his grin became broader-set with every jolt of the bay's pounding stride.

Either Garth had been with Anse Canaday and the bunch which had run off Red Boy, or he had talked to them enough to know the Diamond Butte trail up the south end of the bench. In any case, he knew where he was going.

There was grass and water at the abandoned ranch, and a five-mile view of the country a man had left behind him. A man could rest there, graze and water his horse, have time to roll a smoke and make out for sure if anybody was on his backtrail. Then, either way, there was that good trail up and across the wall behind the ranch, leading out past Camp Verde and north safely to the west of Flagstaff. Yes, Garth Graden knew where he was going.

And so did Frank Rachel.

The only difference was that Frank knew a better and shorter way to get there. He was remembering Jim's long-ago words now, as he took that better, shorter way, "I got a cute way into them Tonto headlands. There'll be times you'll want to remember it."

The half-breed had been right. And this was one of those times. It was a cute way all right.

It's name was Dry Canyon.

The Dry Canyon trail was shorter by ten miles. But the last three of those ten were up a chert-rock goat track as steep as the pitch of a snow-country roof, and Red Boy's blazing speed might possibly outmatch Frank's memory of the half-breed's shortcut.

The thought grew swiftly in the big rancher's mind as he forced the failing bay up the final precipitous mile. Before the mile was out the torment of the suspicion had built into a foreboding certainty. He halted the laboring pony in the rock jumble which clogged the canyon's exit. Seconds late, he was peering across the bench, lean face darkening.

There was harsh memory enough in that first glance to bring the scowl: the lonely set of the empty corrals, the sweep and wave of the heavy grass, the vacant, staring ruin of the burned cabin, the high drift of the cotton clouds above the brooding silence of the granite walls—yes, in these and a hundred other things which rushed unbidden to a man's mind there was memory enough to bring the scowl.

But these were the things you saw with your heart, and they were the things which could kill you only slowly. It was what you saw with your eyes which could kill you in the next five minutes.

And what you saw was Red Boy standing, cinch loosened, in his own corral!

Quickly then, Frank saw the rest of it.

Garth was hunched over a tiny, clear-flamed coffee fire at the corner of the stud's corral. From his position he could see the bench from north to south, and he was seeing it. The shifting, nervous swing of his glance, from the fire to the silent buildings to the open grass of the bench, was never still. A man could get his horse as many as three, possibly four, buckjumps from the head of Dry Canyon before the tall gunman would have him spotted. And once he had been spotted, there was still that wide mile of open grass to get across.

Garth could get mounted up and have time to roll a smoke before Frank could hope to get within long rifle range of him. Then, with the stud under him, he could run any way he liked and have the bay plug headed in the first forty jumps.

Right about now a man wished he had Jim Fewkes with him.

The half-breed would know how to come up on that wary white bastard out there, without him ever knowing there was another human within sixty miles of him. He would do it like the damn Indian he was, naked-footed and bellying back of every gramma clump, outcrop rock or juniper big enough to hide a runt grass rat.

He would start, no doubt, by working north of the cabin ruins, like as not keeping them between him and the man at the corral. That way he would get into the timber at the base of the wall behind the ranch, ease down through it to hit the pasture fence, follow that on his belly to where it angled into the mares' hayshed. Then all he would have left would be to slide along the back of the shed, somehow make it across the open of the feed corral and bring up against the rear of the stud's box. And once to the box, it was three seconds around it to where he would step into the open not twenty feet from his man— and squarely behind him!

The thought of Jim and his savage ancestry was broken swiftly by another thought; the first one grim father to the second. Jim had always said he, Frank, should have been an Indian! Frank's scowl dropped away under the sudden flash of the old grin. Damn. The only shame of it was that the copper-skinned breed could not be there to see his white brother win his warbonnet!

Seconds later, he was in the grass.

Behind him the silent rocks of the canyon's throat stood guard over a little pile of personals which would have gladdened Jim Fewkes' half-red heart: the dust-stained, run-over Texas boots, the short, double-tubed barrel of the '73 Winchester, the heavy, cartridge-studded bulk of the twin holsters, the dull, sun-faded slouch of the black Stetson. Seeing these, his slant eyes would have narrowed further, and his half-breed's heart quickened yet more. Jim Fewkes would never have missed a touch like that.

The righthand holster was empty.

Frank knew how long it took to boil a can of coffee and blow a tired horse. He had no more than fifteen minutes to get to that stud box and make his play.

The open grass part was the easiest. Garth could not know of the Dry Canyon trail and would likely keep his eyes pretty well on the south sweep of the bench over which he had just come. A man had to gamble on it anyway. Five minutes more and he was raking in the first half of the pot. He was in the pines under the wall and Garth had not moved from the fire.

And in three minutes more, he was behind the hayshed and getting his last look at his enemy before he would loose him for those final seconds beyond the intervening square of the box stall. He hesitated in those last moments, his hand dropping to the curved handle of the Colt protruding from the waistband of his Levis, pale eyes measuring the distance. He shook his head quickly, hand pulling away from the gunbutt.

It was a long seventy-five yards, and no matter how Ned Buntline had Bill Hickok lying about it, you did not open up with a beltgun at anything over fifty—and preferably under five! Oh, maybe you might with Indians or Mexicans. Or homesteaders or sodhut farmers. But if you meant to call a fast man and then hit him in the belly with six slugs where you could cover the spread of them with one hand, you got in close enough to powderburn his shirt.

Past the corner of the box, he could see Red Boy moving nervously in the stud corral. He scowled, testing the wind with a wetted finger. The scowl deepened. The wind was wrong, carrying from him toward the stallion. If the big bay should wind him on his way in . . .

It was just another burr in the ratty tail of the horse of his chances. He would have to pull it and hope the horse didn't feel it. Taking a deep breath, he pulled.

His stockinged feet made no sound in the deep dust of the yard. Red Boy did not even grunt. He was behind the box stall then, wanting to gasp for breath and not daring to. He slid to the corner of the building, crouching there to let the passing seconds slow his breathing and steady his hand.

When he was ready, he moved swiftly.

He came two, gliding, Indian steps into the open, the short-barreled .44 held low and four inches forward of his right hip.

It was the first time in his life he had made a call with his gun already in his hand. But he had come to kill a man, not match draws. He had come to see a man die. And before that—before the first slug bucked into him —before he grabbed his guts and went forward into the stable dirt—to see the moment of truth on his face and in his eyes. To let him see the naked gun in his hand. And the man behind the gun. *And the woman behind the man with the gun!*

Yes, and more. To give him time, in that memory-suspended moment before he died, to know why he was being killed and *who* was killing him.

It was the way it had to be. The bitter years would not have it otherwise . . . that dim glow of the Fewkes' cabin lamplight with its first silhouette of that matchless form . . . the moonlight of that same night with its echo of the throaty, taunting laugh . . . the way she had looked at him that grim midnight in Tombstone when he had asked her to come home with him . . . Jim's Christmas tree . . . Red Boy and the sugar lumps and the dried

apples . . . the ominous return of the cough and those
bright stains on the torn sheeting she hadn't thought he
had seen . . . the wild and brooding stillness of her lookout . . . the drifting smoke of the cabin's last ashes . . .

There was no other way.

"Garth!"

He waited for the hiss of the single word to travel the
twenty-foot silence between them, saw it strike the broad
back of the crouching gunman, saw, too, the involun-
tary hunch and following slight sag of the wide shoulders.

Then Garth was standing up.

He made the move unhurriedly. Not stiffly, and not
tensely. But slowly and deliberately and effortlessly. Like
a giant, sun-stretching cat.

He stood with his back to Frank for a full five seconds,
and when he came around it was with the same animal
ease and deliberation with which he had stood up. They
faced each other then, the eternity of coming death stalk-
ing the tiny fragment of time and space remaining between
them.

Neither man was new to death. Both had seen him
before this. Both knew him well, and feared him not. Yet,
each time he wore a new face, and every man saw him
differently. They were seeing him differently now.

Garth Graden looked at death and saw him towering
over six-three in his stockinged feet. Saw him lean and
sunblack and gaunt-boned of face, and wide and cruel and
motionless of mouth. Saw him flaxen and mane-long of
hair, and pale and still of eye. And he saw the naked gun
in his hand.

Frank Rachel looked at death and saw him big shouldered, muscular, heavily boned. He saw him calm and
quiet of face as a mountain lake at sunrise. He saw him
with peaceful, deep blue eyes, widely set and watchful, and
uncreased by tension at the corners. He saw him freshly
shaven, broad of jaw, close-cropped and silvery black of
hair, generous and pleasantly half-smiling of mouth. And
he saw him with his long-fingered hands hanging loosely
and carelessly behind the forward hitch of the double-
belted guns.

"I'm Frank Rachel."

Saying it, and watching him, Frank knew the moment was now. Knew that full time, and dangerous overtime, had already been allowed for the swift course of back-trailing memory to bring the mind of this last of the Gradens up to that final moment of his destiny now held in the right hand of Frank Rachel.

"*She would have wanted you to know it*," he added softly. And let his finger come into and back against the hairline of the .44's let-off.

He had been unable to resist it. He had had to know in that final moment, that the big gunman across from him understood it. It was his first mistake, and with Garth Graden's kind each customer is allowed only one.

The little pause between Frank's conclusion and the tightening of his finger on the trigger, was Garth's opening. Dry-voiced and still smiling, he eased into it. The flat meaning of his statement halted the travel of Frank's trigger-finger for just the calculated, necessary fraction of lethal hesitation.

"You were Frank Rachel," was all Garth said. But in the saying of it, his guns were out.

Frank, like Simm and Jake Bivins before him, did not see the movement of the wrists which brought them there. He only saw the flame of them, and the burst and black pepper blast of the unburned powder grains and shredded wadding behind the bullets. He knew, instinctively, even before Garth's lead came to him, or the twin roars of its discharges followed that lead into him, that his own shot was low and late. He saw its mushroom of spurting earth rip into the ground in front of Garth a clock-tick after the latter's first shot smashed into him.

The bullet hit Frank high in the right lung, spinning him back and around. He fell, twisting for the cover of the box stall corner, Garth's second shot following him. Ricocheting off of the butted logs, it tore through his left thigh. In the second following the three gunbursts, he heard the slam of the stall's front door, and knew that Garth had leaped inside the fortress of Red Boy's box.

In the same moment the wind shifted suddenly and in the corral beyond the box, the excited stallion threw up his head, nostrils belling with the memory stir of a for-

gotten man-smell. *The* man-smell. The smell of *his* man!
The challenging neigh was high and sharp, fiercely savage
with the longing and joy of remembering.

Braced against the bottom logs of the stall's west wall,
mind racing, body writhing with the pain of his wounds,
Frank heard the big stud's call and knew what it meant.
But in the physical and mental agony of the moment, he
ignored it.

He had had his chance. And it was gone. His right
arm and side were useless. His left leg too badly hit to
bear his weight. Garth was in the box stall with two guns
and a full belt of shells. There were no windows in the
stall and the front door was a full door. The only way
into that stall now was the half-door separating it from the
excited Red Boy and the stud corral. All Garth had to do
was watch that half-door and wait.

And wounded like Frank was, the big gunman would
not have long to wait.

The continued harsh neighing of the bay stud rode in
over his dimming thoughts. Again the stallion blasted his
whistling challenge. And then again. The angry, grating
sound forced its way into Frank's mind now, bringing the
wildness of the idea with it. It was crazy, he thought. It
would never work. Never in God's world. Garth had had
the stud a long time.

Still . . . and yet . . .

If Garth had not worked any at gentling him. If he had
used him as roughly as that Spanish spade-bit he had on
him would seem to suggest. If those white-haired scars on
his flanks were Mexican quirt-marks. And if Garth Graden
had put them there. If the big, nasty-tempered horse was
remembering him, Frank, as strongly as that wild neighing
sounded. If the gunshots and the smell of the blood and
the excitement of returning to his beloved box and corral
had him crazy enough . . .

There had been a time when no man dared touch the
stud when Frank was near him. He could be handled by
a hard horseman, but not when Frank was within sight or
smell of him. Libby had been the only one who had ever
done that. Even Jim Fewkes, tophand with any horse as

he was, had known better than to lay a hand on Red
Boy when Frank was around.

Maybe now, by God just maybe . . .

Somehow, Frank reached the closed front door of the
stall and dropped the heavy stovebolt through the hasp
which locked it from the outside. Then he was dragging
himself back around the west wall, hunching foot by
foot on his braced left arm. He turned the corner and
started down the south wall of the box, the pain-racked,
fifteen-foot distance taking him five minutes to cover. It
was the long way around, but that damned half-door was
latched on the south side, making that the side he had
to approach from.

At the south corner of the little building, he writhed
under the bottom poles of the corral fence, inched his
way along the eastern wall toward the closed half-door.
Six feet from it, he stopped. Panting heavily, he lay face
to the ground, waiting for the dizziness to pass and his
strength to come again. As he waited, the thin, bright
trickle of blood from the torn lung came up in his throat.
It filled his mouth, broke free of the compressed lips, cak-
ing his jaw with the dirt and dried manure of the corral.

Presently, it subsided, letting him raise his head and
place his ear against the outer logs of the box stall, listening for the least sound of movement from within. At
first there was nothing, then he heard it—the little scrape
of holster leather against a shifting thigh, the soft rustle
of a booted foot moving through bone-dry bedding straw.
Garth was still in there. But moving around now. Getting
restless with the long crawl of the passing minutes. Frank
had not much time left. If he had any. And he needed
a little more. Just a little more . . .

But the bay stallion, away at the far end of the corral
when he had writhed under the fence, had seen him now,
was coming swiftly forward, ears pricked, nostrils flaring
suspiciously. He was on top of him in another minute,
and in the same minute had gotten his full scent. He was
at once wild with excitement.

Racing the corral fence, he dashed away from, and back
to Frank, rearing over him, lashing out with his forefeet,

racing away again, wheeling and neighing crazily as his
highstrung nerves snapped under the sudden, full impact
of the memories and half memories unleashed by Frank's
familiar scent, and compounded by the actual sight and
presence of the man who had bottle-broken him from his
dam's flank.

Frank waved him desperately away, not daring to call
out to him nor to take his eyes from the opening above the
half-door. But, miraculously, the silence within the box
stall held. Either Garth had failed to interpret the meaning of the stud's sudden excitement or, interpreting it, had
chosen to ignore it and wait out Frank's move.

In either case, it was a lethal indecision.

Frank braced himself upward along the stall's outer
logs, shoved the .44's barrel under the stovebolt which
fastened the door, popped it free of its rusted hasp.

Garth's shot, muffled by the close confines of the box
stall, smashed outward through the door. Its lead ripped
the heavy planking inches from Frank's withdrawing hand.
But in the same instant Frank's foot was in the sagging
crack of the released door, shoving it and kicking it wide
open, and Garth's second and third shots went wild into
the dust of the corral. Frank lurched back against the
wall, free of the opening, his shrill whistle going to the
lathered stallion.

The stud wheeled, threw up his head, thundered toward
the opened stall.

"Inside, you red bastard! Inside!"

He screamed it at him, breathing a prayer behind it as
the stud came racing across the corral in answer to the
remembered command. The big horse was past him then,
ears back, eye whites rolling, sleek body lunging into the
familiar gloom of his box.

Garth tried to get past the stallion, and almost did. The
rearing horse could not turn and wheel from his entering
lunge in time. It happened then. It is given to each man
to make that one mistake. Frank had made his in delay-
ing with Garth. Garth now made his in the manner with
which he attempted to evade Red Boy.

Ducking the first rush of the maddened stallion, he
leaped, cursing, for the side wall of the box, seeking to

slide down along it and thus past the pivoting reach of the great rump, trying desperately to get behind the horse to gain the second of time needed for a killing shot. But that slide down the wall was an old game to Red Boy. An old, and in this case, a deadly one.

It was not a clean trap. The man was already partially clear of it. But the crushing drive of the stallion's haunch caught Garth's left leg and hip, pulping them against the logs. He fell free of the wall, twisting into the forward corner of the tiny stall as the grunting studhorse finished his pivot and came for him.

His entire left side paralyzed, Garth thrust his right shoulder forward, fought the right-hand gun free of its holster. The first of the slashing hooves struck him in the shoulder as he did, cleaving the thick muscle to the bare whiteness of the bone, springing the gun outward and away from the nerveless fingers. The single shot whined off of the metal corner of the feedbox, rocketed harmlessly into the roof timbers.

Outside the stall Frank heard the wild curse, the single blast of the ricocheting shot, the stallion's continual, high, piercing neighs. And after these sounds there were only those of the log-jarring smashes of the great rump repeatedly driven against the box's inner walls, and the angry, sodden drives of the steelshod forefeet lashing again and again into the near corner of the stall.

He closed his eyes then, leaning weakly back against the logs of the outer wall. He felt the weakness grow sickeningly, coming up from the pit of his stomach in thick, slow-pulsing waves. He called haltingly to the raging stud within the stall. "Easy, boy, easy! It's all right now. Cooeee, Red Boy . . ." And with the break in the calls, his head slumped.

His body remained braced against the logs for a moment, then pitched and slid soundlessly forward into the corral dirt.

Presently, the stallion quieted down, came stepping nervously out of the box stall. He put his slim nose under the slack arm, nudging it in the old game. It flopped limply and fell away. Red Boy backed off, cleared his nostrils of the blood smell. He whickered and stomped de-

mandingly. He nuzzled the still form gingerly, not whick-
ering now but grunting softly and eagerly. There was no
reply from the man. The big stallion threw up his head
and trotted away.

Twice more he came back to nose at Frank's body.
Once he started back into the stall where the other body
was, but immediately shied back out and away from it,
snorting loudly. He went away then, to the far end of the
corral. Stretching his neck over the top rail, he watched
the silent ruin where the house had been and where she
had always waited with the sugar lumps and the dried
apples. Repeatedly and insistently, he whickered.

There was no answer.

The flies in the corral droned on. The noonshade crept
out from the east wall of the box stall. Its shadow lengthened, and lengthened again. The crumpled body of the
man did not move.

The fourth horseman

He first heard the whistle of the stallion, wild
and faint and far away.

Then it was loud, close, insistent; the demanding, shrill
whistle of a studhorse calling to his mares.

His eyes opened and he lay for a long minute, not
knowing where he was. He got his left elbow under him,
then the hand, pushing himself up, his mind clearing now.

Red Boy was at the far end of the corral, arching his
neck over the southern top rail, whistling fiercely down
the bench. Through the fence poles Frank saw the mares
coming, cautiously at first, moving up through the junipers to the south, ears pricked, nostrils spreading in uncertain puzzlement.

He recognized the lead mare, first; Libby's favorite little dun, a red-bay weanling colt at her flank. Then, swiftly,
the others—the roan, the three blacks, the chestnut with

the nose-snip, the steeldust with the white front stockings, the little gray—his mares. His and Libby's and Red Boy's. All that was left of them.

They came on now, beginning to remember the bay stud's call, beginning to whicker and grunt in eager answer to its imperious summons.

Frank tried his arm then and could not move it. Hunching himself up the stable wall, he tested the leg carefully. It took the weight. Stiffly and with searing pain at first, but it took it. The blood had stopped, he saw, thick and fly-crusted on his thigh and chest. His strength grew a little as he rested against the wall.

Moving along it after a moment, he turned the jamb of the box stall's open half-door. He peered into the inner gloom of the box a long time, the twist of his wide mouth not pleasant to see. He did not go inside. There was no need.

He rested against the wall again. His glance moved across the corral, and across the grasslands of the bench beyond it. His eyes, narrowing now, traveled upward along the granite wall towering behind the bench. They came to rest on the gnarled juniper halfway up its sheer face. The softness of the words made them barely audible, the little pause which broke them in mid-whisper scarcely perceptible.

"It's done now, Lib . . . and there's more than mud on his boots!"

With the mutter he broke his glance from the juniper, turned and hobbled slowly across the corral. He was a full minute hoisting himself to the top rail of the fence. The stud watched him curiously but did not come to him. When Frank was ready, he called him softly. "Coo-eee, boy. Red Boy. Come along now. Easy, son, easy!"

The big horse came up the fence, gentle and easy as a weanling filly, crested neck arching to the toss of the fine head. Frank let him come. When he was alongside, he knotted his good hand in the long mane, forced his injured leg out and across the sleek back. He sat him a full minute more, closing his eyes and gritting his teeth against the pain and the weakness. His head cleared then, and he turned the big horse quickly away and toward the swing-

latch of the corral gate. In the entire, following time of
the slow jog across the open mile of the bench, Frank did
not look back.

At the canyon's head, he slid off of the stud.

The bay stallion followed him a few steps, then stopped
and looked back toward the mares which had trotted curiously behind them all the way. Presently, Frank came
back out of the rocks, leading the old brown gelding. He
looked more like himself in the high boots and dirty black
hat. Red Boy whickered gladly, trotted mincingly toward
him.

Frank let him come up to him, then circled the proud
neck with his uninjured arm. The stud nuzzled him,
bunting eagerly at the arm. It was the game. Remember
the game? It had been a long time but the stud was remembering it now. He bared his yellowed teeth, nipping
playfully at the silent man. Frank cursed him softly, swallowed hard, tightened the circle of his arm around the
arching neck.

One of the mares, watching anxiously, whinnied and
moved forward from the group. Another followed her,
curious-eared. A third edged forward to join them.

Seeing them, Frank nodded. Quickly, he unhooked the
cinch buckle of Garth's saddle, carefully slipped the cruel
roller of the dead gunman's Spanish bit from Red Boy's
mouth. He dumped both saddle and bridle among the
nearby rocks, hobbled back toward the stud. The tall bay
stepped away, swinging his satin rump, sidling playfully
toward the approaching man.

"Hee-yahh!" Frank yelled suddenly, and swung the big
black hat with the yell. Red Boy leaped away, eyeing him
uncertainly, still not quite remembering that part of the
game.

"Hee-yahh!" Frank yelled again. "Get outa here you
big red bastard!"

This time he threw the hat with the yell, and suddenly
the bay stud remembered. Remembered and understood.
It was the rest of it, the other part of the old game! The
signal to run with the mares, free in the pasture, racing
through the junipers!

He reared, lashing out with his forefeet, whinnying in

mock fury at the man. Frank cursed him then, and with the curse he was gone, galloping across the bench, herding and driving the squealing mares before him. He was free now and with his mares. And at long, long last, home again!

Frank watched him go.

He stood a long time, until the last mare had passed the ranch, until the whole herd was small with distance and lost, finally, in the sunset shadows of the wall beneath Libby's lookout.

"He was always your hoss, girl," he said at last. "Feed him good . . ."

The rising wind whipped the low words away and across the lonely bench. The big rider turned to go. He came to the old bay, climbed stiffly up on to him. The piled rocks of Dry Canyon closed quickly behind them. Frank Rachel did not look back.

Thus passed the last horseman from Apache Bench.

And, passing thus from the bench, he went down and through the canyon's gorge to the nightfall gloom of the Basin's floor. And eastward across the floor, through the thickening shadows toward Cherry Creek. And beyond the creek, south-turning at last, toward Jim's cabin and Mulvehey's waiting men.

The big rider's thoughts were his own. They were not turning on horsemen. He would not have known the last horseman from the first. Nor the second from the third. He had never heard of the Four Horsemen. And had he done so, he could not have known that he was one of them, and the last one of them.

Old Jim Stanton, though. He could have told him. He had known from the beginning. From the moment of his first uneasy look into those pale, lion-still eyes. Even then he could have told him.

For Peaceful Basin, and for all of those so long since and silently departed from it, Frank Rachel was the Fourth Horseman . . .

He passed John's cabin, hunching his shoulders to the building chill of the night wind. The empty windows stared at him, black and lifeless. The wind whimpered keeningly around the sag of the open, swinging door, whirled across the deserted dust flats of the corral, drummed startlingly along the rusted iron belly of the empty watertank, fled away to die, thinly lisping, in the pines.

Frank shivered, feeling sick again now. Feeling the cold flow of the weakness and the pain. Knowing one moment the rage and ache of the fever. And the next, the shake and sweat of the chills.

He rode on, hurrying the old horse now.

The lamplight, once in those other years so warm and dear, fell wan and foreign now from the main cabin windows ahead of him. The oaks stood black and gaunt against the lesser darkness of the night, their broad trunks backing the uncertain shadows of the many saddled ponies standing in the yard.

The plank door opened and he recognized the thin ramrod of the silhouette—Mulvehey.

He stopped the tired bay, letting him stand facing the converging shadows of the dismounted possemen. He heard Mulvehey's low command, "Hold up, boys . . ." and then his soft query, "Rachel?"

"One name's as good as another . . ." His own voice sounded strange to him. Strange and far away. Like it was not him it was coming out of.

Mulvehey was standing by the bay horse then, peering up at him, his deep voice softening as his eyes narrowed.

"You all right, Frank? We thought you wasn't comin' in. We was about to ride without you."

Frank swayed, caught at the horn. Straightening in the saddle, he fought back the blackness and the cold that was roaring in his ears now.

"We made a deal," he said. "I'm here."

Mulvehey caught him as he fell.

ABOUT THE AUTHOR

WILL HENRY was born and grew up in Missouri, where he attended Kansas City Junior College. Upon leaving school, he lived and worked throughout the Western states, acquiring the background of personal experience reflected later in the realism of his books. Currently residing in California, he writes for motion pictures, as well as continuing his research into frontier lore and legend, which are the basis for his unique blend of history and fiction. Ten of his novels have been purchased for motion picture production, and several have won top literary awards, including the Wrangler trophy of the National Cowboy Hall of Fame, the first Levi Strauss Golden Saddleman and five Western Writers of America Spurs. Mr. Henry is a recognized authority on America's frontier past, particularly that relating to the American horseback Indian of the High Plains. His recent books include *Chiricahua, The Bear Paw Horses, I, Tom Horn* (a major TV movie) and *Summer of the Gun.*

BANTAM'S #1
ALL-TIME BESTSELLING AUTHOR
AMERICA'S FAVORITE WESTERN WRITER

THE SACKETTS

Meet the Sacketts—from the Tennessee mountains they headed west to ride the trails, pan the gold, work the ranches and make the laws. Here in these action-packed stories is the incredible saga of the Sacketts —who stood together in the face of trouble as one unbeatable fighting family.

☐	14868 SACKETT'S LAND	$2.25
☐	12730 THE DAY BREAKERS	$1.95
☐	14196 SACKETT	$1.95
☐	14118 LANDO	$1.95
☐	14193 MOJAVE CROSSING	$1.95
☐	14973 THE SACKETT BRAND	$2.25
☐	20074 THE LONELY MEN	$2.25
☐	14785 TREASURE MOUNTAIN	$2.25
☐	13703 MUSTANG MAN	$1.95
☐	14322 GALLOWAY	$1.95
☐	20073 THE SKY-LINERS	$2.25
☐	14218 TO THE FAR BLUE MOUNTAINS	$1.95
☐	14194 THE MAN FROM THE BROKEN HILLS	$1.95
☐	20088 RIDE THE DARK TRAIL	$2.25
☐	14207 WARRIOR'S PATH	$1.95
☐	14174 LONELY ON THE MOUNTAIN	$2.25

Buy them at your local bookstore or use this handy coupon for ordering:

Bantam Books, Inc., Dept. LL3, 414 East Golf Road, Des Plaines, Ill. 60016

Please send me the books I have checked above. I am enclosing $_____ (please add $1.00 to cover postage and handling). Send check or money order —no cash or C.O.D.'s please.

Mr/Mrs/Miss_____

Address_____

City_____State/Zip_____

LL3—3/81

Please allow four to six weeks for delivery. This offer expires 9/81.

"REACH FOR THE SKY!"

and you still won't find more excitement or more thrills than you get in Bantam's slam-bang, action-packed westerns! Here's a roundup of fast-reading stories by some of America's greatest western writers:

Bantam Book Catalog

Here's your up-to-the-minute listing of over 1,400 titles by your favorite authors.

This illustrated, large format catalog gives a description of each title. For your convenience, it is divided into categories in fiction and non-fiction—gothics, science fiction, westerns, mysteries, cookbooks, mysticism and occult, biographies, history, family living, health, psychology, art.

So don't delay—take advantage of this special opportunity to increase your reading pleasure.

Just send us your name and address and 50¢ (to help defray postage and handling costs).

BANTAM BOOKS, INC.
Dept. FC, 414 East Golf Road, Des Plaines, Ill. 60016

Mr./Mrs./Miss_____
(please print)

Address_____

City_____ State_____ Zip_____

Do you know someone who enjoys books? Just give us their names and addresses and we'll send them a catalog too!

_____

Mr./Mrs./Miss_____

Address_____

City_____ State_____ Zip_____

_____

Mr./Mrs./Miss_____

Address_____

City_____ State_____ Zip_____

FC—9/76